MW01226482

"❝❝This is what's go
sounded a lot m
this lift-disk. As soon as it
way to the that small shuttle. We will have to run since the walkways have been turned off. That shuttle is our last hope to rescue
the Colony kids. Ready?"

"What if somebody sees us?" Rio said.

"Pray to the gods of the universe."

They were all silent as the lift-disk rose slowly to the first level
and stopped with a creak.

Without a word, Marlo started off down the walkway at a fast
trot, Fan and the others right behind him. Almost there, Marlo's
foot slipped through a gap in the railing and he lurched forward,
only saved from falling by the bulk of the small ship. Pain ripped
through him as his leg jammed between the shuttle on its cradle
and the walkway. Unperturbed, Fan stepped over him. Marlo stifled a scream as Triani and Rio crashed into him, jerking his leg.

"Shit! Move!" shouted Triani.

"I can't!"

By now, our of them were safely behind the high wing of the
runabout, but there was no room for Eldred to get past Marlo who
was stuck in a sprawl on the narrow track.

"I'll go back," he whispered. "You might need a decoy."

He was gone before Marlo could stop him.

"You down there! Freeze!"

THE COLONY DANCERS
THE MERCULIANS BOOK 5

CARO SOLES

ONE

Everyone in the Merculian capital was talking about the Colony Dancers. Even those like Marlo, who were not as mad about dance as his compatriots, were intrigued by all the hype, the contrast between their sweet, childish looks and their accomplished professionalism as shown on the many dance clips being broadcast everywhere. It was the first time the Merculian children from the Colony were coming to visit their home planet and their every appearance was already sold out.

Their arrival coincided with a city-wide holiday named for some centuries-old councilor whose name would have been forgotten long ago if not for this festival. No one could tell you what he had done to deserve such celebrity. His name only meant that everything in the city was closed down and the citizens took advantage of this to line the streets near the SpacePort, waiting for the arrival of the children, who would parade through the main avenue of the city to the Theater Residence, where they would be staying.

Com Marlo Dasha Bogardini was in charge of the security for the event. It was supposed to be an easy job, since he had only just reported back for duty after a lengthy absence due to a work-related injury, but now, standing on the glass balcony beside his lover Calian, he was beginning to wonder. He hadn't expected such a huge turnout for one thing. Below him packed three and four deep were Merculians of all ages, laughing and talking and carrying flowers and ribbons wrapped around messages. The whole avenue was lined with welcome signs and large party balloons filled with confetti.

"Quite a crowd down there," remarked his Terran female friend Boothby when she arrived. She was wearing high heeled boots which made her tower over her Merculian friends. "Thanks for inviting me."

"Calian's place has the best view," Marlo said.

"All this for a couple of dozen kids!" She obviously didn't get it.

"Merculians love children," Calian said, slipping an arm around Marlo's substantial waist.

"And dancing," Marlo pointed out.

"So dancing children hit the jackpot, right?" She leaned over and inspected the crowd. "Not much in the way of crowd control down there."

"It's just children walking by," Marlo said, miffed at the hint that he might not be doing a good job. "You're not with the Black Circle anymore, remember."

"Thank God," she said and laughed heartily.

From their vantage point, they could just make out the glittering SpacePort far in the distance where the company had landed about an hour ago. As they watched, a column of children swung into the street marching two by two, and headed towards them up the wide avenue. The crowd broke into frenzied cheers. Hand in hand they came, all dressed alike in high-waisted lace tunics with short, full skirts, white leggings and shiny red shoes. Their long curling hair was caught back from their shining faces with a bright red comb, the rest so long down their backs they could probably sit on it.

"Holy cow!" Boothby exclaimed. "They're so cute! Do they ever cut their hair?"

"Our children don't cut their hair until they're older," Marlo explained. Boothby hadn't been on Merculian that long and he kept having to explain the strangest things. At least she was finally accustomed to the use of 'he' to translate the pronoun referring to them, even though they were all hermaphrodites.

"So it's sort of like a puberty thing?" she said, still watching the children as if mesmerized.

Marlo nodded and pulled out his high-power glasses to study them. The rest of the group, all adults dressed in dark blue, were moving quickly to walk on either side of the children now. The baggage floats followed behind. A band wheeled smartly into place at the head of the little procession, instruments gleaming in the sunshine as they played a jaunty tune. The children quickly switched their steps to march in time with the rhythm.

Calian leaned on the railing. "They're not really smiling."

"They're probably overcome," Marlo said. "I don't think they've ever been off their own planet before so I imagine it's all a bit overwhelming."

"I don't think they look overwhelmed, exactly," Calian said thoughtfully.

"Awww, they're just like little dolls," Boothby gushed.

Several of the more enthusiastic people in the crowd flung flowers and message-bundles at them, causing a momentary confusion and a wavering of the line of children, who were obviously not prepared for this custom. Marlo saw the blue-clad caretakers snap their fingers and clap, and the children fell back into place. Well trained, he thought, wondering how they could hear anything over the noise made by the crowd.

Marlo was doing one more swing across the crowd with his glasses when an explosion shook the balcony. Screams and shouts shattered the air and the music stuttered away in confusion. Boothby grabbed him and pulled him down just as another explosion made him clap both hands over the thick curls covering the auricular membranes of his sensitive inner ears. Through the glass floor he saw the crowd below try to scatter, pushing and shoving desperately to escape the confines of the street but they were packed too tightly in the narrow space. Then he saw some familiar faces moving like eels though the panicked group, all heading against the flow.

"So that's it," he murmured. He pushed Boothby away and hauled himself to his feet, relieved to know what to do. "It's okay," he said. "It's not serious."

"It sure looks serious!" cried Boothby, jumping to her feet. "Look at all that black smoke."

"Fireworks, I think." Calian sniffed the air.

Marlo took out his com-dev, pushing the official contact button for his team. "El, it's a code 39. Just a diversion. I saw Big Stendi's crew working the crowd in this sector, perfectly calm. Get unit 6 over here and round them up, will you? And get crowd control to the eastern area."

"On it. And I'll check the usual Stendi hangouts right away."

"Good." Marlo slipped the com-dev into his pocket

"All under control?" asked Calian, peering over the balcony.

"It will be. I'd better get on over and sooth the Colony people."

Down below It was utter chaos. People were pushing and shoving, trying to get away from the smoke. The children's caretakers had closed ranks around the kids and they were fast disappearing down the avenue, their way cleared by El's unit. He saw some of his other people herding the crowd back to the open areas around the port where there was more space.

Boothby was about to leap over the balcony when Marlo grabbed her arm and shouted, "No!"

"I can see better over everyone's head from down there," she cried. "I can help!"

"Relax. It's not what you think," Marlo said, "but thanks."

Calian touched Marlo's wrist for a moment to pick up his feelings. "Boothby, let's go inside and have a drink," he suggested a moment later, turning away.

Sometimes it's very handy being a touch empath, Marlo thought. Even though Calian couldn't have picked up much, he'd figured out enough to get Boothby out of the way.

Marlo's com-dev buzzed. "Dasha Bogardini."

"What in the name of all the stars is going on down there!" exploded his boss, Old Livid. "This was supposed to be a simple job any rookie could handle!"

"Not to worry, boss. It's just Big Stendi showing off, using a diversion to cover his pickpocket crews at work."

"You'd better reassure our guests. They wanted the Black Circle to handle security you know, but the top brass assured them we could handle it."

"We can, I tell you."

"Then get to it! Handle it!"

Marlo hurried down to where he had left his Regulator hoverbike. He rarely used the thing and it took him a moment to remember how to start it. Then he almost fell off when he turned a corner too sharply. He eased up and headed after the Colony group, using side streets and alleys.

They were almost at the Theater Residence when he saw them, surrounded by a whole crowd of gawkers and vidsters, their bright light-halos bobbing with excitement. He slowed down, stopped and slid off the back of the bike as gracefully as his rotund body allowed.

"Flying farts," he muttered. He knew the group wouldn't want publicity after their frightening experience. They would only want to get the children safely inside. They didn't know they had never been in any real danger.

Marlo held up his Regulator insignia and was about to wade into the crowd when one of the Colony kids burst out of the group and ran right into him. Automatically his arms went around the child and held on tightly.

"It's okay, dear. You're safe now. It was just a small malfunction of a couple of the party balloons."

To his surprise, the kid pushed away. Hard. He was trying with all his wiry muscled might to get away from Marlo and into the lane to his left. Marlo could pick up his fear and some pain, but didn't loosen his hold. Maybe the child was injured? Marlo held on tighter, relieved to see one of the dark-suited Guardians hurrying up to them.

"Corvin! It's alright. It's time to come inside. Now, Corvin!"

"There really was no danger," Marlo assured the new arrival, who scooped up the red-haired dancer easily. "I apologize for the technical malfunction that caused the noise that frightened you so," Marlo went on. He was pleased to notice a Regulator under his command wading into the vidster group, waving them away.

Corvin seemed to have slumped in the guardian's arms. "They've never been in such a big city before," the older Merculian said, giving Corvin a shake and setting him on his feet like a large doll. "It's easy to get disoriented. Thanks for the reassurance, *Com* Bogardini." He slipped an arm around the kid's shoulders and half-marched, half-pushed him back to the Theater Residence and through the door. It snapped closed at once.

Marlo stood there staring after them. The child was very strong, much stronger then he had expected. It rattled him how hard it had been to hold on to the kid. Of course they were dancers, he reminded himself. They had to be strong. But the child had been very scared, too. Terrified, more like it. And angry. Perhaps he didn't believe Marlo when he said there was no danger. Would he even know Marlo was a Regulator? He wasn't in uniform. As a class

A investigator he didn't wear one. And the insignia around his neck on a wide ribbon would mean nothing to the child.

Marlo shook his head, strangely unsettled. He could still smell the flowery scent of the child's long red hair in his nostrils, could still see that pale wide-eyed face in his mind. Was there something familiar about it? Marlo was famous among the Regulators for his memory for faces, but nothing came to mind as he thought about this one.

Slowly he made his way back to his hover-bike and climbed on. Calian would be waiting. Marlo felt a warm sweep of pleasure all through him. Maybe Boothby would be gone by now. Maybe Cal had been cooking. Maybe…

Marlo licked his lips and started up the bike.

TWO

"Come on, Triani, you must be just a little curious about the kids?" Eulio sat up on the weight bench and wiped the sweat from his neck and shoulders.

"They're just a gimmick." Triani pulled off the sweat band holding back his black curls and ran a slim hand through his hair. "Why would I want to see them? Where's the soul in kids dancing like trained animals?"

"*Soul*?" Eulio grinned at his dance partner, his round blue eyes sparkling. "You're jealous, is that it? Because you weren't that good at that age?"

"What? I was good enough never to be in the chorus! In any company! Ever!"

"What's that got to do with soul? And anyway I was only in the chorus for a month!"

"If you say so."

"Ancient history!"

Triani grabbed his towel. He wasn't sure just what it was about the Colony kids that bothered him so much. He didn't like his art form reduced to the status of side show, but it was more than that. He had seen the clips. He had been in the Dance Bar across the street a few days ago watching, seeing the fans, *his* fans, transfixed as they watched, their faces softening, smiling dreamily as if falling in love with the Colony brats. Maybe Eulio was right. Maybe he was jealous. Of course he knew the fans would come back to him, that they hadn't really left, but still, it rankled. And he did feel that what the Colony kids were doing cheapened everything he stood for. On the other hand, he had to admit they were technically incredible. That didn't make him feel any better about them.

"What's the matter? The new one in the chorus didn't give in to your incredible charms last night?" Eulio teased.

"Shut the fuck up!" Triani sat down and put his head in his hands.

"There's no need to be rude!"

"It's Giazin."

"Oh. What's that child done now?"

"I don't know. The school won't tell me till I get there."

"That sounds bad."

"You think? Holy shit, Eulio, I'm at my wits end with this kid! And he's only seven!" Triani got up abruptly and grabbed his dance bag. "I better get going. See you later."

"Good luck," Eulio called after him.

Less than an hour later Triani stepped out of his late model air-car onto the landing pad of Giazin's school. Dressed in tight black velvet pants and an emerald-green satin shirt under a vest embroidered with jet beads, he looked the picture of what he was, one of Merculian's greatest dancers. His image was everywhere, his beautiful country home much photographed and talked about, his tempestuous love life a source of never-ending gossip.

Gateway was one of the city's top schools for youngsters expected to be the next leaders in their chosen field. The children of many of the city's top celebrities in the arts and in government went here. Right from the beginning Triani had been determined his child would attend this prestigious school, which he himself could never have gotten into. It hadn't been easy, especially since Giazin was a willful child, used to getting his own way and clever at figuring out ways to achieve it. Whatever he had done this time Triani would have to be diplomatic and ready to appease the school leaders. Again.

The main door snapped open and he walked through a stained glass hallway into the Grand Room, filled with sunlight and shadow, long windows open to let in the sounds of children singing and the heady scents of the spectacular flowering rope trees. Triani looked around regally, as if he had grown up in this sort of place, then walked over and bowed to the three school leaders, standing in a row behind the long, floating table.

"Thank you for coming, *Chai* Triani," said the one in the middle.

Sibalian, his name was. Sibalian something Morana.

"I am always here for my child." That was not strictly speaking true but it sounded good, he thought, and Triani needed it to sound good now.

"If we had the contact for Giazin's other parent, we would have contacted him, too."

Shit. This must be really serious. "As you know, we are no longer together," he began carefully, "and right now, Savane is in the process of moving back to the city."

"Please sit down."

All three sat down at the same time. Triani tried to remember if the other two had ever spoken to him in this room but couldn't. The visitors' chairs were not meant to be comfortable but Triani tried his best to lean back and look at ease. His rings flashed red and orange in the sunlight as he waved one hand in the air. "Well, here I am. Have at it."

Morana cleared his throat. "I'm afraid your child has gone too far this time, *chai*. The Colony Dancers are visiting us here today and earlier they performed for the whole school. Afterwards they were to have a meet-and-mingle time with the Middle Circle group, who are about their age. But Giazin insisted he be allowed to go to that, too. We said no. Firmly. Later someone noticed Giazin was not in the Junior Circle room and went looking for him. We found an older student shut in a closet where Giazin had pushed him and locked him in. Giazin had taken his bracelet pass for the event and had managed to get into the Middle Circle meet-and-mingle without anyone noticing. He was there for about twenty minutes before we found him and took him away, much against his will."

He sat back and looked at Triani, waiting for a reaction.

Triani stared back. "So, you're telling me you lost track of my child for about a half hour before finding him. And this is why I pay these high fees?"

"I think you have missed the point, *chai*."

"I don't think so," Triani said icily.

"Giazin has lied, stolen and physically attacked a fellow student. That is what this is about." The Head Leader stood up. "We cannot tolerate this behavior, *chai*. This is why we have, reluctantly to be sure, decided to expel him."

"What?" Triani sprang to his feet and reached for the jeweled presentation dagger at his waist. The gesture calmed him, but not much. "This is as much the school's fault as Giazin's. If you hadn't lost track of him he wouldn't have been able to do any of that!"

The Head Leader just looked at him without expression.

Triani sat down again. "Look, I know he can be a handful. But a lot of it is my fault because I'm away so often on tour and making guest appearances all over the known universe, practically, so he acts out for attention."

"That may be so but it is not relevant. He cannot be allowed to disrupt the running of the school."

"Surely that's a bit of an exaggeration."

"No, it is not. I'm afraid he has to go."

Triani swallowed. This couldn't be happening.

"There are other schools, *chai.*"

"Not for my child," Triani said firmly. "Look, I don't have time for games. What's it going to take?"

"This is far from a game. We have given Giazin chance after chance and he does not improve. In fact, he is getting worse."

"Then he needs help, not expulsion."

"In that case, hire a Child Specialist. We can give you a list."

"Done. Hand it over. And Giazin stays put, right?"

"No."

Triani felt the anger and frustration but held on to his temper. It was a major effort, but Giazin's future was worth it. His brain scrambled for something he could offer as a bribe, something that would tip the scales in his favor. But he sensed that credits alone would not work any magic this time.

"I know you have many parents here who are celebrated in their field," he began carefully, an idea beginning to form. "I also know that now and then some of them come here to talk to the students." He paused.

"That's true."

"I have never had the time to do this but at the moment, it's possible I may be able to clear a morning to come and talk to your senior dance students." He paused again.

The Leader held both hands out as if balancing two different weights. "One morning," he said quietly. He shook his head.

"Look," said Triani, beginning to feel desperate. "Giaz must be made to realize that what he did was wrong, I know that, so I suggest suspension as a good way to do this." He watched the Leader, but his expression did not change. "During that time," Triani went on, inspired, "the Child Specialist you mentioned could visit and do some work with him."

The Leader nodded slowly. "One morning would not be nearly enough to make a difference to our senior students who are even now preparing for their first competition."

"As you may remember I was a judge at the last Laurel Rose event," Triani reminded him.

"I realize that, *Chai* Triani, but they need more than one ninety-minute time period of coaching. I would suggest three weeks as a reasonable period."

"What?" Triani bit his lip. "Three days. And Giaz stays."

"Three weeks coaching and Giazin is suspended for two weeks."

"One week coaching." Triani watched the Leader's face. There was no change. He sighed. "Okay, you win. Two weeks."

The three Leaders stood as one and bowed. "Giazin has already been sent home with his governor, *chai*, since we had no idea when you might get here. We will send you the senior class schedule and will let them know the good news."

Thinking it best to say nothing, Triani bowed his head briefly and left.

He strode through the archway and across the playfield, feeling good that he had achieved his goal of keeping Giaz in the school, even at the cost of some time for himself. He smiled with satisfaction. He had just reached the main gate when a child rushed up to him and pulled his sleeve.

"Triani, wait! I'm Rio. I need to talk to you!"

Triani looked down into the anxious face of one of the Colony Dancers. "Sweetie, I'm sure you've heard I'll jump into bed with practically anyone but I draw the line at children."

"No! No! I don't want that! I'm family! I'm Rio, your—"

"You think you're the first one to try this con on me?" Triani pulled his arm away roughly. "Claiming to be a long lost relative? Wanting credits or intros to famous people, anything to grab a piece of what I've got? Fuck off!"

"But—"

"Rio!" One of the dark-suited Guardians accompanying the Colony Dancers came rushing up and grabbed the child roughly. "I'm so sorry, *Chai* Triani! They get excited, you know."

"Keep that one away from me!" Triani turned away. The nerve, he thought, smoothing out the satin material the child had grabbed. The fucking nerve!

He climbed into his air-car and initiated the contact button for Savane. His ex wanted to be a parent, then he could fucking act like one and take some responsibility! He conveniently ignored the fact that he had kicked Savane out of his life to begin with when Giazin was very young. Of course Sav was falling apart then. Now he was back on track. Or seemed to be.

THREE

The murmur of voices died down as the youngsters from the Colony filed into the large rehearsal hall, dressed in red tank tops, black tights and short frilly white socks under their dance shoes. Their long hair was tied back with red ribbons. Eulio smiled. Triani, he noticed, paid no attention as the kids took their positions along one wall. As if on cue, they turned all together and stood facing forward, their feet in the first dance pose, backs arched, shoulders back. Two of the blue suited Guardians who were always with them sat down at the front to watch.

"Those kids are like little robots," murmured Alesio beside him.

"Just well trained," Eulio responded, moving into position beside Triani, who seemed miles away. Eulio poked him, something few others would ever dare do. "I need to talk to you after class."

Triani glared at him, annoyed. Then he noticed the Colony kids. "What the hell are they doing here?"

"Hush."

The music blared out the opening chords that always sounded the beginning of the company workout, then stopped. Mal, who was the class leader today, stood rubbing his hands together, smiling. "I'd like to welcome our guests, the Colony Dancers, who are joining us in class while they're here. I understand they have already warmed up in the small rehearsal hall assigned to them so let's begin."

The class proceeded through the usual formula dance steps and combos, then advanced to the more complicated combinations and then the diagonal solos, where each dancer got to soar across the room, doing the assigned steps in between, then return, doing more or less the same thing but with a partner while everyone else watched.

Eulio gazed, mesmerized, as the children matched the professional adults step for step, leap for leap. Even their partner dancing looked just as good as the adults'.

"You have to admit they're amazing," he said to Triani as the music died away.

"I never said they didn't have technique," he answered, grabbing a bottle of water from his dance bag.

Eulio ran across the room to congratulate the kids and grabbed the arm of the pale blond on the end of the row. He almost dropped it again when a wave of pain hit him. He patted the child on the shoulder. "You were really good, really professional."

"Thank you. I'm a principal with the company." He bowed his head and joined the dark-clad guardian who had moved up beside him.

"Of course! Forgive me. I don't know who's who yet. And I am looking forward to your performance tonight." How awkward, Eulio thought as he headed back.

"That kid is really hurting," he told Triani.

"Aren't you? I am!"

"Not like that!"

"They've got their healers with them. What did you want to talk about?"

"How did it go with Giazin's school?"

"Shit, Eulio, I don't have time to go into it all. Let's just say I've called in Savane for help."

"Really? I didn't know you two were still talking."

"Sort of. I've given him legal access to our kid so he may as well help. Want to be a parent, act like one. So, what do you want to talk about or do you just want gossip you can dine out on for a while?" Triani grabbed his dance bag and threw it over his shoulder.

Eulio took a drink of water and followed him along the hall towards the dressing rooms. "It's about the wedding."

Triani groaned. "Now what?"

"Manilo is driving us crazy with his grandiose plans and complicated charts, insisting on meetings when all he has to do is let us know and we can send a message yes or no. I think he likes to hear himself talk in that lovely low voce of his."

"What's he want now?"

"A meeting with you, me. Orosin and his Wedding Witness."

"Oh? Who's standing up with him?"

"Some old friend from his music school days. He's coming in all the way from Nercalo and he'll be here tomorrow."

"Holy shit, Eulio! I have so much going on right now. This Giazin thing is big! I'm supposed to be home tomorrow to meet the Child Specialist we have coming over."

"Didn't you just say Savane is there? And where's Parla?"

"Parla doesn't know, okay? And don't you fucking tell him!"

"God's teeth, Triani, I do have some sense! He's *your* lover!"

"And he's *your* cousin. You tell him everything!"

"Oh shut up. Not about you. Anyway this wedding meeting won't take that long."

"I've got to change and get out of here." Triani paused outside the ivory door with the pulsing gold star above it. "Look, one hour for your precious Manilo and then I'm outta there," he said, and went inside, snapping the door shut behind him.

Realizing he had forgotten his legwarmers, Eulio turned back to the rehearsal hall, and found the Colony kids still cooling down. The one with the long black hair caught his eye and held the look. Surprised and a little curious, Eulio went over to him, picking up his legwarmers along the way.

"I always forget something," he said, smiling.

"As long as you remember again." The child wasn't smiling, Eulio noticed. His dark eyes gazed at him steadily. One hand made a subtle gesture, the symbol of pleading.

"I hope the child is not bothering you, *Chai* Adelantis. They have been told not to."

Eulio began to pull on his legwarmers. "Certainly not. As a matter of fact, I came over here to invite him to lunch in my dressing room. I'm having a light meal brought in and there's plenty for two."

"I'm afraid that's not possible, *chai*."

"Nonsense. It would be good for us both to have a little professional exchange. Don't worry. I'll bring him back in plenty of time. Come, child. Bring your dance bag."

Out of the corner of his eye Eulio saw the guardian reach to stop the young dancer but he slipped out of his grasp and ran lightly into the hall after his savior.

"Thanks," he said simply.

"They work you pretty hard, don't they. You don't seem to have much down time."

The youngster shrugged and stepped into Eulio's large luxurious dressing room.

"Wow! What a great room!"

"Triani's is just like it."

"Honestly, it's Triani I really need to talk to. It's urgent. They watch us all the time so I haven't had much chance."

"He's gone by now, dear. By the way, what's your name?"

"Rio Porvan Erlindo."

Eulio stared at the young dancer. He was one of the very few people who would recognize that last name. He swallowed. "Really?"

The child nodded. At that moment Eulio was reminded sharply of Giazin. This one was a few years older than Triani's child, perhaps, but an unmistakable family resemblance now that it was pointed out.

"So that's why you want to talk to Triani? You're some sort of relative?"

"He's my sibling. That's why I worked so hard to come on this tour, why I have some hope I won't have to go back. If I can talk to him, I mean. I need to stay here! I want a normal life!"

"A dancer's life is always hard, physically."

Rio took Eulio's hand in both of his own small ones. "Do you feel that? Do you have that kind of chronic pain to deal with? Do you get a constant stream of drugs pumped into your body in order to keep you going?"

Eulio pulled his hand away, tears welling in his eyes. "God's teeth, child, we have to get you away from these people! Now!" He jumped to his feet.

"No! Please!" Rio grabbed Eulio's arm then let go. "Forgive me. I shouldn't have touched you like that, but—"

"No, you shouldn't have." Eulio sat down again. "But you made your point." He reached for the wine. "Tell me what's going on."

"May I eat while we talk? I'll have to leave, soon. We have a tech rehearsal in half an hour."

Eulio handed him a plate of berry bread and poured some *pamayo* juice in his glass. "Triani doesn't talk about his childhood, but I gather he doesn't know about you?"

Rio shook his head. "I was born on the Colony."

He made short work of the layered bowl Eulio had handed over. Then he wiped his mouth and swallowed. "I'm sorry. I shouldn't eat so fast."

"You're hungry." Eulio poured some more sugared *celerin* into his bowl. "Drink it! It's what I do when no one's around."

"I can't imagine you ever doing such a thing!" Rio smiled impishly.

The angle of his head, the high cheek bones, the glint in his eye, so like Triani, Eulio thought, but without the sexual heat. Maybe that would come later as he matured.

"Tell me why you have so much pain, Rio," he said.

"Well, it's complicated," Rio began. "Everything was fine until just a year or two ago. I was happy there, even though I rarely saw my parents anymore, partly because they had moved to Minacordia and it's quite far away, and partly because, once you join the company, they discourage visits from outside our little world. We grow up there very, very isolated from the outside world. It's to help us concentrate, they say. Even on tour, we're kept apart although it's not usually as strict as this," he added.

"That's not how we do things here," said Eulio.

"We had no way of knowing. We thought it was like this everywhere, if we thought about it at all. Anyway, I want to stress that I had a happy childhood. I don't know what Triani says about—"

"I told you, he doesn't talk about his childhood," Eulio interrupted.

"Honestly, I loved the school. I was overjoyed when I was accepted into the company and I was thrilled when I became a principal."

"When was that?"

"Five years ago. But I—"

"Wait! How old were you then?"

Rio put down his glass and took a deep breath. "*Chai* Adelantis, I warned you it's complicated. Honestly, I'm afraid I don't have time to explain it all now. If you could just set up a meeting somewhere so I could talk to Triani…"

"What are you saying, Rio? I don't understand any of this."

Rio clasped his hands together and frowned in concentration. "Honestly, I don't know how to do this without help and I realize I'm asking a lot, but I've tried on my own. Three times I've tried and it won't work. I can't get away long enough."

Eulio poured more wine. What the child was saying made little sense to him, but there was no doubt he was sincere. "Just tell me this. What do you want Triani to do?"

"I want to stay here, with him, for a while, till I figure things out and get some medical help. I don't think they can stop me from visiting my family. But they can't know about our relationship or they might send me back right away."

"Why?"

Rio blushed. "I don't want to boast, but I'm as well-known back home as you and Triani are here. They don't want me to leave while they still have a few years left before I...well, age out of the company, shall we say."

"I see. Well...it sounds as if this may take a long time to explain. And Triani may not react well."

"*Mertsi* says he has a temper."

"Your *mertsi* is right. We'll have to go somewhere outside the theater but I think I can arrange it. Not tomorrow. We have a meeting. I'll let you know during the class warm-up."

"Oh thank you! Thank you, *chai*! You are literally saving my life!"

I guess melodrama runs in the family, Eulio thought, but he was worried and still very confused as he watched the young dancer bow and then almost skip out the door. The time line made no sense. No sense at all. He looked about eleven or twelve at the most. How could he have been a principal for five years? And why all the pain?

FOUR

Marlo had never actually met Big Stendi. Everyone knew the gangster's name and Marlo's team had spent countless hours tracking down Stendi's various crews who were involved in his nefarious schemes. He was rumored to be very rich yet everyone swore he still lived in the River District, a dilapidated part of town inhabited by those who scoffed at laws and rules of any kind. Off-worlders and Merculians lived cheek by jowl in an uneasy truce here where Regulators went only when intel was solid and they could find the miscreants they were after without spending too much time there.

Today, however, Marlo's early recognition of Big Stendi's gang of thieves meant that most of them had already been picked up. There was no need to cross the bridge into the River District at the moment. He could stay at HQ and question some of the main perps in the comfort of the interview bubble, referred to as the 'quizzer' by the miscreants.

"Where did you get the baby, Cushna?" Marlo asked, sitting down opposite the dapper Merculian who clutched a tiny child in his arms.

"Where ya t'ink babes come from, ya razzer," he countered, pushing back his long blond hair.

"Not from you, that's for certain," Marlo pointed out, noting the lack of breasts and general sallow complexion. This one had not had a baby in many a long month, if ever. And Marlo would know. He had questioned him on several occasions.

Cushna was one of Big Stendi's best pickpockets and when the uniforms picked him up earlier today, he had been in possession of three jeweled daggers, five cred disks, two rings and four pouches, neatly sliced from the belts of their owners. Not bad for about twenty minutes work. Marlo knew the baby had been used as a distraction only and the child was duly turned over to the care officers who would track down the parent. His mother had probably been paid. Imagine renting out your child, he thought indignantly. And some people had lost their children and had their hearts broken. His mind went to the missing persons file on his desk, what his friends in the office called his "hobby" case. Four small children gone missing fifteen years ago. One had been found dead, apparently of a broken neck from falling from a tree in the woods where he had been playing. But the other three seemed to have disappeared into thin air. Many hours of Regulator work had been poured into the case under his lead but no trace of the three had ever been found.

Marlo knew he probably wouldn't get anywhere with the seasoned veteran but he tried for half an hour. It was only when he was about to hand the surprisingly well-dressed thief over to the guards to take down to the detainment rooms that Cushna began to talk.

"You want to know somma, nah, razz?" he said suddenly, lifting his head and grinning at Marlo.

"Only if it's important."

"Depends, don't it?"

Marlo sighed. Flying farts!

"So, if I spill the tea, what's in't fer me, nah?"

"Look, I can't deal in the dark. What have you got?":

Cushna scratched his short upturned nose and looked down at the table for a moment. "Okay, but I want ta go home soon?"

"Define soon."

"Like soon! Nah, razzer, this is slaps so you gotta make sure I stay up!"

"What's he talking about?" whispered Tabor, who had come in halfway through the interview.

Marlo began to stand up.

"Okay, okay. Wait!" Cushna straightened up in his chair. "I found out somma. Before you razzers grabbed me I was with a friend—a total snack he is, too."

"We're not interested in your sex life. Get on with it."

"Your loss!" Cushna grinned. "So anyways he showed me a few cases. Silver, they are, one small, one a bit bigger, ya know? They fell off the baggage cart of them dancer kids, nah? When the balloons went off, like."

"I see." Marlo ran a hand through his hair and looked at Cushna closely. One of the reasons the pickpocket got away with so much was that he looked so respectable. He was well-dressed, hair long but clean, his small hands manicured. But his eyes gave him away. They were shifty, always glancing about him. Like right now.

"What's in them?" Marlo asked.

"Didn't have time to find out, did I? They was locked, nah!"

"I see. So where are they now?"

The thief shrugged. "Depends."

"Come on, Cushna, you're running out of time, here!"

"Okay, okay. I think he may have ditched 'em inside the river grate behin' the old alien casino."

Marlo remembered the place all too well from a painful mission there about four months ago. He nodded. "Okay, we'll hold you till we see if this all checks out. Just one more thing, Cushna. Where were you supposed to meet Big Stendi after this was over?"

"Who?" The thief stretched his round eyes wide in innocent incomprehension.

"Take him away, Tabor." Marlo motioned to the youngest member of his team and left the room. He hadn't really expected much else.

He was glad to have the chance to return the stolen luggage to the Colony people and earn some kudos for something after their fright earlier in the day. He sent two of the younger Regulators to see if they could find the cases. "Just bring them back and put them with the other evidence." he said. "I'll check them to make sure they really do belong to the Colony people." After all, you couldn't believe much of what Cushna said.

Marlo picked up a handful of *chaico* chips from his desk on the way to the evidence room and munched a few as he examined the haul laid out on three tables. The crew had been fast and very efficient. Some of the objects would be easy to return like the cred disks and one of the daggers, which was a *cimbola* dagger and therefore had the owner's name engraved on it. Other things, like jewelry, would take a lot more time and the pouches might be impossible, since they rarely held ID, just recreational drugs and handkerchiefs and other similar items.

Leaving El in charge, Marlo dusted his hands briskly and headed for the door. He wasn't looking forward to this next chore.

Every year about this time he paid a visit to the parents of one of the children who had gone missing all those years ago. In the beginning, all three families would turn up at Regulator HQ trying to get any news of their children. But as the months and years passed, they became discouraged. Marlo was eventually moved to other cases and had to keep his search for the children on his own time. And then he began his visits to their homes. At first it was to reassure them that he was still working on the case no matter what his boss had decided. He and two others labored on, but no headway was made. Now, it was only Marlo, working alone.

Two years later one of the families moved away from Cap City; four years after that, the other family asked him not to come any more. They were "moving on". They didn't want this yearly ritual of ripping open the stiches from their wounds and having to staunch the blood all over again. So now he only visited the Arcili Magorana family—the only ones who had neither moved out nor moved on. When Marlo had suggested a few years ago that they might be better off without his yearly visits they seemed to almost panic. Now it was as if Marlo was the only remaining link they had to their child.

He took a deep breath and walked up to their door. It was open, waiting. As he walked through he felt swallowed up by the sadness of the house, the unseen shadows in the corners of the rooms. Even the generous spread of baked goods and *rolinis* was not enough to lift his spirits, but he smiled as he walked in, steeling himself for their eagerness. He was their one chance to talk freely about Pendorin. All their friends had grown tired of their ceaseless pouring out of memories: Pendorin at three years old, look! Wasn't he sweet? Wasn't he smart to be able to dance that well at that young age? And look! Here we all are at his first recital at four. Everyone was talking about him afterwards. There was only so long people would listen. But Marlo, he still listened, because he felt guilty. It was his job to find the child and he had failed.

He sat in their reception room, the walls crowded with images of the family of three, the ornaments and water wall and everything just the same as he remembered it at every visit. Time had stopped for them when Pendorin disappeared.

Marlo smiled and listened and looked at the new age-enhanced images Dorli had had drawn up, aging their missing child by one more year. The face looking at him was older, the childish plumpness honed away, but he still looked sweet and oddly innocent, longing to come home. He would be just past his age of majority ceremony now, would be wearing his *cimbola* dagger, have his own song, might even have the beginnings of a good dance career. Marlo winced.

"I suppose any person would have done what the others have done, don't you agree, Marlo?" Cisorin said, almost wistfully.

He wants to stop, Marlo realized, but the spouse isn't ready to let go yet. He shrugged. "I'm not one to judge such things. You are the one going through this."

"You are too, in a way."

Marlo shook his head.

"Look, here's something I found just the other day in a box I was clearing out. Look!" Dorli held out yet another image, this one of a group of young schoolkids lined up in two rows and grinning. "Have you seen this one? There's Pendorin in the front row."

"I think that was the time the Junior Circle went on a school trip to the Art Wall, remember?" Cisorin squinted at the image then reached to take Dorli's hand. His eyes were moist.

Marlo concentrated on the picture, more to keep from looking at the misery of the older couple than out of any real interest, but as he looked, something caught his eye. Or someone. A child with reddish hair, standing in the back row, grinning mischievously at his friend in front, who was turning to laugh back at him. A tickle of memory. His famous gift for recognizing faces must be playing tricks on him, he thought. "What year was this taken?" he asked.

They looked at each other. "Well," Dorli said, counting on his fingers, "it must have been about sixteen years ago. About a year before they—Well…"

"May I take a copy of this one? It's just that it's a little different from the ones I have."

"Help yourself, but it's not that clear of our Pendorin." Dorli looked at him curiously as he copied the image to his com-dev.

"By the way, what's the name of the kid in the back row? The one with red hair?"

"He was a great friend of Pendorin's, they were together all the time. And he was very gifted in dance, too, I remember that. What was his name, dear?"

"I don't remember. Does it matter?"

"Just curious," said Marlo hastily. "He reminds me of someone, that's all." I must be wrong, he thought. It's way too long ago. But it doesn't hurt to check.

FIVE

Triani strode into the small dance space and looked around at the eight students waiting there. They stopped talking at once. He was in his dance clothes, the only difference being he had chosen a white blouse cinched in at his narrow waist with a wide purple belt instead of the bright tank top he usually wore. They were a handsome group, he noticed, and they looked ready to work but it was already clear to him, just looking at them, who thought he was at the top of the class, who was worried about criticism and who was just hoping not to make a fool of himself. So like the new youngsters coming into the chorus at the company, although the chorus kids were a few years older.

"You know who I am," Triani began, "but I don't have a clue about you, not even your names. I wanted to come into this blind, not swayed by anything in your past record, your family history or anything else. So you have to show me who you are. Now."

"But *Chai* Triani—"

"You don't speak. You dance." He reached into his bag for the music cube he had prepared and set it on the small table by the window. "Places for a shortened version of the morning class routine, variation one."

"But we already—"

Triani glared at him. The youngster dropped his eyes at once and went into the first pose to begin the routine. Triani called out the order of the steps, the linking movements, the tempo, then started the music.

It was clear that the students were not prepared for this. Good, Triani thought, watching them. He began to nibble his lip to keep himself from shouting insults at the three who had looked so smugly secure when he came in. A few of the students were at least following his directions, but they looked stressed and two were completely lost. He reached over and stopped the music.

"That was shit."

"We were expecting to show you our solos for the competition. That's what this class is supposed to be for, isn't it? Coaching?"

Triani folded his arms and stared at the kid. Of course. The one who had started to complain at the beginning. The one confident enough of his standing to not even use an honorific when addressing him. The insult infuriated Triani. "Do you want to be a dancer?"

"Of course. That's why I'm here. Isn't it obvious?"

"Obvious? Not to me, sweetie, especially after that performance, so let's go through the whole routine again. Maybe this time it will be obvious!"

Triani went through the instructions once more and this time he noticed they were paying closer attention. He also noticed the startling amber eyes of the short kid on the end, and the sensuous curves of his young body, the half-smile. Shit. He started the music and watched as the group managed to keep together better and get most of it, at least. Maybe it was too hard, but they were supposed to be the top senior class, for fuck sake.

The mouthy kid looked even more sullen at the end of the exercise but Triani ignored him and walked over to a kid in the back, the one who had gotten completely lost the first time but this time had managed to get to the end without a slip and even with a dash of style. He touched the top of his head and tapped it lightly with a finger. "Up. Higher. Taller. There! Stretch your spine. Now, move to the front where I can see you better."

This meant that someone had to move back. Triani pointed to the complainer. "You. Move back. Now we're going to do diagonals. Line up and back row, take your partner from the one in front." He saw the complainer open his mouth and clapped his hands loudly. "Now!"

This exercise went better than he had expected but he still refused to let them dance their solos. In fact, he took them back to a more basic routine. He heard a muttering when he announced this but they took their places and listened as he went on. "You are probably used to taking this simple exercise quickly. Today we are going to slow it down. You'll find it's much more difficult. It's useful to learn control."

He watched them, how their legs began to tremble with the effort to control the slower movements. "You've got to learn it's not all about solos, sweetie," he murmured as he passed the complainer, who was struggling, just like the others.

After the class, Triani went to change in the room assigned to him, avoiding the amber-eyed kid who tried to follow him by closing the door in his face. That kid could be trouble which was the last thing he needed here. And the rest…well, not what he had expected. He thought back to himself at that age, but he was already dancing with a professional company, albeit illegally. The comparison wasn't fair, he knew. Still, he needed to let the school know his feelings. He was pretty sure some of the little darlings had already sent in their complaints. He shrugged into his jacket and dropped his dance shoes into his bag.

He clapped outside the Leader's door and it opened at once. He grinned. They were probably expecting him. He nodded briefly to the trio on the other side of the table and sat down.

"Look, I'm not a miracle worker," he began. "I thought I was getting an elite group all at the same level. This bunch is barely ready for the senior circle, let alone a competition. Two of them shouldn't even be there, one of them has a superior attitude that does nothing but hold him back. One kid, who actually has some talent, seems to have given up for lack of guidance."

"I hear they didn't dance," the Leader said.

"They danced alright, just not what they wanted to dance. If they don't have the basics down cold, how can they do a fu– a solo?" Triani cleared his throat. "So someone complained. What did *you* say?"

"Something along the lines that if they wanted to stay in the class they would do what they're told." The Leader raised a thin eyebrow. "One youngster sent a message saying you didn't know anyone's name."

"That's true. I'm sure some are from dance families and I'd rather not know until I decide what they can do."

"Interesting idea. I look forward to tomorrow's messages."

Triani laughed as he got to his feet and bowed. He had to hurry to get to the wedding meeting and hoped the amber-eyed kid was not lying in wait along the way to his air-car.

Parla met him at the entrance to the Benvolini-Adelantis home. "Glad you made it. Eulio is eating tranq sticks like candy and Orosin is heavily into the sherry, and it's only been half an hour."

"Sounds like fun." Triani followed his lover into the large reception room which was filled with piles of sample material, ribbons of different colors and widths, flower arrangements made of wax (also samples, presumably), images of different views of the huge Salinda Estate where the event would be held. One whole wall was covered with a long complicated-looking timetable of the three day event, marking out each section where different parts of the ceremony would take place in blocks of different colors. To one side was the list of restrictions on media coverage, the exact placement of float cams, the list of alien delicacies needed for various alien emissaries, friends of the Benvolini clan, and headshots of the wedding party with a cryptic note about security.

"Holy shit," muttered Triani looking at it all. For the first time he began to get a glimmer of the scope of the wedding of a First Order family member who was as famous as he was himself. Two thousand invited guests. The first day open to the public, so probably another few thousand. No wonder they had the City's Special Event Coordinator as their Wedding Counselor.

"Sherry?" Orosin asked with a wide smile. His face was unusually flushed.

"Sure, sweetie. I think I'll need it."

Eulio laughed and handed him a plate of strange-looking spiky fruit, all of different colors. "We're just getting to the good part," he said and winked. "By the way, the great Tulini just pulled out for health reasons."

"I told you not to ask any of the Greats," exclaimed Triani. "Too old."

"I know but otherwise there's the jealousy thing to contend with."

"Not if you invite someone from off-planet."

"Brilliant! The Colony kids."

"Ah, Euli, dear, they'll be gone soon." Orosin had been paying attention after all.

"I was thinking of the Ultraati rope dancer who happens to live right here," Triani said.

"Could we discuss this later? Triani, I want you to meet Lucaron, my old friend from Music School who is standing up for me as my Witness."

A short, portly Merculian with straight fair hair falling to his shoulders, stood up and bowed. "I think we're going to be busy," he remarked, glancing at the dark-eyed youthful Manilo who came gliding in at that moment with an armload of pale ivory lace.

"Triani," he said. "Glad you are here."

"Wouldn't miss it, sweetie."

"I should hope not." Manilo's soft musical voice managed to sound a note of reproof. "I expect you have already chosen the site of Eulio's two-day retreat?"

"Of course," said Triani, who had, in fact, given the job to his recently hired assistant. It was such an odd custom, the two about-to-be spouses each escorted off to a secret retreat where they would be left on their own for two days, no one but their Wedding Witness and his second even knowing where they were.

Manilo began to go through the ritual of picking the retreat, taking the wedding person there, leaving him, picking him up and bringing him back, suitably dressed, the morning of the third day.

"Okay, we know all that," Triani interrupted.

"Don't," whispered Eulio. "He'll just start all over again."

Which was exactly what happened.

"But I know all that," Triani muttered to Parla.

"Hush dear, or we'll never get out of here."

Eventually Manilo spread the lace material out on the large table in front of him. "These are the wedding veils," he said, gesturing to them in case they weren't sure which material he was talking about. "Three each, remember. The first one is removed after processing halfway to the wedding pavilion by their Witness. Hand that one to your second. Then there is chanting, singing etc. and you process up to the pavilion and remove the second one. Then more chants etc. When you step inside the pavilion, the walls become opaque, remember and nobody can see in. Then you assist the High Priest to remove the final veil."

"Hey, Eulio, what are you wearing under that last veil?"

"Guess you'll have to wait and see," his dance partner replied and smothered a laugh with one hand.

Manilo gave him a reproving look.

Triani sighed. "I am never getting married," he said firmly.

"Good to know," murmured Parla.

SIX

"What's the matter?" Beny sat up and looked down at his lover anxiously. "I thought you liked that?"

"I do! I really do! Don't stop now!"

"Do you think that after all these years together I wouldn't notice that niggle of worry under your skin? Or that you were trying to shield me from it?"

Eulio sighed deeply. "I'm sorry, love. I really was enjoying it, I just couldn't let go."

"What's wrong?" Beny arranged pillows behind his head and reached over to fluff up Eulio's cushions, too. "I know Manilo is a pain but he *is* getting it done and no one else has his experience with such large events. People are falling all over themselves to donate their services, by the way, just because we have the City's Major Event Co-Ordinator as our Wedding Counselor."

"That's nice, dear," Eulio said, but it was obvious he wasn't listening. He sat up and looked at his lover, his blue eyes troubled. "Orosin, I think I may have gotten myself into something…difficult."

Beny reached for the sherry, conveniently nearby. "Tell me."

"It's about Rio, one of the principals with the Colony Dancers. He gave me a signal…Well, in dance it means 'help', so I invited him to my dressing room for lunch. He's in a lot of pain and wants to stay here after the tour is over to get medical help. And he's Triani's sibling, so he wants me to arrange a meeting with him."

"Wait a minute. I thought Triani doesn't have any relatives."

Eulio shrugged. "He doesn't know about Rio, although they look so much alike I can't believe nobody's noticed. Anyway, there's something really wrong about all this. Not that I think he's lying but he's not telling me everything, either. He says it's complicated and I believe him!"

"But why all the secrecy?" Beny asked, scratching his head. "Can't the child do this himself?"

"They never leave the kids alone. Even in class with us there are at least two Guardians, as they call themselves, always there watching. I think the company is afraid one of their principals will defect. Apparently Rio's very well-known on their planet."

"They're all Merculian citizens, though. How could they 'defect', unless they hide in the Serpian Embassy, which I would not advise."

"Maybe that's not the right word. Rio didn't use it. The main problem is I promised to set up the meeting with Triani and now I'm really worried about what might happen."

"Like what?"

"Triani is going to hit the roof about this and he'll be furious at me! Remember, he has carefully hidden the fact of his single last name all his life. If Rio is his sibling, the name will come out."

"Surely the parent realized this?"

"From the little I've picked up about that bastard of a parent, he may not have even thought of the effect on Triani."

"Or he might not even know what his younger child is planning."

"True. I hadn't thought of that."

Beny took another sip of sherry. "You know, dear, the Colony Planet has been in a rebellious state for some time now and from what I gather from diplomatic gossip things are very bad there. The Mining Group pulled off a coup of sorts years ago and seem to be running things with a hard hand. Everything they do is about credits. They even made the work day longer for the miners."

"I thought they used 'droids for the mining."

"The hard physical part, yes, but some people still have to be down there with them to make sure nothing goes wrong. Mining *troxite* is complicated. And there are a lot of Elutians around, for some reason, a few even part of the Signet."

"I don't pay any attention to politics." Eulio leaned against Beny and sighed.

"If you decide to go through with this, dear, make sure you have others with you. And you may need a witness. Triani won't do anything too drastic if you have someone there like Marlo Dasha Bogardini, for example."

"The Regulator? That's a good idea. And he knows about the secret of Triani's shameful birth."

Beny shook his head. "I don't like this. I don't like this at all!"

The next morning, Beny watched as Eulio took off in their faded blue air-car with his usual carefree abandon on his way to the theater. Beny was about to go back inside when he caught sight of Manilo approaching from the other direction. Without thinking about it, he fled around the first dome of the house, across the courtyard and through to the garden. He paused only a few seconds to check his right hand to make sure he was wearing his cred ring, then opened the gate and hurried outside, almost running into Thar-von Dell, his Serpian friend.

"I take it Manilo is coming?" The tall blue male raised a silver eyebrow.

"Yes, and I'm just not ready to face him all alone. I'm sorry if you were planning to swim, though. We can go back and—"

"No, no. I would prefer not to run into him either. Let's just walk down to the park."

They began to stroll, Thar-von adjusting his steps so that Beny wouldn't have to run to keep with his usually long stride.

"Von, you know I would have chosen you to stand up with me at the wedding if I could."

"I understand, Ben. There is no need to keep referring to this 'no non-Merculians' rule in the wedding party. I am aware of it. And I am also aware of the honor of being invited to the Third Day. Thank you."

"You know that includes coming to the Second Day when the ceremony actually takes place, don't you?"

"Indeed. I will be there."

"Are you bringing that gorgeous female I saw you with at the embassy gala?"

Thar-von cleared his throat. "That is unlikely," he said. "She is my boss."

"It looked more the other way around to me," Beny remarked with a grin. "By the way, does the off-planet celibacy rule apply when you're with another Serpian?"

Thar-von didn't answer. Bloody damn, Beny thought. I must have stepped across that line. Again.

By now they had come to the park and Beny sat down on a bench carved from tree trunks. After a brief hesitation Thar-von sat down beside him, leaving plenty of room between them, and stretched out his long legs.

Around them the flowers and birds and chirping plants were waking up in the sunshine. They sat in companionable silence for a while, but Beny couldn't help thinking about Eulio and what he may have gotten himself into.

"Von, what do you know about the Colony Planet?"

"What sort of thing do you want to know? I've never been there, by the way. These days they make it very difficult. You need special papers and they ask a lot of questions I don't think they need to know. They charge a considerable fee, as well. You aren't thinking of going there for your wedding trip, are you?"

"No, no, nothing like that. It's just that with that children's dance group making so many waves I realized I know nothing about the place except it belongs to Merculian."

"'Belongs' is not a word I would expect to hear from a diplomat."

"Slip of the tongue. I know we invaded way back in the dark ages when we, apparently, still did that sort of thing."

Thar-von shook his head. "Hard to imagine," he murmured, "but you know why it happened, don't you? They have the *trox-ite* mines, remember. Merculian and others needed a lot of it and sources elsewhere were drying up."

"Not a part of our history we usually bring up."

"All peoples have those dark periods in their past. The original people who lived there went underground, where they stayed. There were encounters now and then, mostly in the mines as you would imagine. I think they eat the stuff. For the most part, the Merculians who live there never meet the Originals."

"Don't they have a real name?"

"I imagine so, but they never tried to communicate. They just... vanished."

"They may have died out by now. It was a long time ago."

"True."

"I remember hearing about some kind of a quiet revolution and some group taking over running things."

"True. Merculian didn't interfere because...Frankly it was just easier. They wanted to keep the *troxite* flowing. Other planets felt the same way, so now the Colony Mining Organization runs everything. As far as I can find out, they basically rule as the major part of the Signet of Seven, with a small well trained council, and they're very hard line. That might not be completely up-to-date intel, though."

"That's fine. It's better than I have. What about the dance kids? Do you know anything about them?"

"When they arrived I was curious so I looked them up. They are big earners for the CMO and the three directors of the Colony Dance company. It's like a large village, completely self-sufficient, shut off from the world behind high walls. There are about thirty-five members of the company at last count, and one group or another is always on tour on the Colony and around the few trading stations nearby. They demand very high fees—and get them, too—and charge a lot for the performance clips they sell. And then there's the school they run to feed the company."

"Well, we have big dance schools here."

"Are they isolated? Secretive about their methods?"

"Well, no." None of this was making Beny feel any better about Eulio. His lover's big heart was leading him into trouble, Beny felt sure of it. He turned to his friend and told him what Eulio was setting up.

Thar-von shook his head, his silver hair stirring. "The *horvax* raised with song birds will spend a life time trying to sing," he said at last.

"I imagine that may be true," said Beny, but he had no idea how this applied to Eulio and his efforts to help this kid. But no surprise there; in his experience, Serpian proverbs were never very illuminating.

SEVEN

"**H**oly shit!" Triani grabbed his ankle after bashing into a pile of travel boxes in the dark hallway. "What the hell is going on? Why is it dark in here?"

The Keeper arrived at his side with his usual swift glide and coughed. "This…person arrived insisting he was moving in but I would not allow him to move anything, since I had not been informed." He sniffed.

"Oh for fuck's sake." Triani hopped past the boxes. "You *know* Savane."

"Yes, but he has not actually lived here for many years, *chai* and I was not informed—"

"Yeah, yeah. I should have told you. It's been a rough day." The Keeper loved the power he wielded in Triani's chaotic household a little too much, but he was good at what he did, if not necessarily how he did it, and Triani restrained his temper. "Just get it cleared out of here."

The words were barely out of his mouth before two house 'bots rolled up, raised the boxes into the air on a magnetic float and rolled away with them.

It's getting awfully crowded in here, Triani thought, as he set off to find his ex. He already had a staff living on the premises, the Child Specialist had moved in last night and here was Savane. A good thing Parla had suggested building another dome area beyond the second courtyard. He had showed Triani the plans just last week. Still, neither one of them had ever mentioned the possibility of Parla moving in. Yet.

He found Savane on the floor outside Giazin's room, picking up toys. He looked so happy, his face flushed with laughter, his hair tousled from play.

"Triani!" Savane jumped to his feet and flung his arms around him.

"Don't get carried away, sweetie." Triani pushed him off, but more gently than usual. "You sure acted fast. It usually takes you a few days to get rolling."

"Not when Giaz needs me. Thanks for calling."

"Don't thank me yet. And why all the luggage? You're only staying a week, two at the most, remember!"

"I know. I know, but I need something to wear, don't I? You're the last one who should lecture me on having too many clothes!"

Triani had to admit Savane had a point. He leaned one shoulder against the wall. "Where is the little bastard?"

Savane stamped his foot. "Don't call him that! Even as a joke!"

"Okay, okay. Simmer down. So where is the little angel?"

"Well, things were going well until Big Doc By-the-Book Ardian told him he could only have half an hour free play time this afternoon because of something he had done before I got here. So Giaz ran away somewhere and it took quite a while to find him. By that time he had disconnected the light system in the hallways and wouldn't tell us how he did it. They're still trying to get it going again."

"Shit. I may be coaching at that damn school the rest of my life if this goes on. Where is he now?"

"The doc took him in the small salon for a serious talk."

"Best of luck to him. You'd better unpack. First guestroom on the right okay?"

Savane moved close enough for Triani to feel the heat from his willowy yielding body.

"Hey, sweetie, what are you doing?"

Savane said nothing. With a quick motion he leaned over and kissed Triani on the lips, then turned and strolled off to unpack.

Triani watched him go, suddenly reminded of why he had ever fallen for Sav in the first place. He sighed.

Just then the lighting system hummed on. It was time to do some more work on his wedding present, that one special dance that only he could perform for the happy couple on their special day. Much of it would be wasted on Benvolini but it was Eulio he was dancing for. He was the one who would pick up all the little touches and pieces of business from dances they had done together on stage. It would, he hoped, amuse his partner and with luck, bring a tear to his eye. Of course, Benvolini would enjoy the music, so that had to be just right, too. It was a lot of work for such a short piece.

He was just coming up from his studio when the peace and quiet was shattered by screams and yells. Triani began to run. Outside Giazin's room he found Savane arguing with the famous child Specialist, Ardian.

"Triani, tell him Giaz should have some toys, will you? It's cruel to take everything away from him at once." Savane turned to Triani, tears running down his cheeks. He was holding a box of 3D puzzles.

Those tears had done him in so often years ago but now, remembering what was at stake, he steeled himself against them. "Is this true?" he asked, staring into the round grey eyes of the doctor.

"I am here for one reason only: to change the behavior of your clever, willful, and very spoiled child," Ardian began. "If I am not left free to do my job, I will leave. Now."

Triani shifted uneasily. He wanted to tell the nasty character to go, but realized that Ardian was part of the deal he had made with the school. There was nothing he could do. "Surely a few puzzles—"

"No. He must be made to see that he has to earn things. Earning his toys back little by little is one step to this. First, he has to settle down and stop these tantrums."

Triani and Savane looked at each other.

"This is always hard on the parents," Ardian went on, his voice now more soothing. "But the rules must be followed. Here. At school. And later at work. You must agree, no?"

"Shit," muttered Triani, who had never been one for rules.

"It hurts my heart to hear him cry," said Savane, his voice breaking.

"Then I suggest you move out of earshot," said Ardian crisply. He sat down on a chair and crossed his arms. It was obvious he was not moving.

At that moment an earsplitting shriek came from behind the locked door. Savane reached for Triani's hand. "Let's get a drink."

Triani led the way to his private sitting room but they could still hear the frenzied cries. "Grab the glasses, Sav, I'll bring some bottles." Rattled far more than he cared to admit, Triani grabbed the two closest bottles along with a bowl of buzzers and headed towards the garden. Out there it would be quiet, at least.

Clouds were gathering overhead but at least they could no longer hear the shrieks of their furious offspring.

They sat down on the first bench they came too, under an arch of whispering flowers. Triani set the bowl of buzzers down between them and opened the first bottle. It was not the mild mint he had thought, but *lim*, a much stronger drink.

"Shit! I didn't know it was going to be like this," he said, pouring the *lim*. His hand shook and a little splashed over the side. He popped a buzzer in his mouth and leaned back, noting the faint ray of sunlight just touching Savane's golden-brown hair.

"Where'd you find this quack anyway?" Savane took a long drink, one hand plunging into the bowl and taking out a few buzzers.

"I told you—"

"No, you didn't. You shouted that Giazin was in trouble, about to be kicked out of school for some shit and, and I quote, 'You'd better get your ass out to Hanging Rock and do some fucking parenting, for a change,' unquote." Savane glared at him and grabbed the wine bottle for a refill.

"Okay, so I was upset. Anyway, the quack was recommended by the school."

"Why are you so insistent he goes to that school anyway? Is it because Eulio went there?"

"What? You idiot! I didn't even know!" Not at the beginning, anyway, he added to himself. When he had found out, he was even more determined that Giazin get in, and stay in, which was proving even harder.

They sat together, lost in their separate thoughts, staring morosely at the beautiful garden as the night birds began their evening salute. As the cloudy sun began its slow descent, the evening flowers released their intoxicating scents. Triani breathed deeply and opened another bottle. He was finally beginning to relax.

"How did Giaz get like this?" Savane said suddenly, turning to face his ex.

"Are you accusing me of something?" Triani shot back, sitting up straight.

"Oh for fuck sake! I never could talk to you! I just asked a simple question, because all I remember is sweetness and love from him. He was such a charming child."

"Yeah, sure. I'm surprised you can remember anything about him back then, you were so wrecked half the time."

"I had a difficult pregnancy! Of course you wouldn't know any-thing about that since you were hardly ever there when I needed you!"

"You knew what to expect! You knew I was on tour a lot! You were even on tour with me once so don't tell me this was all a big surprise!" Furious, Triani jumped to his feet.

"You just can't stand criticism, can you, even when it's true. Especially when it's true."

"You had everything you could possibly need!" shouted Triani.

"Except you!" Savane wiped his eyes with the back of his hand and emptied his glass. "Are we out of wine?"

Triani tipped up the last bottle. "I can go get more, if you want."

"It's okay." Savane sniffled again.

Triani sat down and reached over to lift a lock of hair off Savane's cheek. "It wasn't all bad, was it?" he murmured.

Savane looked at him through his tears and shook his head, smiling. He slid over and laid his head on Triani's shoulder. Triani pulled him closer, his fingers playing with the long curling hair. He felt the sudden hot wave of emotion, felt his own response. He swept Savane up in his arms as the bowl of buzzers went flying. "Pull them off," he whispered, and began to wriggle out of his own pants. In moments they were both naked and on the ground, Savane's hot fingers dancing over the erogenous triangle of flesh above Triani's hard muscled ass.

"You could always turn me on," Triani murmured.

Savane laughed. "Anyone can turn you on, hon."

"Stop talking." He slid his tongue inside Savane's warm mouth. And then the rain came. Sudden. Loud. And heavy.

"Shit!" Triani jumped up and pulled Savane after him into the house. "In here." He pushed open the door to his sleeping chamber.

"My clothes!"

"Get them later. You have plenty of others." Triani pushed the damp Savane onto his bed and jumped on top. "Hmmm." He began to lick the warm damp stomach, savoring the forgotten taste of that moss-scented skin, the hint of rose gel mixed with sweat. He could feel the swell of his own masculine sex, the trembling of Savane as he opened himself, the heady waves of pleasure.

"How long has this been going on?"

Triani froze. He felt his sex jerk and begin to shrivel, the sharp pain as Savane tried to pull away, grabbing for something to cover himself.

"Parla! I didn't think you were coming tonight."

"Clearly." Parla stood in the doorway, staring at the sweaty couple, his green eyes slits of anger.

Triani jumped up and pulled the naked Savane to his feet. "Get out," he hissed.

Savane ran past the elegant Parla, covering his emerging sex with one hand as he squeezed by.

"It doesn't mean anything, you know that," Triani said. "It just happened."

"In the bed I considered *our* bed? With all these rooms and acres of grounds you have to do that here?"

"But—"

"What *does* mean something to you?" Parla turned on his heel and walked away.

"Parla, please! It's nothing! That room was closest, that's all. It's just a room!"

"Why is your ex here in the first place?" Parla called over his shoulder.

"He's just here to help with Giazin! I needed the kid's other parent here for the school. Shit! Giazin's in trouble and—"

"Giazin is always in trouble. I guess this time you didn't bother to tell me." Parla stopped suddenly and turned to face his lover. "Does it ever occur to you that I might come here for more than sex?"

"What? Of course!"

"No, Triani. It's clear I'm not an important part of your life. This whole thing with you has been nothing but a charade from the beginning." He turned and stalked out through the colonnade.

"That's not true! Parla! Come back!"

But Parla kept going, the lights glowing on as he progressed and fading as he passed by.

"It's just a room!" Triani shouted. He slumped against the wall. "This is not all my fault! And besides, it's my house," he added.

He rested his forehead against the wall, shaking with anger and sexual frustration. Damn Parla anyway. He's the one who always wants to talk, but does he ever listen? Holy shit!

Triani marched through the house, passing a group of humming 'bots gliding over the wall outside the guest chamber where Savane was getting into a sleeping robe.

Striding into the room through the open door, he shouted, "Take that off. We're not finished."

Savane turned slowly and let the gown slide down his body to the floor. He fell back on the pillows with a smile.

EIGHT

"Look at these two images, El," Marlo said, reaching for a handful of *chaico* chips from an open container on his desk. "Does this look like the same kid to you?"

El glanced at the wall where the images hung. One was brightly colored, the young face smiling, red hair blazing in perfect ringlets around the oval face. It looked professionally done, the lighting bringing out the red-gold glimmer in the hair, but it couldn't hide the hint of sadness in the light brown eyes. The other image was dimmer, perhaps having been taken in overly bright sunlight, and showed a younger child about 4 or 5 years old, grinning at someone just out of range. This child, too, had reddish hair and the face was the same shape.

"They look very similar," El said cautiously. "Siblings, maybe?"

"Or the same person a few years apart?"

El shrugged. "Could be. As I said, they look very similar, but the one in the second image isn't clear enough to tell for sure."

"I cropped it from an old snapper."

"The first kid looks like one of the kids who vanished fifteen years ago. In other words, part of that cold case you're not supposed to be working on."

"I'm not exactly working it, but don't you see how similar they are? The second one is a publicity shot of one of the Colony Dancers named Corvin something."

"So it obviously can't be the same kid. Leave it alone."

Marlo sighed. "I wish I could find a better picture of that first kid. I don't even know his name."

"Do you know the school?"

"You're a genius!"

"It took you long enough to notice," El said. "It's a waste of time anyway, like I keep telling you. Anyhow, I have to take this stuff to the tech unit upstairs. See you later." He picked up the green box off his desk and walked out, leaving Marlo still looking at the photos.

Marlo sighed, switched off the images and opened a drawer, rifling around to see if there was a sweet snack in there somewhere. Nothing. The second drawer, however, revealed a pink biscuit, still dusted with colored grains. He slipped it into his mouth and bit into it, closing his eyes to savor the burst of heavenly flavor.

"Are you having an orgasm or just thinking about your last meal?" Old Livid sounded right beside him.

Marlo's eyes snapped open and he swallowed the biscuit hastily. He coughed. "Just thinking I should go and check the silver cases we think may belong to the Colony people," he said, and coughed again. The biscuit had not gone down smoothly. "A few of my team finally found them."

"I see. Don't let me keep you." Old Livid made a harrumphing sound and headed to his own office.

"Flying farts!" muttered Marlo. He grabbed some water and took a drink. Why couldn't his boss stay in his own office and stop snooping around in his?

The main room of their unit wasn't busy today and most of the work spaces were empty. But Marlo found two of his team in the room being used for the evidence from the Big Stendi haul. Some of the surfaces formerly piled high with loot had been cleared, the various pieces identified, tagged by Reg-image and returned to their owners. But the two silver cases he was looking for lay on a table by themselves, waiting to be opened and inspected.

"Someone has been with them all the time?" Marlo asked, though he was pretty sure of the answer.

Ferdalyn nodded. "I took delivery of both of them half an hour ago and Tabor was here with me. Both our images are on record."

"Good. Let's take a look." Marlo lifted the bigger case, weighed it in his hands. "Not very heavy," he remarked.

Ferdalyn handed him a laser key. "I think this will do the least damage," he said. "It's set at the lowest range."

It was a simple lock and it sprang open right away. Inside was crammed with small transparent boxes, each with a first name written in glitter on the top. The name Corvin caught his eye on the end of the last row. He popped the box open to see what must amount to the child's precious possessions: two gold rings with tiny stones of different colors around one side, several sparkling bracelets, a few folded papers, a cred disk, a pin with the logo of the dance company in gold and a medal on a long crystal chain with PRINCIPAL written on it in red. He flipped open another box and found similar things, but no gold medal. This child had not yet made it.

Marlo closed the suitcase feeling slightly guilty. It made perfect sense that the children's valuables should be all in one place when travelling. But these small items were private and somehow a little pathetic. The last box he had looked into had only a pair of small dance shoes, blue hair ribbons and the company pin. Maybe they had more personal things in their own luggage.

The small case was heavier and the lock much more complicated, forcing them to call in a techie from upstairs to solve its mysteries. The contents made Marlo stare. The case opened in layers, each tray filled with different colored bottles and syringes. On the bottom were blocks of large, square containers, each a different color and each with an injector on the side. Nothing was labelled.

"Medicine?" suggested Ferdalyn.

"Not like any medicine I ever saw," Tabor said.

Marlo pulled out his com-dev and pushed the contact for Charlo, the post-death specialist, and asked him to come up. Surely he would know something about drugs, even though his patients these days had already passed onto a plane where drugs were of no more use.

"Sure, sweet cheeks. I jump at the chance to see my favorite person!"

But once he arrived and looked at the contents of the case, Charlo sobered up quickly. Without a word, he sat down and proceeded to sniff, then test samples with the drug kit he had brought with him.

Marlo sat down to watch.

About ten minutes later, Charlo looked at Marlo, his face flushed. "I don't know what they're giving these kids or why, but one thing I can say for sure; this is not the usual drug stuff Healers carry around with them to help the sick. Some of this stuff is very powerful, and some doesn't even register with my kit so I'll have to take it to the lab for further analysis."

"Anything obviously illegal?"

Charlo pursed his lips and stared at the rows of bottles. "Talking about the stuff I've checked, not really, but these doses of painkillers, for example, are way too strong for kids. Unless they dilute them, of course. They might have brought the concentrated form since they'll be here so long and may not have wanted to have to restock. But some of this other stuff? I have no idea why they would want it or even what combining these drugs might result in. I'm going to have to bring in a specialist, one who knows more about the living." He snapped his kit closed. "You know…" He paused and looked at the younger Regulators who were listening avidly.

Marlo waved them out and muted the room. "Tell me."

"Listen Marlo, this is not official, get it? For you only, so don't quote me!"

Marlo nodded and made soothing noises, waiting for the usually ebullient and forthcoming Charlo to continue.

"I'm troubled by some of this. Seriously troubled. I managed to separate a few known elements, mostly benign, from that large yellow square container, but they're mixed with something I don't recognize and it worries me. From what I can see, one of them appears to be a hormone of some kind, not a drug at all, but I'm no expert at this stuff. Another seems to be something that's used, or used to be used, to repress sexual activity, but they're far too young to have to worry about that sort of thing! Look, how far do you want me to go with this?"

Marlo looked at the colorful vials and bottles that now appeared so suspicious. He remembered the pain and terror he had felt coming from the red-headed Corvin, the child he had caught on that first night. "Call in whoever you need, Charlo. Just make sure they take the oath of secrecy. We don't want the Colony Guardians to get wind of this."

"Have they reported the case missing?" Charlo asked, pausing at the door.

"Not yet."

Charlo hitched the strap of his kit up over one shoulder. "If I lost my drug case, the first thing I'd do would be to report it missing, that's for damn sure."

It was late when Marlo showed up at the Theater Residence where the Colony group was staying, the large silver case by his side. He hadn't told them he was coming, hoping to catch thm unawares, with no time to prepare any polished answers. The door was opened by an older Merculian who ran the place for visitors.

"They're in the main reception room, *Com* Bogardini. And a right commotion they make, too. It's a nice change from the usual adult professionals who are always wanting service of one sort of another. They look after themselves, so we leave them to it. They've got almost half the place to spread out in, since there are no other visitors here this time of year. The door's right here."

He clapped vigorously.

The door swung open almost at once and a short child in a long sleeping gown grinned up at them.

"Hi! Want to come in? We're just having rec time."

"Sutini! You should check who it is, first!"

"Why? You're not the boss of me!"

"You little turd. Shut up!"

A taller child with long straight pale hair leapt gracefully over a foot stool and pulled Sutini away from the door. "He'd let in Serpian Pirates if they clapped politely," he said, pushing the smaller child back to his chair.

"Luckily it's just me, *Com* Bogardini," said Marlo, walking in and looking around.

It was a large, airy room, hung with pale silk drapery at the large round windows with many images of famous dancers from history hanging on the walls. The room was filled with comfortable chairs and footstools which had probably once been arranged in some sort of order but were now scattered all over, most filled with small bodies, sometimes two to a chair, chatting and fixing each other's hair. There must be about 20 of them, Marlo thought, Several chased each other around the room, calling each other rude names. A few were curled up near the far wall, reading. Two just sat on a large footstool holding hands and watching the others. One of these was Corvin, the red-head Marlo had caught in his arms the day of their tumultuous arrival. His friend had long black hair, now in a thick braid over his shoulder. The others were all wearing sleep gowns with the deep lace ruffles, all except the two hand-holders, who wore black briefs and nothing else. Their heavily muscled thighs were almost obscene.

"You've brought the case with our boxes!" cried another child rushing up to Marlo and reaching for the case.

The blond slapped his hand away. "We're not all barbarians, *Com*," he said apologetically, "but they're excited about tomorrow's outing and some of us have cred disks in that case."

"We're going to a Snack House," said Sutini, grinning from ear to ear.

"Oh I recommend them," said Marlo, with enthusiasm. "Try the *chaico* chips."

"They're probably not allowed." That was Corvin. "Things are rarely allowed that might be fun."

"Old sour puss," muttered someone else.

"Just let them have their expectation of fun, at least." That was one of the readers.

"Shut up!"

"You shut up!"

"Make me!"

"Probably bad for the diet," Marlo said quickly, sensing something ugly in the air that had not been there before. He was about to suggest someone go call an adult when one of the Guardians Marlo hadn't seen before came running in through a side door. He looked tired.

"I'm *so* sorry. No one told me you were here," he exclaimed, bowing and ushering Marlo to a chair. Then he raised his head and shouted "You two, stop running around and go to your room. Where's Briden?"

There was silence for a moment. Then Corvin's friend spoke up. "He crashed, *chai*. I took him to bed."

"Good. Too much excitement." He sighed. "I probably shouldn't have left them alone so long. Children overdo it sometimes."

Corvin snorted.

"All right, out! All of you! Time to rest. And you, Sutini. You'll have to remove all color polish from your fingernails and toes tomorrow, remember."

"But no one will see my feet!"

"Alright, just your hands, then. And no makeup!"

Sutini scampered off after the others.

Corvin and his dark-haired friend remained. "We'd like our boxes now, Nibtin," Corvin said.

The Guardian sighed. "Don't push your privileged position, you two. Being allowed to dress as you like in private does not mean wandering around half naked, and you know it."

"Our boxes, please, Nibsy." The dark-haired one held out his hand imperiously.

Nibtin retrieved two boxes from the case and handed them over. "Now go to bed," he said, and watched them saunter off.

"Problem?" Marlo asked, curious.

"They're both principals, and they both have swelled heads." The Guardian sighed. "The night shift gets a little out of hand sometimes. Over tired, over excited and childish energy needing to let loose. Anyway, not what you came for. Thanks for bringing over one of our cases. How may I help you?"

"I'm Marlo Dasha Bogardini. I wanted to bring the case as soon as possible."

"Thanks so much. That saves me a trip. We just realized it was missing today. Because of the outing tomorrow, the children want their things, you know, hair ornaments, bracelets that sort of thing. And credit disks, of course. They want to go to the dance stores your pros go to."

"Yes, of course. It took a while to locate it."

"There's a smaller one, too, heavy, with a serious lock. It's our back-up pharmacy. I noticed when I was looking for the other one today that its missing, too. Lucky we didn't have an emergency."

"There are Healers at the theater, I understand, and plenty of others not far away."

The Guardian smiled and smoothed the material of his long blue robe over his bony knees. "Some of the children have physical problems and we've pre-mixed medicine for them before we left. We have our own healers with us who know the children intimately. I'll send someone over tomorrow to pick it up."

"That won't be necessary, *chai*. When it's gone through our system I'll bring it to you myself." Marlo got to his feet and bowed. For a moment, he thought he saw the dark-haired young principal watching him from the door to the other rooms but when he looked again, the face was gone.

NINE

"It's not a military maneuver, dear," Eulio said, and patted Beny's cheek reassuringly. "Tell him, Von."

The tall Serpian gazed thoughtfully into his drink. "It sounds more like an ambush to me. Perhaps not military, precisely, but still..."

"Big help you are," Eulio muttered. "Anyway, I'm off. The 'ambush' is scheduled for after company class."

"How do you know Triani will go to his apartment then?" Beny asked.

"He won't right away because he has an appointment with Nevon about the guest principal who now says he won't partner with Triani. He thinks Triani's style too wild or something. Personally I just think he can't handle those huge dramatic leaps Triani does. Anyway, that won't take long, I expect, and then he'll go to his apartment, as he always does. Wish me luck!"

Eulio ran out of the garden and through the house, almost tripping over a pile of tiny sculptures suspended by ribbons. More samples. What was Manilo planning now? He didn't bother to check, figuring he'd know soon enough. The wedding was edging closer.

He had talked to Rio only a few times since their disturbing lunch but the youngster had made a point of telling him about the half-day break the group was getting today so this was the perfect time to act. He had to get something settled between the kid and Triani before the wedding, after which Rio's story would be the furthest thing from his mind.

As he entered the rehearsal hall, Eulio saw at once that the Colony dancers were much more animated than usual, whispering to those close by and using rapid hand signals to those farther away to avoid notice. Probably excited about finally getting out in the city. Triani, on the other hand, looked absolutely morose. Giazin's regime must not be going well. Eulio felt a tinge of guilt thinking that he would soon be loading more worries on his dance partner's shoulders but there wasn't enough time to do this properly. The Colony kids would be leaving town soon, returning only to dance on the last day of the wedding and then off home. He had to act now!

"The kids look happy for a change," remarked Alesio, taking up his place beside Eulio. He bent over to adjust his shoe.

"They have some time off, I think," Eulio said.

"I guess it doesn't take much to cheer you up when you're that age."

Eulio glanced at him. "You ever wish you were that age again?"

Alesio grinned. "Well, we had a lot of fun but there wasn't any sex, so there's that."

Eulio laughed, then got into position for the start of their daily routines.

It seemed to him time went more slowly than usual. He found himself glancing at the ancient time-piece high up on one wall, something he rarely did. As the minutes crawled by he began to feel almost short of breath, his active mind calling up some of the bad scenarios Orosin had hinted at that morning, the very things he had laughed off at the time. He glanced over at Rio, the child's face total concentration, his small body technical perfection. Eulio noticed the rehearsal director looking at him, puzzled. Eulio snapped his mind back to business and soared into the air on cue.

When everyone had cooled down, Triani headed out at once but it wasn't as easy for Eulio to get away. Everyone seemed to want to chat about the wedding; what to wear, what delicacies had been chosen, how many people were invited for the Ceremony. When he finally made it, he found Rio outside his dressing room and ushered him inside.

"Are you sure you want to do this?" Eulio asked, yanking off his tank top and pulling a loose-fitting blouse over his head. Forget the shower. There wasn't time. "Hand me my hair brush."

"I'm sure, *chai*. Is this the one?"

"Thanks." Eulio pulled the brush through his dark blond hair, grabbed a pair of shoes and stepped into them. He smiled at the young dancer, noting his colorful full skirted jacket made of many-colored ribbons. It was a hopelessly old-fashioned style, like most of the Colony group's clothes, but it suited the kid. "You look very nice," he said kindly.

"Thank you. I made it myself for a party when Libalin was promoted to principal last year." He swallowed. "Honestly, how mad do you think Triani's going to be? I mean not warning him we're coming?"

Eulio shrugged. "I guess we'll soon find out. Let's go."

Eulio had been asking himself the same question. Another thing he was worried about was running into Triani before they all got to the apartment. He wanted the Regulator, Marlo, to be with them and Pom, the company healer. He needed witnesses and a healer to check the kid's overall health.

Luck was with them as they hurried through the corridors to the side door of the theater but outside a crowd of fans and vidsters had apparently been waiting for some time. Waiting for Rio. How had they found out? The questions began raining down at them at once.

"*Chaisalin* Rio!"

"What's it like being in Cap City for the first time?"

"Hey, Rio!"

"*Chai* Adelantis! How do you two know each other?"

"Rio! Do you know Triani, too? You look a bit like him."

"You have any new solos coming up, *Chaisalin* Rio?"

Rio jumped back on the top step, beaming at them. He was obviously used to this sort of fame. He kissed the tips of his fingers and made a scattering gesture over the crowd. "Thank you! Thank you for the warm greeting!" His childish voice was surprisingly strong. "I hope to see some of you in the theater tomorrow night where you can see my interpretation of the Night Bird. And then—"

"Yes, but right now we're rushed for time," Eulio broke in, reaching out for Rio's hand and bracing for the pain he knew he would feel. To his surprise, he sensed very little.

"I took extra blockers this morning," Rio said as they crossed the street and walked to Triani's building. "It's something they let us do when we're going out in public for rec time."

Eulio nodded.

Marlo and Pom Roni Dalia, their company's healer, were waiting outside Triani's white and gold door. They both looked anxious, their foreheads creased with worry.

"I'm not quite sure why I'm here, *chai*." Marlo stepped forward, pushing back his hair with one hand. "I'm not an expert on the law but if I understand things here, the youngster is a relative of *Chai* Triani, right? So this is not kidnapping. Quite the opposite."

"I know. I know it looks like way but this is complicated, *Com* Bogardini. Believe me, you help by just being here and I appreciate it." Triani is going to kill me, Eulio thought, as he placed his hand on the carved door frame to let the system recognize him. The door snapped open.

"Oh, this is gorgeous!" exclaimed Rio, walking slowly into Triani's sumptuous turquoise and black space. "It's almost like a stage set."

Eulio glanced around him absently. "I guess so." And in a way, I think it is, he added to himself.

"Holy shit!" Triani appeared dramatically in the doorway on the top of the three steps leading to the sleeping quarters, his black curls damp from the shower, his tight black top gleaming with sequins. "What the hell are you doing here, Eulio? Did Parla talk to you? Is the Adelantis army of morality invading? Hope you brought some good drugs. I'm nearly out. Hah! You didn't need to bring the *razz*, for fuck's sake!"

"There's no need to be rude," said Eulio.

"Says the one who barged in with his posse without an invitation. And what is that little shit doing here?" He pointed to Rio. "Trying to con you, too?"

"If you let me get a word in edgewise I'll tell you. I'm helping him get a chance to talk to you. You need to listen, Triani."

"Why? Because the little con artist pulled on your heart strings? How much does he want, have you got that out of him yet?"

"What are you talking about?" Rio's young voice almost cracked with emotion. "I'm a principal dancer. I get paid well! And I'm not trying to con anyone, least of all you."

"Applause for you, sweetie. Then what the hell are you doing here?"

"I need your help."

"Aha. Here it comes."

Eulio tensed. "Tell him your name," he said to the youngster.

Rio cleared his throat and straightened his narrow shoulders. "I am Rio Porvan Erlindo, and—"

"Just a minute." Triani stared at the youngster, his eyes narrowed. "Sure," he said at last. "If you are who you say you are, you would know enough never to come anywhere near me."

"But I am!"

"Look at him," said Eulio, moving closer. "Just *look* at him!"

Triani walked around the youngster, slowly. "I see a kid with black hair like mine, wearing a ridiculous out-of-date outfit not even an eight-year-old would be caught dead in, trying to look like my kid. All part of the con. Right kid?"

"There. Is. No. Con." Rio blinked back tears.

Eulio felt the urge to rush over and give the child a hug but he restrained himself. The youngster had to handle this himself.

"*Mertsi* said you wouldn't welcome me with open arms," Rio said, staring up at Triani.

"Open arms? *Open arms!* Holy shit! You have got to be kidding!" He laughed again and grabbed a bottle of Crushed Emeralds. "Shit. I need a drink."

Rio touched the wide bracelet he wore and an image sprang into life on the one blank wall: A tall Merculian, looking exactly like an older Triani, stood with one arm around a smiling Rio, who wore an old-fashioned high-waisted lacy tunic similar to what the troupe had worn on their arrival.

Triani spun around and hit the wall, spilling some wine. "Turn that off! Now!!"

Obviously frightened, Rio did as he was told.

"The nerve! The utter fucking nerve! That bastard had the sheer nerve to send you *here?* To *me!* And all this time I was hoping the bastard parent was dead! But no! He just goes on, ruining more lives! Heaping more shit on me! Why doesn't he just fucking die" He dropped into the white chair nearby.

"You take that back!" shouted Rio, leaping forward, one arm raised.

"Oh, so this is what the bastard parent taught you? To hit people?"

"No! Our parents don't do that. You should know."

"*Our* parents. Fuck. You really don't know shit about me, do you?"

Rio brushed tears out his eyes and backed away. "Well, he never told me about you until the tour to Merculian was announced. Then he did and some things made sense. I suspected I had a sibling, but…"

"I'm not surprised he kept me a secret," Triani said, leaping to his feet again and beginning to pace. "Once he needed me, I'm sure he painted a lovely happy picture of my childhood amidst the illegal drugs and drunken lovers he slept with in exchange for bubble dust."

"You're lying! He loves us! He said so!"

"Not to me he didn't!" shouted Triani. "Not when I came home to find him lying in his own puke and nothing to eat in the house but—"

"Triani, stop!" Eulio ran over and grabbed his arm.

Triani pulled away. "What? You expect me to turn off all that rage burning inside me for most of my life? Just like that? Because I now have another family member I never wanted?"

"Let's go." Rio turned and marched to the door.

Eulio pulled him back. "Forget all the family history, Triani, for god's sake, and just listen to him."

"No more shit about the Bastard Parent." Triani sat down again. "Wait. I have to cancel my lunch date." He pulled out his com-dev and sent a message. "Okay, So, kid—"

"My name's Rio."

"So, Rio, what's the plan? If you don't need credits—By the way, where does your salary go since you're so young, and such a hot shot principal and all? To the…parents?"

"*Mertsi*'s been holding the credits for me."

"I bet. You can kiss goodbye to a big chunk of it in that case. I'm surprised he wants to let go of his nice little earner."

"Triani!" Eulio felt like slapping him.

"Why are you here, Rio? In my home?"

"Honestly after the way you're behaving I don't want to be here anymore than you want me to be, but I need medical help. I'm not the age I look. I've been a principal for five years, and it's taking its toll on my body."

"Ah," said Pom, moving over to stand beside Rio. "At last something that makes some sense. They use puberty blockers on the children?"

"They use a lot of things on us. I don't know exactly what they all are. We're in pain a great deal as we get older and have to leave once it gets too much to bear. They call it euphemistically 'aging out of the company.' I figure I have maybe two years left, at the most. But I don't want to go to the cottages. I want to dance! It's all I can do! It's what I love. So I need help. *Mertsi* said the medical healers here are much better then on the Colony. And anyway, the ones we see all work for MinaCor."

"What's that?" Eulio asked.

"The mining company."

"I thought that was the CMO."

"They have lots of names but it's all one thing. Honestly, the mining companies control everything now, my parents say. So this was my one chance to get away and get help. So he sent me to you."

"Must have been high," muttered Triani.

"How old are you really?" asked Pom.

Rio dropped his eyes and clasped his hands so tightly his fingers went white. "I'm not sure exactly, *chai*. They don't want us talking about our age and we never celebrate the Birth Day feast I used to have when I lived with my parents."

"What a crock of shit. Of course you remember how old you are."

Rio's head snapped up and he almost spat at Triani. "That proves you don't know shit about me, either!" he shot back.

Triani shrugged, a faint smile curving his lips. "Point to you. Go on."

"Honestly, every day is the same. There are no celebrations to mark the ending or beginning of a year, only the ending of a tour or major show, so these are irregular. Once we're accepted into the company and go through the probation and initiation phase, our parents or friends, if we still have any on the outside by this time, are strongly discouraged from coming to visit. Sometimes they even say we're on tour or sick or something when parents visit. This happened several times to me but *mertsi* kept coming back. Until they moved, of course. A lot of the kids are orphans and have lived in our compound a long time, so they have no clue."

"Excuse me." Marlo stood up and moved closer, his curiosity getting the better of him. "Do you know Corvin? Do you know how old he is?"

"Who cares about him?" asked Triani.

"I do," said Rio, throwing back his head. "He's my lover."

"Holy shit. I guess we're related after all." Triani downed the rest of his wine. "So, stop pissing around and tell me how old you are."

"I would if I knew for certain, but I don't. *Mertsi* didn't have time to get hold of the birth registration."

"Make a guess, for fuck's sake!"

"Oh sure! So if later on you find out I'm off by even half a year, or more likely a whole year, you can hold this against me and say I lied so maybe all of it was lies!" Rio burst into tears.

"Fuck!" Triani poured himself more wine.

"I can help with the birth reg," Marlo said.

"Yeah, yeah." Triani waved his words away irritably. "So what's the plan? What did the perfect parent think I would do for you, for some reason?"

Rio glared at him, his black eyes blazing. "If I'd known what you're really like, I wouldn't have agreed to this," he said, "but I need a relative to stay with. It's the only way I can break the contract, I think, and I want to leave the company so I can start medical treatment to try to help me grow, and get…better. So I need a place to stay while this is happening. I have credits—"

"Oh shut up about the credits!"

"I can pay my way!"

"Okay! So if you want to leave the company, I can get my crack legal team on it to break the contract for you to your advantage and if it makes you happy, you can pay them. Anyway, who signed it?"

"*Mertsi.*"

"Of course! Why ruin just one kid's life! Two is always better!"

A tense silence filled the room. Rio's face flushed red with anger, but he controlled himself. "Thank you," he said icily, "but right now it's better if the company knows nothing about our relationship or my plans. They'll stop me the minute they find out."

"Oh really," Triani drawled.

"Honestly, you don't know what these people are like. I do, and take it from me, they *will* stop me. Whether you believe it or not, I'm valuable to them. So I'll do the rest of the tour, finishing at *Chai Eulio's* wedding. After that, the company is leaving to go back to the Colony right away."

"And you want me to help you get away, hidden in my crowds of fans."

"I have crowds of fans back home, remember." Rio wiped his eyes.

"Turn off the tears, for fuck's sake. You've got what you wanted so get the hell out! All of you! I have a headache."

TEN

Triani lay on the floor staring at the ceiling. His stomach churned and cramped. He had kicked out all his uninvited guests about twenty minutes ago and he was now exhausted. Reaching for his com-dev he cancelled the rest of his appointments for the day and lay down again. Damn Eulio and his bleeding heart!

Triani's stomach cramped again, hard. He rolled onto his side and threw up, splashing the greenish contents over the thick-growing rug. He lay back a moment, feeling slightly better, then summoned the closest house 'bot to clean up. He crawled to his feet and walked unsteadily up the few steps to his sleeping chamber to change his clothes and take a pill to settle his nerves. The image of the haggard-looking Parent with his arm around Rio haunted him. That face. That dancer's body exactly like his. The half-smile. And Rio, looking so much like Giazin, only a few years older. But was he? The kid had refused to say precisely, finally breaking down in tears. Triani wanted to know how old he himself had been when the kid was born. How quickly had the hated parent forgotten all about the child he had abandoned on Merculian?

He sat down at his dressing table and stared at his pale face. The shock was still in his eyes. He winced and began to dust his cheeks with color. His lips with a touch of red. Sparkle dust in his hair. He needed to talk. He wanted Parla but wasn't sure he would accept Triani's call. So far he hadn't. Triani would have to go to his house and hope to hell he was in.

By the time he arrived at Parla's place, he was feeling better physically but strangely nervous about his reception as he clapped at the door. He knew he could open it with a wave of his hand but he thought that might not be appreciated. And besides, he didn't want the humiliation of finding out Parla had wiped his DNA from the house system.

"You look tired." Parla stood in the doorway, his green eyes serious and a little sad.

"Yeah. Look, Parla, I'm sorry."

"I know. So am I." He turned and lead the way to the beautiful room under the glass swimming pool that was the roof.

No kiss, Triani noted, following him. Parla always kissed him, or touched him in some way. Shit. So that's the way it was going to be. No forgiveness today. He sprawled back in the moss-colored chair and looked up at the ceiling, through the dappled blue water above their heads. Parla had designed and built every inch of this house since moving back to Cap City. It was a marvel, jutting out of the rocky cliff into the northern part of the city, looking as if it had just grown there. From some angles, it was barely visible. Architects came here to see the place and exclaim at its wonders, but Triani had never felt completely at ease here and that was another bone of contentio between them.

I suppose I could make myself like it more, he thought, and then noticed there was a naked swimmer in the pool.

"Who's that?" He pointed to the ceiling.

"A cousin."

"Eulio?"

"I have many cousins, you know. This one will be gone in a few minutes. He just brought me some news."

"Good news, I hope."

"No. Not really."

Shit. Triani shoved his last tranq stick into his mouth and placed a hand over his still tender stomach. As he looked more closely at Parla, he realized he didn't look much better than he did himself. "What's the matter?"

"No, Triani. You come to the party but you never stay to clean up."

"Why would I? There's staff and 'bots for that. What are you talking about?"

Parla smiled. "So there is. How silly of me."

Triani narrowed his eyes. "What the hell is going on with you? I said I was sorry."

Parla got to s feet." Come on. I want to show you something."

Intrigued, Triani followed him out into the inviting corridor under a waterfall, leading to the steps up to the pool. Halfway along in a lighted alcove he stopped surprised, gazing at a large image of himself and Parla, dancing down the stairs at the Gala opening of the new Wave Entertainment complex Parla had designed.

"We look so happy," Triani said.

They stood together now looking at the image, the way they were looking at each other, the electric connection at the tips of their fingers as Triani twirled under Parla's arm. Of course, that was before the Savane incident.

"See that narrow bridge over your shoulder, to the right?" Parla said now. "Someone fell from there this afternoon. Luckily he didn't die."

"Accidents happen."

"I know, but they say I'm to blame."

"Why? Did you push him off? Come on! He slipped. He was probably high or something. Who knows? It's not your fault."

"It might be more complicated than that."

"Shit. You're an Adelantis. It should be easy to get out of that with your legal team."

"Oh, Triani dear. Never change."

"I don't intend to."

Parla slipped an arm around the dancer's narrow waist and hugged him. "It's been a rough day."

"You have no idea," said Triani. He tried to pull Parla closer but he slipped away again.

"Let's do some smoke."

"Works for me," said Triani, although he was a little surprised. Maybe Parla really was worried about the silly accident.

Back in the beautiful reception room, Parla produced two globes from the serving cupboard and handed one to Triani. The dancer glanced up and noted that the pool was empty now. Not a ripple disturbed the greenish hue of their ceiling. He slipped lower on his spine as he relaxed from the first deep breathes of the fragrant smoke.

"I have a sibling," he said after a few moments, tasting the words on his tongue for the first time.

"You have a what?"

"A sibling. His name's Rio."

"How did that happen?"

"Well, for him it happened the normal way, Parla." Triani laughed bitterly.

"But that's wonderful! You must be so happy!"

"Do I look happy?"

"Well…tell me why not."

Triani took another long hit of the smoke. "You don't know anything about me really," he began, the words sliding out with the smoke mixed with his breath.

"Only what you've told me."

"I don't know what 'family' means, Parla. I see you and Eulio with your siblings and cousins and parents and grands and it's like watching something completely alien to me."

"Who is Rio and how did you find him?'

"He found me. He's one of the Colony dancers." Triani slid lower and closed his eyes. "He thinks we have the same parents." After a few moments the words began sliding out easily, with the occasional long pause. He had never told his lovers anything about his childhood, his secret birth as a result of illegal self-insemination, the neglect and disinterest and occasional cruelty of his self-centered parent, but he told Parla. Everything. Well, almost everything. Not the sex part, the part where he was selling his very young ass for enough credits to feed his craving for luxury. Not the part about Brolio, his much older mentor whom he paid with sex on demand and who had betrayed him so cruelly. It took a long time to tell all this and after a while he became aware that Parla had slid in beside him and had one arm around his waist.

"So what am I going to do with a sibling?" He looked up into Parla's green eyes.

"You're going to love him, and help him get the care he needs, whatever that entails." Parla stood up and pulled him to his feet. "And we're going to eat something and then go to the theater later and see your sibling dance."

"Why?"

"Because you said you haven't seen him on stage and if he's anything like you, he will only show his true colors there, pouring his soul into his dancing."

Several hours later Triani and Parla took their seats in the VIP section of the theater and waited. Triani was still pretty relaxed from the smoke, though not enough not to feel a tremor of nervousness at the thought of seeing Rio up there where *he* usually held sway. "Just don't fuck it up," he muttered as the curtain went up.

The first part was cute but bland. The children engaging and sweet, and dancing like wind-up toys, just as he had expected. Rio was nowhere to be seen. And then the second part of the program. Several minutes into this, Rio burst onstage to a round of applause and the kind of energy that draws the eye and holds it. He had style and flair and he danced with the kind of wild joy that cannot be faked. Rio was right. He was a star. His red-headed dance partner had a lyrical style that worked well with Rio. Sort of like me and Eulio, Triani thought. When they took their curtain calls, Triani smiled and applauded with the rest. Rio saw him and smiled even wider. Triani nodded, but remembered the kid wanted to keep their relationship under wraps, so no visits backstage.

"I didn't expect him to be that good," remarked Parla, as the curtain came down.

"Holy shit," muttered Triani. For the first time it occurred to him he might have some stiff competition from Rio Porvan Erlindo.

ELEVEN

Marlo was glad that Boothby had resumed her routine of bringing him a small coffee with whipped cream every morning. He was only allowed one cup because the caffeine went straight to his Merculian head and he became very high, very fast. There had been a few embarrassing scenes in the past, one of them ending in both of them being ejected unceremoniously from a tony restaurant. Now he contented himself with a small cup only.

Marlo knew that the Terran female had had a mad crush on him early on in their work relationship but that seemed to have waned. He hoped she had found another Merculian, preferably younger then he, to explore hermaphrodite sexuality with. There was one evening neither could really remember when they may have done some exploring of their own but since neither wanted to bring up the topic, they left it alone.

As she brought his old data system up to date with the latest from the IPA office where she worked in cyber security, he began telling her about the Colony Dancers and that very emotional meeting between Triani and his newly discovered sibling, Rio, just the day before.

"The whole scene made me very uncomfortable."

"I bet. So they're not really little kids? That's fraud!"

"I don't know, Boothby. Some of them are. I think it's the soloists and principals who may be...well, a little older somehow. When I find Rio's birth registration we'll know for certain how old he is. It's a start."

"Super! Let's get right on it!" She cracked her knuckles and switched screens deftly.

But Marlo held up one small hand and cocked his head, just

as Orosin At'hali Benvolini appeared at the open door. Boothby instantly switched back to a gaming screen.

"I do hope I'm not disturbing you," the new arrival said, smiling widely. "I was in the neighborhood and thought of some things I would like to discuss with you. I hope you don't mind."

"Of course not! Please, come in. You know Boothby?"

"Yes, Miss Boothby. I do remember you. And it's Beny, between us."

"And it's Boothby, all the time," she said.

"*Do* you have a first name?" Marlo asked. It had never occurred to him before.

"I hate it. Case closed."

"Well then, Boothby," Beny said, moving in to sit in the only other chair. "You must be a help to our friend Marlo, with all your cyber expertise."

"I keep his ratty system updated as best I can."

Marlo shifted his substantial body uneasily. What did Beny want? He remembered another time when the musician/diplomat had appeared suddenly with knowledge he should not have had and suggested some actions to him he should not have suggested. Should he ask Boothby to go?

"Do you want to discuss something about the wedding?" Marlo asked, unable to restrain his curiosity. "Security, perhaps?"

"Yes, that's part of it. You're in charge?"

"Of the inner grounds, yes. The Black Circle is handling the perimeter. It's a big place. We're going to work on that tomorrow, I believe. We need to pull in a number of officers from the outlying areas for such a big job. But traffic is already on their bit."

"I see. Had you thought of using some of the Serpian raider troupes stationed around the city? You wouldn't need as many of them."

"Well, I guess that's true." Marlo bit his lip. The very thought of the tall muscled blue aliens standing around in a wedding party was unsettling. What was going on? "They are a bit...intimidating, though, don't you think?"

Beny shrugged. "It was Thar-von's idea, so I expect he didn't think of it that way."

"They sure couldn't go undercover," Boothby remarked, snickering. "Sorry."

Beny laughed. "That's true."

"Are you expecting trouble at your wedding?"

"I certainly hope not, but there will be alien representatives there who are not usually close to each other. And Eulio's plans for Rio are a bit disturbing. I'm afraid my beloved is all heart when it comes to helping those in distress, and gives little thought to consequences. All he sees here is a broken dance contract. All I see is reprisals."

"But the youth is Merculian. Born on the Colony Planet, which is part of Merculian."

"Technically, yes, but in reality the Colony has only symbolic bonds with our government these days, since it has been taken over by the group owning the mines. They appear to run everything now, including the dance company where the children live and perform. These people appear to be worse than the Elutians from whom they have learned much. Nothing seems to matter but credits."

"But why does the Merculian government not march in and kick them out?" Boothby asked, true to her military training.

"Sounds easy, doesn't it? But we don't do that sort of thing nowadays. We tend to take the easy way out if possible, I'm afraid. And we need *troxite*. A lot of it. We use it in everything, from air-cars to building materials. And we're not the only ones using it. We do have some mines here on Merculian but they're old and very deep and therefore expensive to run. Theirs are more numerous, the ore nearer the surface and the product quicker to arrive. Nobody wants to interfere with the *troxite* source."

"I didn't think Merculians were like that!" exclaimed Boothby. "I mean just turning a blind eye like that."

"We aren't perfect." Beny tucked one foot under him and settled back in his chair. "Many years ago we used to send our rowdy, uncooperative citizens to the Colony for a cooling off period. Unexpectedly, most of them decided to stay and they prospered."

"Sounds like a prison colony." Boothby crossed her legs.

"Of a sort, perhaps, but there was nobody there to crack the whip, as it were, and we sent supply ships up every month until they were settled and didn't want us 'interfering' anymore."

"So, like, they went rogue."

Beny nodded. "I guess they did."

Marlo sat there quietly, thinking about the Originals who had lived there all along and who had disappeared, going underground, rarely seen now, if ever. What was their name for their home planet? What did they think of all this? Did anyone know? Or care?

"None of what this youth Rio says has been substantiated in the legal sense." Beny studied his toes thoughtfully.

"But you're going along with the great escape?" Marlo asked, curious about Beny's ambivalent stance.

Beny sighed. "Eulio wants this to happen at our wedding. I want to make Eulio happy, so there you have it. Unfortunately our Wedding Councilor is the lover of my *tan* Pamiano, who is on the Inner Council, so Manilo *cannot* know about this."

"You have a plan?" Boothby cut through the fog of words, as she often did.

"On the third day of the wedding, the Colony Dancers will perform, among others, of course. Eulio pulled that one off without a hitch, so Rio will be there. We thought the best time would be near the end, when we make our way to the air-car that will carry us to our transport and off on our wedding trip. Things tend to get a bit disorganized at this last stage so we were hoping Rio might slip away then."

"That's all you've got?" Boothby asked incredulously.

Marlo smothered a laugh with his hand. He suspected that was not all Beny had, but said nothing.

"What would you suggest, my dear."

"For starters you can't leave it all up to the kid. He needs help, no matter how old he is, right, Marlo?"

"I would suggest a diversion." Marlo was remembering Big Stendi's stunt at the Holiday arrival parade.

"Yeah! Right on!"

"Very good indeed," Beny agreed. He tapped his wrist band and a map of the estate grounds where the wedding would take place appeared on the wall. "This is the latest from Manilo, showing where everyone will be just before we leave. And here is a mock-up of the actual farewell walk."

Marlo watched the animated crowds waving goodbye to the animated married couple who were moving along under a canopy of fluttering flowers. By chance, the route took them quite close to the table where the Colony kids sat. "He's certainly thorough," remarked Marlo, who knew Manilo from his organizing of city events.

"He is. And he's constantly making small adjustments that I'll send along so you have the latest."

"Those flower thingies," Boothby asked, leaning forward. "Are they real or programmed?"

'Programmed, as I understand it."

"All rightie! How about if you add more and they..."

"Malfunction?" suggested Marlo, grinning.

"Yeah! Exactly, bro! I mean Marlo."

"Excellent!" Beny was all smiles now, too. "I guess I better try to get you the plans for the things, or charts or whatever Manilo calls them so you can have a go. Oh, and you do have an invitation to Day Three, don't you? I can't remember."

"I'm going with Marlo because Calian will be out of town. I'm really excited. Especially now!"

Beny left soon after that, leaving Marlo wondering if they had played right into his hands. It didn't really matter, as it sounded like a good idea.

Boothby got down to business right away. "Okay, I'll be very busy once I get that program so let's get that birth reg done." She cracked her knuckles again and switched back to the government screen. "Just like old times, right, boss?"

Marlo sighed. "Not really. This one shouldn't be difficult to find. I could do it myself, you know."

"I know but I'll do it faster."

And she did.

They both stared at the screen where the document was highlighted.

"Are you sure you've got the right name?" Boothby asked, still staring.

Marlo showed her the program notes he had saved.

"But he can't possibly look like he does and be that old!"

"Flying farts," murmured Marlo. "He should have had his coming of age ceremony two years ago! Poor child! What have they done to you?"

And then he remembered the red-headed kid. "Look up Corvin Denini Vorson," he said.

But there was no document under that name or any other spelling of that name. On a hunch, he spelled out the other principals' names. Only Rio seemed to exist legally.

"What the fuck!" muttered Boothby. "What's going down?"

Marlo lay back and closed his eyes, holding back tears. Whatever it was, it was most definitely not legal!

TWELVE

Two days later the Colony Dancers moved on with their tour of the major Merculian cities and the focus of the vidster news hounds swung over to the Adelantis-Benvolini wedding. News channels splashed images of Eulio and Beny, trying to go about their business, Triani, wearing dark glasses and looking unusually pale and drawn and Beny's friend Lucaron, though he got off lighter because he wasn't famous.

The usually peaceful Salinda Estate now hummed with activity as large carriers shunted in with building materials, and work crews arrived to erect large parking-pad towers at strategic points around the grounds, special areas for VIP guests, platforms for entertainers in different areas, dance floors for the professionals and miles of moss-turf and ribbons and the mauve and yellow decorating drapery for the arches.

A troop of Black Circle Guards began patrolling the walls around most of the perimeter of the estate, checking for weak spots and setting up look-out towers for crowd control, while their Merculian counterparts went about trying to dress up the somewhat military look with ribbons and flowers, featuring the couple's chosen unity image. Tech crews arrived to set up the equipment needed to handle the official broadcast, and hundreds of fanciful white towers crowded with technical equipment. Bubble floats and confetti balloons had to be assembled and thousands of silver chairs and tables put in place. The airspace above the huge estate had been declared a no-fly zone for the duration.

Meanwhile, many members of the Adelantis family began streaming into the city from far flung regions of Merculian, and the Benvolini relatives, mostly coming in from diplomatic postings, were gathering together in one place for a great show of family pride. Along with the relatives, came their friends, names celebrated in the dance world, the music world and the diplomatic corps. Alien ambassadors already in the city were anxious to come and show their planet's support of two important Merculian families.

Dance fans, eager to spend any amount of time and credits to get this once-in-a-lifetime opportunity to attend their idol, Eulio's, wedding—*the* event of the year—had begun to set up camp outside the main gate, determined to be among the first guests to arrive. They wanted to scoop up wine from the wedding fountains with both hands and eat amazing creations not usually available. Something to tell their children, they said, the day they danced at Eulio's wedding and saw Triani and some of the other big stars up close

In another part of the estate almost the entire traffic division of the Cap City Regulators was being drilled on the finer points of their upcoming job, while several units of Serpian Raiders were quietly settling into the old main building to be ready in case of need. Some of the alien VIPs did not get along with others and although Manilo and his team had spent many hours trying to set things up so that the warring parties were as far apart as possible, no plan is ever foolproof. Marlo had reluctantly okayed the Serpian presence, realizing that if things did get out of hand, they were the best chance of restoring peace quickly. He had been assured that they would be wearing colorful outfits and would look festive enough to disguise their true purpose. Marlo had a hard time imagining Serpians looking festive, no matter what they wore but remembering Beny's suggestion, he signed off on it.

A week later, on Day One of the wedding Triani stood in the midst of the happy crowd, amongst the banners and music and laughter, holding Giazin firmly by the hand and greeting everyone with a smile and nod of the head. The child was ecstatic to be here at all, especially with his *tatsi*. It was a reward for being so well behaved lately, now that he was back at school. Savane had finally moved out, Parla was at least answering his calls if not his many invitations to bed and things were gradually getting back to what passed for normal in Triani's household. He was concerned about what might happen when Rio arrived, but for now, all was well.

The first day of the wedding was a relaxing time for Triani, whose only duties today were to be seen and to mingle, two things he enjoyed. Tomorrow morning he would ride off to pick up Eulio, taking with him the hair-stylist and Eulio's dresser from the theater who would help prepare him for the shimmering outfit, jewels and veils required for the ceremony. Tomorrow would be full of ritual but today was just a huge party.

Triani was just about to make his way to the children's area where he could drop off Giazin when he heard his name called urgently. He turned, smile in place.

"*Chai* Triani! We're so happy to run into you!" The red faced Merculian was well dressed but disheveled, his sparkly sash undone and trailing behind him. He must have been running to cut off Triani's retreat.

"Are you enjoying the Adelantis-Benvolini First Day?" Triani asked, remembering his job.

"Oh yes. But I wanted to speak to you." He paused to catch his breath. "I wanted to thank you for helping our Delantio at school. He had just about given up before you arrived."

Triani looked away for a moment, running over the faces of his former students before settling on the shy one who had put himself in the second row and rarely looked Triani in the eye.

"He shouldn't give up," Triani said. "He is a dancer, *chai*." Unlike one or two of the others, he added to himself.

He remembered clearly how Delantio had rushed out of the room in tears that last day when Triani shouted at him for wobbling on a toe step. It was near the end of the class and everyone had danced their solo, with Triani giving a final critique. Every one of them was better than they had been at the beginning and he had told them so. "Which does not mean you'll walk off with any prizes," he added.

Five minutes later Triani had walked down the hall looking for Delantio. He found him in the last small classroom before the garden door. "You should have waited," Triani said, striding in and sitting down beside the sniveling youngster. "I was about to tell you that apart from the wobbles, your solo was not bad. You may not be technically brilliant but you have style and a grace that some of the others lack. You feel the music."

Delantio looked up at him. "But none of that matters if I wobble."

Triani didn't answer for a moment. "Okay, sweetie, get up and show me the first six bars."

"But—"

"Do it!"

Delantio got up and wiped his eyes. Triani reached into his bag for the music cube and gave him the cue. Delantio danced. Grace. Soul. And wobble as he went onto his toes.

"Stop!" shouted Triani. "Were you taught to roll up onto your toes like that?"

The youngster nodded.

Triani adjusted his dance shoe and got to his feet. "Watch." He went through the same sequence and stopped. "What did you see?"

"You don't wobble."

"Watch again." Triani went through the steps again slowly, this time and stopped, looking at Delantio intently.

"You don't do the roll up into the toe position."

"Right. Look. Heels on floor. Slide. Hop up. Balance. See? Try it."

When Triani left a few minutes later, the kid was beaming with joy.

His parent was beaming at him now. "Delantio was in the top ten at the competition, *chai*. Thank you for your encouragement."

"It was a pleasure, *chai*." He bowed and strode away, tugging Giazin with him. The child was getting tired and beginning to whine. He would soon forget all the patient training of the last several weeks. Triani glanced up the hill and noticed Marlo pacing and talking into his com-dev. Two buttons were missing from his light-colored tunic, which was a little too long. Triani shook his head. Some people had no sense of style.

Marlo tucked the com-dev into his sash and looked up at the sky to see if Merculian's two moons had made an appearance. Alas, not yet. He sighed. His feet were hurting and he was quite peckish. Every time he sat down and tried to enjoy a snack, some other emergency demanded his attention. Luckily thus far these had all turned out to be minor: someone fell into one of the wine fountains and had to be hauled out by a passing Serpian; a team from the Drugged, Drunk and Disorderly squad discreetly helped several groups of inebriated revelers off to their air-cars; an Elution had spilled half a can of lube over a Merculian musician. Marlo suspected off-world drugs in these last two incidents. It was hard to keep all illegal drugs off the premises, in spite of all the high tech sniffer probes and the menacing Black Circle types at the gates.

And then there was this last call. Apparently a group of youths had high-jacked the programs of a bunch of server 'bots and sent them all off at high speed to the other side of the main pavilion where they fell down the hill, emitting high-pitched beeps and squeals as they landed wheels spinning in the air at the bottom. Marlo gazed at them sadly and dispatched tech Team 4 to attend to them. As he made his way to the Haberdashery Aid station to get his buttons sewn on, he took in all the music and laughter, the snap of colorful pennants and jingle of tiny bells on the intricate white tech towers dotted over the grounds. Tomorrow it would be another group, smaller in numbers, even better dressed and more aware of decorum; invited guests, friends and family all waiting for the wedding couple to appear and clasp hands in the wedding tent to be blessed by the high priest of Merculian.

THIRTEEN

"**Y**ou are *not* wearing that!" shouted Eulio, flinging open the door of the sunny Retreat Cottage.

Triani sauntered up the wide walkway wearing a very short-skirted sparkling red tunic that barley covered his crotch, his long dancer's legs encased in sheer tights. "God's teeth, Triani, if you upstage me at my own wedding I'll never speak to you again!"

"That might be a relief," Triani countered, with a wicked grin.

"And I won't dance with you ever again, either! I don't care how many contracts I have to break!"

"Don't get carried away, sweetie."

Eulio burst into tears.

"Holy shit. Come on! I wouldn't do that! The rest of my outfit's in the car."

Eulio punched him. "You…you…ass."

"It was worth it to see the look on your face." Triani gently pushed Eulio back into the cottage, noting as he did so that the love jewel around Eulio's neck was glowing deep red. "Did you really think I was going to wear this?"

"I wouldn't put anything past you." Eulio punched him again, but lightly this time. "Don't tease today. I'm nervous enough."

"Look at it this way. It's just another performance."

"A once-in-a-lifetime performance. How was Day One? You didn't insult anyone, did you?"

"Nobody important. Everything went fine."

The door sprang open and Loradi, Eulio's dresser, and his hair stylist Fritori, barged in, their arms full of the tools of their trade. They were followed by Triani's taciturn driver, carrying the boxes of veils and jewelry and the tall crown the veils would be resting on.

The next hour was filled with chatter. Eulio sat still while Fritori brushed and jelled and braided his hair, twisting in chains of pearls and crystals and one large, blue *mantino* stone right in front. Meanwhile his dresser spread out the veils, and steamed out any faint trace of crease in the delicate pleated gown to be worn after the last veil came off. He also took all the wedding bangles out of their boxes and spread them out on the dressing table.

"They're beautiful," he said, looking at the gleaming silver and gold, some studded with tiny gems, some elegantly carved, some with tiny bells attached. "I've never seen anything like them."

"They're very old," Eulio said. "They've been in my family for many, many generations. My big sibling Josna was the last one to wear them at his wedding a few years ago."

"Another reason not to get married," said Triani.

"You'll have to buy some if Giazin wants to marry someday. Or Rio. Which reminds me. Are you clear on what's happening tomorrow with Rio?"

"Yeah. Yeah."

"Tell me!"

Triani sighed dramatically. In a sing-song voice he recited his instructions: "When the music starts for your farewell procession, I go to the white tower behind the head banquet table and wait for what's her name to cause a shit storm with the humming flower things, during which Rio arrives and we just head to my air-car and take the hell off like a firecracker to Hanging Rock. See? I've got it."

"Good." Eulio popped a tranq stick in his mouth. "Are my parents there yet?"

"How should I know? I'm not on the top of their contact list."

Eulio shrugged. It was true. Although he had never told Triani, some of his relatives were offended when he had asked his flamboyant, brash, often vulgar dance partner to be his Wedding Witness instead of some First Family friend. But they did not know Triani the way he did.

"God's teeth! I'm so nervous," Eulio picked up a make-up brush, then put it down.

"Why? What's really going to change?"

"If you don't get it, there's no point in talking about it. Fritori, is that curl supposed to hang down in my eyes like that?"

Eulio watched at his stylist twisted the curl out of the way. These last two days completely alone had been unexpected torture. Several times he had been tempted to walk down the hill to the pleasure resort he sensed was there. From time to time he had heard laughter and splashing of water as the breeze shifted in the right direction which reminded him that the isolation was only contrived. He realized too that what he longed for was not just any company but Orosin. Even though they had been apart many times for long periods during company tours and Orosin's own trips, they always talked sometime during the day, if it was at all possible. And he had always been surrounded by friends and other dancers from the company. Now he had been forced to look inside himself, to really think about what he was doing, to appreciate this most important step in his life's journey. The scents of the lotions and oils spread out on the dressing table now brought a rush of images of his lover so strongly to mind that he could almost feel Orosin's presence.

At last he banished Triani from the room with orders to get properly dressed. He stood up and dropped his own robe to let the others anoint his naked body, dust it with gold and slide on the short misty lace tunic he would wear under the veils. He was used to people fussing over him and had learned to turn off all emotion when touched this way. When all was done, his dresser stepped back to admire his handiwork.

"What about my *cimbola* dagger?" Eulio asked, touching his waist which felt odd without the gold chain belt of the First Order of Merculian where his dagger should hang.

"Triani will clip that on over your wedding robe once you're in the tent. Before that, Parla, his second, will carry it. Stand still now. We need to fit the crown."

It took both of his attendants to fit the crown on his head and attach the long veils in the right order, lightest one first and then the other two, each one thicker than the one before. By the time he was ready the world looked hazy. He was glad to hold Triani's hand as they walked slowly to the waiting air-car.

The driver looked at him almost in awe before sliding the door open and murmuring the traditional wedding day good wishes. And then they slid under the bubble of the air-car and were on their way.

About a mile and a half away, Beny was going through exactly the same routine. He had not found the two day retreat as difficult as Eulio since he was more accustomed to being alone and even found it refreshing. It gave him time to think about his music, though he kept being interrupted when some musical phrase reminded him of something he had written for his lover, some phrase that had made Eulio smile, some similar tune they had played together. And he would touch the love jewel he wore, that would soon be marked with the sign of their union, and smile.

But he was not used to being fussed over; primped, powdered and anointed with sweet-smelling lotions by people he was not emotionally close to and he found this part very difficult. They had to stop several times to let him gain possession of his emotions enough for them to continue. He was relieved when it was all over and he stood in his long wedding veils and sparkling bangles and crown, ready to leave.

The sun beamed down on the wedding guests from a cloudless sky as the two participants in the ceremony arrived at the same time, at opposite ends of the long flowered path leading to the wedding tent where the *Praetan*, High Priest of Merculian, and his acolytes stood waiting in his long purple robe. Along the way stood the *epicantare* singers in the pale blue robes with bows down the front of the traditional *Meshdravi*. They were there to sing the Mercoli chants and the personal *cimbola* song of each participant.

Eulio blinked back tears of relief when he saw his parents waiting for him. He couldn't touch them and wouldn't even try, knowing they were sticklers for protocol, but their smiles were so full of warmth and love he could feel it. Parla was there, too, holding the dagger, waiting to take his place behind Triani as his second. Eulio looked around at the gathered throng. It was all quite hazy through the thick lace but he knew hundreds of his relatives, friends, admirers and fellow dancers were all here wishing him well. In the distance, on the other side of the gilded pergola where the High Priest stood, he could just make out the veiled figure of his beloved, standing with his parents and attendants, waiting.

And then the low rumble of the long twisted golden horns used only on occasions when the *Praetan* was officiating, sounded like distant thunder, sending their shuddering tremors through everyone present. Eulio straightened his shoulders and reached one hand back to make sure Triani was right behind him. He felt his dance partner's fingers, felt the jolt of support, the expectant emotion he often felt at the theater when they were about to go onstage. And then his parents started the long walk along the flower-strewn path to the wedding tent. He waited, listening to Triani behind him, doing the countdown before they began the slow processional.

The long procession was supposed to mirror the stages of life, starting out with birth, when they stopped for a long chant about moving into the world while the first veil was removed, revealing the deep blue one underneath.

The long horns blew again and they moved forward as bells tolled and music swelled. The next stop was longer and they stood at first still as statues as the second veil was removed. Then they swayed with emotion while the *epicantare* singers sang the song first heard on their coming-of-age ceremony, written just for each one, the song sang at every major event in their life ever afterwards, that would be sung in the end, when they closed this circle of life. Tears ran down Eulio's cheeks as he listened. His song was cheerful and bright, a dancer's song and it was followed by Benny's which was slower, more lyrical, with a hint of a minor key change in a few places. The emotion could be felt all through the crowd watching and listening, reliving their own *cimbola* ceremony, some their own wedding.

Then the horns bellowed again and they moved forward, closer and closer to the gleaming pergola where they would become united.

A breeze sprang up, moving the pennants on top of the wedding tent, and catching Eulio's remaining veil so that it billowed out on one side. Triani reached out to hold it down, unsure exactly what might be underneath but confident it wasn't meant to be seen by the assembled crowd. The parents were now at the tent and had moved off to the side, waiting. The couple kept moving at a stately pace and the music rolled over them in waves and the singers chanted the final chants.

And then they arrived.

Triani stared at the High Priest, never having been that close to this near mythic being before. He was very old, as they had to be,

Triani supposed, his pale face surprisingly free of wrinkles, but his bright green eyes were sunken so far back in his head they looked like tiny lights. His hair was bone-white and held in place by the purple band of his stiff, round hat that was studded with gems. Under the purple robe he wore a sparkling white shirt, visible over his thin wrists and up around his neck. Conscious that he was staring, Triani dropped his eyes and let go of Eulio's veil.

With a final flourish, the horns stopped. It was the signal to enter the marriage tent. Triani took the dagger from Parla, prepared to set in on the small table inside. Eulio nodded to Orosin, now so close on the other side of the tent and together they and their Witnesses stepped inside. Instantly the invisible walls on all sides of the sparkling edifice turned black, blocking all light except that flooding down from above them through the large clear dome. No one was to see what happened here. Even Triani felt a frisson of excitement as the High Priest spoke.

"You are here to become one in a union never to be broken. Is that a true thing?"

"It is a true thing," the couple chorused.

"You are here to become one so that there is no other for you?"

"It is a true thing."

"If one is cold, the other will bring the warmth of his body. If one falls, the other will lift him up. If one weeps, the other will dry his tears. Are these all true things?"

"They are all true things."

The rest was lost on Triani, since it was in Mercoli. He was still stuck on the realization they were now supposed to be monogamous. Marriage was definitely out for him.

And then he heard the music, his cue to help the Praetan remove the last veil. It came off easily enough, leaving behind the last part of the crown, now just a tiara of flowers and ribbons. Eulio stood nearly nude, his airy lacy tunic flaring out over his hips and stopping well above his knees. The fine pale gold lace was handmade, embroidered with tiny green leaves. Triani held the veil in his arms and watched as the couple clasped hands and faced the High Priest who took a short wand from his sleeve and held it to the middle of the love jewel of each one, chanting as he did so. Triani saw Eulio tremble and reached out a hand to steady him, receiving a jolt up his arm for his trouble. Whatever the High Priest had done it was powerful. And quickly over. When the couple turned to face their wedding Witnesses, Triani saw the Eternity symbol engraved on the love jewel, which glowed white. He had never seen one white before.

The rest was easy. Triani was handed the wedding robe, which he slipped over Eulio's head. It slid down easily, its iridescent folds flowing nearly to the ground in one easy motion. Then he fastened the gold chain and attached dagger around Eulio's waist. There were green embroidered leaves on each shoulder of the robe and Triani hooked the veil to each clasp, hidden under the flowers, so that it flowed out behind like a train. The couple was now dressed identically, although Beny had purple flowers embroidered on his shoulders. They joined hands and turned as the black walls disappeared and the crowd burst into cheers.

As the wedding party walked down the mossy slope to the dance floor, the music swirling around them, Triani stepped close to Parla. "Am I going to have to go to the Pleasure Gardens tonight?"

Parla shook his head, took his hand and squeezed it. "It's way too far," he whispered, grinning.

Triani leaned against Parla as he watched the happy couple perform their wedding dance. Benvolini was surprisingly good, though Triani reminded himself that the pair often went dancing together at the Balio, so they'd had lots of practice. But all Triani wanted now was for it to be over for the day so he and Parla could retire. They had a lot of catching up to do.

FOURTEEN

The final day of the wedding event of the year saw tendrils of fog twisting around the windows of the great estate and crawling along the ground, covering the mossy grass with a dense gray blanket. The air was heavy with mist but few in the great house were aware, except for the early-rising Serpians who were there to guard those within.

Marlo had stayed on the grounds as well, and having found a willing *epicantare* singer to warm his bed was more cheerful than he had any right to be, considering what lay ahead for him to keep an eye on. He had watched the last stragglers leave after the social dancing was over last night, had seen the arrival of the army of workers with their 'bots ready to transform the place once again. The imposing wedding tent sank to the ground under their guidance and slid in sections into the waiting containers, to be floated off to the storehouse. The long flower-strewn wedding path rolled itself up and was likewise stored away. Then the new gilded tables and chairs arrived for the banquet, a new dance floor was installed in front and areas set up for the VIP alien guests, well-spaced out. Marlo had also caught sight of the arrival of the Colony Dancers during the evening but they had been whisked away quickly to the guest house to one side of the estate. They probably needed more sleep than the adults.

From his point of view the Ceremony Day had gone very well, the only problems being expertly looked after by the Haberdashery Aid station, especially during the dancing. Several couples had been found in the bushes and one Elution had to be rushed to the Healing station when he fell asleep and his scales dried out. It took quantities of lube to revive him.

But today, although there would be fewer people, there would also be more aliens, including the quarrelsome Uzoi. And of course, Rio's Great Escape, which was scheduled to take place near the end of the day just as the new spouses were leaving.

As the day wore on, the sun burned away the mist and fog and dried the ground and by the time everyone arrived near noon it was as if it had never been there. The banquet began a little late but after that everything progressed smoothly. Special guests, close friends of the couple, gave their gifts; singing, dancing, even air-painting, all presents for the married twosome's enjoyment. And at the end, Triani appeared and performed his mesmerizing eight-minute tribute to Eulio, danced to Beny's music and brought the house down, as he had hoped.

Unexpectedly, two Uzoi leapt up with a strangled hoot, nimbly jumping over the colorful barrier that had been erected to discourage this sort of thing. Smaller than the Merculians, they made up for it with their sharp, spiky forehead horn and oddly bent legs.

"Us jump!" announced one in a strangled voice.

"Us jump high!" the other one added.

Marlo buzzed his team to be on alert. He wasn't sure what to expect but he knew they were notorious for attacking those who did not appreciate their strenuous jumping contests. If this was a contest it might go on a long time and would probably not end well. From where he stood, Marlo couldn't tell if the caps supposed to be covering their razor-sharp horns were on or off. The music had died away, the musicians not sure what to do.

A tall figure with wavy silver hair strode up and bowed to the two. Thar-von Dell. His deep voice reached easily to Marlo as he said gravely: "Do you wish a contest or an exhibition, *zzylabs*?"

"Already we say! Jump-lyy!" The first one now sounded irate.

"Ah. Forgive me. A demonstration as a gift." Thar-von bowed again and withdrew towards the banquet table where Beny was watching uneasily.

Marlo drew closer, noting that many of his team were also moving nearer. And then the hairy Uzoi began to jump. And they were certainly experts. They jumped higher and higher, almost floating into the air with seeming ease, the long red ribbons they wore around their skinny necks streaming after them, and a high humming noise becoming louder with each leap. And it went on. And on. Twenty minutes passed and people began to stir uneasily. When would they ever stop? Marlo located Manilo in the crowd and noted his look of consternation. This was not part of his meticulous plans.

Then, just as unexpectedly as they had appeared, they stopped, turned and hopped back over the barricade to take their seats.

There was a moment of stunned silence and then Beny rose to his feet and thanked them.

After that, the charming performance by the Colony Dancers was a welcome relief. When they were finished, the children returned to their table and happily tucked into the exotic food that they had not been allowed to eat until then.

By now the sun was sliding towards late afternoon and the guests were gathering on the dance floor to take advantage of the music. Triani found himself face to face with the amber-eyed youngster from the senior class at Giazin's school.

"Shall we dance?" the kid said, looking up at him through long lashes. "You're not going to slam the door in my face again, are you?"

"Do you see a door, sweetie?" Triani took the kid in his arms and swung him onto the dance floor. "But you have to let me lead," he added.

"With pleasure."

The kid leaned into Triani's body, and he could feel a jolt of desire so strong Triani stepped back a little. "You know you shouldn't play with fire, don't you, sweetie?"

"Why?"

"You might get hurt."

"It would be worth it."

Triani laughed. "Not really, sweetie."

They danced on until Triani suddenly caught sight of the married couple already halfway along the farewell path to their transport. But the dance music should have stopped well before this! By now, he should be waiting for Rio up by the white tower.

"Holy shit!" He dropped the kid abruptly, pushed his way off the dance floor and rushed towards the tower. He couldn't see who was there until he came around the end of the banquet tent. Leaning against the base of the white tower was a large Elutian, pouring some lube over his shoulders.

"Have you seen a young kid, about so high? Long black hair? Looks a bit like me?"

The Elutian just stared, then shook his head.

Over his shoulder Triani saw the wedded couple almost to their transporter. He saw the cloud of flowers that was supposed to be over their heads already swarming uncontrollably around the table where the Colony Dancers had scattered in all directions. He glanced at his time piece. It had all happened too soon. Somebody had screwed up!

Triani ran up to a group chatting close by.

"Have you seen a youngster, about this high, long black hair?"

Several shook their heads. One wearing a feathered hat said he had seen a youngster like that a few minutes ago. "He seemed to be waiting for someone. But then he ran off."

"Which way?"

Feather Hat shrugged. "I think it was that way."

But 'that way' was already crowded with people ambling to the parking pads or to the Estate where some were staying.

"Rio!" shouted Triani, heading in that direction. "Rio!" He stopped, took out his com-dev and tried to contact Parla, but there was no answer. "Shit, Parla! Pick up!" But several more tries were equally unsuccessful. Triani felt like howling in frustration. Last night had been so good between them, though Parla had wanted to talk at one point and Triani had stopped him. Still…

He was relieved to see Marlo up ahead. "I can't find Rio," he said at once, catching up to him. "What was the fall-back plan?"

Marlo shook his head. "There wasn't one, I'm afraid. Unfortunately, the music cues that run everything are all on automatic, controlled by the clock from the tower back there. Everything was twenty minutes late thanks to the sudden appearance of the Uzzois, so the recession started too early, while people were still dancing."

"Can you contact Rio's com-dev for me? I don't have the code."

"I'm afraid the children aren't allowed to have them," Marlo said.

"Well do something!" shouted Triani. "He has no idea how to operate in Cap City."

"I've put a call out to my people and the Serpian Troupe. Corvin is missing, too, along with two other youngsters from the company."

"I don't give a shit about them. Where's Rio?"

FIFTEEN

Marlo was trying to keep calm under the pressure of Triani on one side and the constant stream of lost child alert updates coming in on his com-dev. At last he persuaded Triani to join one of the active search groups while he checked the main parking pad towers, which were rapidly clearing out. Merculians were very protective of children and he wasn't too worried anyone would harm them, but on the other hand, the people running the company were Merculians and appeared to be doing a lot of harm, so it was best to check everything, including the host of air-cab drivers. He put a unit of traffic officers on that and took a stimulant. This was going to go into overtime.

Reinforcements were pouring in from everyone who had heard the child lost alert, even those who were supposed to be off shift, and a few who were technically retired. Marlo put El in charge of the newcomers and set off into the bushes with another group. He practically fell over a nearly nude couple sound asleep in each other's arms.

"Up! Up! Time to go home!" he shouted, pounding the ground beside them with his long search staff. The couple had the decency to look embarrassed as they struggled into their grass-stained wedding finery and staggered off to find an air-cab.

Time passed and Marlo finally persuaded Triani to get some sleep, assuring him he would wake him the instant Rio was found. The estate grew eerily quiet as the tech unit rolled out the float cam heat searchers and the flood lights rose onto the tops of the tech towers. The rolling fields, now bleached of their color, looked more like a cold and alien landscape, the long lines of quiet searchers resembling a tired army. It was the many patches of shrubbery and bunched flowers where Marlo was concentrating now, helped by the heat-searching probe 'bots. The problem with them was they kept getting stuck in the thick *twyla* vine ground cover.

"Flying farts," muttered Marlo, untangling yet another one. He would have preferred more actual people helping out but they were stretched thin already. And then he saw the bag. He lifted it from under the vines where it had obviously been hidden and saw the Colony Dance Company logo on one side. There was nothing inside but the frilly outfit the children had all been wearing for the performance. Rio was smart. He must have changed clothes somehow in the bushes, maybe even changed his hairstyle, tucking up those long black curls so he wouldn't stick out so much. Marlo wished he had found this out sooner. There really was no telling where the dancer could be by now. But he said nothing to the others. Instead, he ordered El and a few of his own investigator team to check out the National Dance Theater downtown.

"Keep this quiet," he said. "We don't want to alert the Colony Guardians and there's still Corvin to look for, although they might be together," he added. "And that other one."

Marlo decided to let Triani sleep and went in search of a hover-bike. He wanted to check out closer to the Main Gate, an area so obvious it had been virtually ignored. There was a large parking-pad near there along with an air-cab area and a lot of foliage. As he approached, a slender figure rushed up to him from the shadows.

"Will you help me, please? I need to get home." The youngster's white-blonde hair was long and straight, and he wore the unmistakable outfit of the Colony dancers. His hands were clasped together in front of his chest.

"I remember you," Marlo said gently. "I met you in the residence that time I brought over the case with your personal boxes, remember?"

"Yes, I know. I'm Varsili." His pale eyes looked strained and close to tears, far from the composed youngster Marlo remembered. "I want to go home, please, back to the Theater Residence downtown where we're staying tonight. Can you take me?"

"Of course. Just give me a minute."

Marlo pulled out his com-dev. Varsili. Another principal from the troubled troupe. He contacted various search groups with instructions, then spoke on a private line with El, who was already on his way to the theater.

"Why not send him in an air-car?" El sounded testy. Everyone was getting tired.

"Look, these kids are quite fragile. This one needs reassurance so I'll take the midnight route, it's faster and it's safe this time of day. See you soon."

Marlo led Varsili to one of the Regulator cars left outside the gates. The kid seemed to have gathered himself together once he knew Marlo would take him home and was much calmer, but he was not a talker. Marlo let the silence settle.

It was about ten minutes later that the little dancer finally turned to Marlo and smiled. "Thank you so much for doing this for me. I made a mistake. A big mistake. I don't know what came over me!"

"Rio and Corvin, perhaps?" suggested Marlo.

"Perhaps." Varsili pushed one thumb into the palm of his hand. "Truth to tell, I have no reason to go and every reason to stay."

"And they don't?"

The kid shrugged. "Who knows what's going on in their heads or what strange tales they may have told you. They're troublemakers. All I know is I want to go home."

After that, he sat in composed silence for the rest of the way.

At the Residence, the Merculian he remembered from his last visit opened the main door to them, welcoming them in. As Marlo clapped politely, the door to the dancers' apartment burst open and the guard who had been on duty the last time rushed past, opening his arms wide with a cry of joy.

"Varsi! I thought I'd lost you!"

The kid flung himself into the other's arms and kissed him passionately. "I couldn't leave you, Nibsi! I love you too much!"

Marlo drew back as the door suddenly snapped shut on the odd pair. "Flying farts," he muttered, rummaging around in his pocket for a snack. He reminded himself that the youngster who looked all of twelve at the most was probably well past his coming of age year, but the image was disturbing. Very disturbing.

Back at the Estate, no progress had been made and Marlo, exhausted, enlarged the search area beyond the grounds, adding that the kid might be dressed differently. He then put another

Regulator of his own rank in charge and took the hover-bike back to the main house to get some sleep.

Dawn was breaking when he woke up to the sound of his singing alarm and he was plunged back into reality. Checking his messages it was clear no dancer kids had been found. Not one. He checked the news feed, to see if any of this had leaked out. The first banner he saw made him gasp. He struggled upright, drank a big gulp of wake water, gobbled down half a protein bun, icing and all, and rushed to Triani's suite in his bare feet. It wasn't until he was inside the large room that he realized he was still in his sleeping gown.

Triani was sound asleep, his arm wrapped around a satin pillow, one long muscled leg outside the covers. The black curls covered most of his face. Marlo cleared his throat. He was long past the *chai* form of address with the dancer but nowhere near the actual touching stage. Still, the importance of this news went way beyond protocol. Triani had to know.

Marlo went close to the imposing bed, built against the colored glass wall that stained the sheets wine-red. He bent down close to the dancer's face and called his name.

"Go away." Triani pushed his head under the pillow.

Marlo sighed. "You have to wake up!" he shouted. He reached out and shook his arm gently.

Triani shot out of the bed and shouted. "Get the hell away for me!"

Marlo jumped back, relieved that at least the dancer wasn't completely naked. "I'm sorry to be so rude but –"

"You found Rio?"

"Not yet. We're still looking."

"Then what the fuck are you doing here?" Triani looked Marlo up and down, taking in the sleeping robe with the crumbs down the front, the bare feet, the unbrushed hair. He reached over and slipped into a painted silk robe. "Tell me. What happened?"

"It's in the news. I hadn't checked until I woke up this morning." Marlo handed over his PortaPad.

The headlines screamed: "PARLA SERLINI ADELANTIS ARRESTED AT COUSIN'S WEDDING!"

"Holy shit! What is this crap?"

"Keep reading."

Triani sank back down on the bed and read the short piece:

"Well-known architect and member of First Order family was arrested at the extravagant wedding of his cousin yesterday for 'High crimes against the state, Section 221, failure to secure safety to life and limb' when a visitor fell from the ornamental bridge of the brand-new Wave Entertainment Complex designed by the architect because of a structural fault. 'It's sheer luck he wasn't killed, a fall like that,' exclaimed one of the healers who rushed to the scene. The unfortunate person remains in hospital with serious injuries. Adelantis has been taken to the High Court Containment center, where he will remain until taken before an Advocate at Council."

"It's true," Marlo said, sinking into a welcoming chair. "I checked."

"No wonder he didn't return my calls," muttered Triani. "Fuck! What's that place like?"

"Much better than our detainment areas. But if you're there, you have no right to a com-dev or any other communication with the outside. And the Advisory Council is closed for the three-day Court Pause so nothing can be done to get him out before day four, It's that time of month, unfortunately."

"What crap!" Triani felt around for his com-dev. "Okay, I've got to contact my legal team and make them work for those high fees I pay them! Thanks, Marlo."

Marlo nodded. "When we find Rio, I'll keep him with me till you get back."

As he made his way back to his chamber, Marlo suddenly thought of Calian. He had the urge to contact him but it was far too early for anyone to be awake at an *Epicantare* SongFest. He sighed, dug out another protein bun and ate it, thinking about his absent lover and how he would feel if the stocky, fun-loving singer were arrested.

SIXTEEN

Triani looked at the few clothes he had with him, all of them specially designed for his role in the wedding party, and swore. He had nothing appropriate for where he was going now but he had no choice. He pulled on the black satin pants, ripped the lace off the collar of the black sparkle top and pulled on the finely embroidered short white jacket he had arrived in. It was wrinkled but it would have to do. What was the dress code for visiting your lover in the big stony lonesome anyway?

Outside he helped himself to Marlo's hover bike which he rode across the perfect lawn in a direct line to the parking pad where he found his air-car exactly where he had left it. It looked as if it had been searched, probably looking for Rio. Of course the kid had no idea what his air-car looked like or what its ID was. A few minutes later he was on his way.

It took a while to get there and another five minutes looking for a parking pad. This was an older part of the city, where those who frequented the area knew it was easier to walk or catch a ring car. There weren't many people about at this early hour and finally Triani just landed in the open square in front of the Court House. Throwing back his shoulders he marched into the building.

An older Merculian was snoozing behind the information screen. Triani leaned over and shouted an obscenity in his ear. The oldster leapt to his feet, shocked.

"I could have you arrested for that!"

"I could get you fired for sleeping on the job!"

The oldster smoothed back his thinning hair and looked more closely at Triani. "What's your business here this early anyways? The offices are closed."

"Show me where they're keeping Parla Serlini Adelantis."

"They don't have visiting hours down there. Go home."

"Now you listen to me, you piece of shit. Do I have to call Chief Oderlini himself and tell him what a good for nothing ass-wipe he has working for him?"

"Like you know him," said the oldster scornfully.

"You don't know who I am, do you?" Triani gave him a scornful stare.

He shrugged, but he seemed to be finally aware of the dancer's beautiful though inappropriate clothes, the expensive rings flashing on his fingers and the elaborate dagger at his waist. Something stirred in his dim eyes. "Wait a sec. I seen you in the vids somewhere."

"No doubt. Now, which way?"

"Your funeral." He pointed to the left.

Relieved not to have to go through with his threat, since he had barely spoken three words to the Chief at a party ages ago, Triani strode off along a wide corridor, lined with portraits of city dignitaries looking self-important. He came to a narrow stairway and followed the arrow down to the floor beneath where the walls were a startling white glare with no ornamentation whatsoever. Ahead of him was a room where a few middle-aged Merculians lounged around a table in uniforms that were unbuttoned and sloppy, playing a gambling game with large spinning dice.

"We're not open to visitors," one said, glancing at him, then back to the game.

"You are now, sweetie, and right behind me is a legal team from C and C. Where's Serlini Adelantis?"

"Get lost."

"Wait." The younger one bent close to his friend and whispered something.

Triani tapped his foot impatiently. "I'm waiting."

"Well, it's early," the first one said as if in his defense, "but come on. I'll take you."

Triani assumed that they recognized the legal firm or perhaps recognized him, but his money was on the famous legal siblings. They didn't seem like dance fans down here.

He followed the very overweight guard through a locked gate, turned right and another door slid back with a clang. How old was this place, Triani wondered. Then he saw the wide corridor stretching in front of him, lined on either side with darkened glass. It looked like a seamless wall except that light leaked out under a crack in a few places on the right side.

The guard hesitated, consulted a list on the small PortaPad attached to his waist, then punched in a number on the wall board. At once light appeared in the nearest pane of glass and Triani saw Parla, pacing inside, still dressed in his wedding party clothes.

"Open it!"

"Keep your shirt on," muttered the guard, but he dialed the right code and the glass door disappeared. "You got twenty minutes."

Triani rushed inside. "What the hell happened? Why didn't you call me? Don't worry, it'll be all right. My legal aces are coming and they've gotten me out of some really tight spots. This will be nothing." He slid his arms around the apparently stunned Parla and pulled him close. "Everything will be fine now, baby, you'll be out of here in no time."

Parla shook his head. "I don't think so, Triani dear. This is a High Crime they're pinning on me and anyway, no one can get me out until the fourth day. It's the three-day Court Pause. Nothing legal can be done. But thanks for coming. I couldn't call because they took my com-dev. And my dagger," he added resentfully.

Triani pulled him down on the surprisingly comfortable bed. "Don't you worry," he said soothingly, rubbing his lover's back gently. "If anyone can do it, they can. Or they could contact your people. Whatever you want."

"My people just do contract law. Useless for this kind of thing." Parla let himself relax against Triani. "How's Rio?"

"The little shit managed to get lost, but don't worry. Marlo and half the city are looking for him. You just think how to make all this go away."

Parla took a deep breath and set up again. "I'm afraid it's not that simple. They're charging me with high crimes leading to the endangerment of the public and saying my design for the Wave Complex is flawed. As if no one would have noticed during the hundreds of checks and studies me and my team, plus the City Inspectors have done over the last year or so while it was going up."

"I thought he fell over the balustrade?"

"Apparently not. A person is in the hospital because part of the ornamental bridge actually collapsed. That's a fact. I have no idea how that could have happened. But I've been going over and over it all night long and I'm beginning to think this has nothing to do with the structure or design and everything to do with my rivals in the business who objected strenuously when I won the contract in the first place. Too young, too inexperienced, too small a company, and too well-connected, etc., etc. And whoever it is has real clout. Look when they pounced on me: in public where I couldn't cause a fuss, and right after all the courts closed for the three day pause."

"But your family knows everybody, Parla. And what about Whatshisname, Eulio's sib who got married a few years ago?"

"Look, my parents left town to visit old friends off-world right after the ceremony. My sibs are sweet and talented artists but totally useless for something like this. I know craftsmen and guild leaders but this comes from higher up. This comes from the Merculian Living Safely Board with jurisdiction over the whole planet, not just the city, so Josna will be no help. He's Cap City Council only."

A commotion at the door heralded the arrival of Triani's legal advisors. One was very short, the other very young, but they were both dressed smartly in the black, white and grey of their profession.

"We started making notes as soon as you contacted us, *Chai* Triani," the older one began, "so we're up to speed. Just a few questions—"

"Can you get him out of here now?" Triani interrupted.

"Not all the gods of the universe could get him out during Pause days. Besides, it's a High Crime you're charged with, *Chai* Adelantis. But at least we can make sure you're treated with the utmost respect and supplied with what you need."

"Thank you," said Parla, "but what I'm worried about even more is my reputation. All the time I'm here, in whatever semi-luxury, my name is being trampled in the dirt."

"We can do something about that," the young one said brightly. "We can slap a ban on any publication of your name and this charge until you get out."

"That's the best you can do?" shouted Triani.

"Hush, dear. Let me talk to them alone. You go home in case Rio is back and needs you. I'll be fine."

"You sure?"

"Positive." Parla took Triani's hand and squeezed it. "I'm sorry for saying you only come for the party, *chaleen*. I was wrong."

"Yeah, what I really come for is the after-party." Triani winked.

He emerged into the square just in time to see a Traffic Regulator stamp a no parking seal onto his air-car, which meant it would be locked until he paid it.

"Ah come on, sweetie! I'm having a really bad day here. Can't you just delete it?" He smiled seductively, but it had no effect on the serious-faced youngster who just shook his head and walked away.

"Shit!" Triani fumbled with his cred ring, peered at the seal and paid the very high fee. "Everyone seems to think I'm made of credits," he mumbled, climbing into the large car. It was bigger than his usual sporty runabout, since it had been used to bring Eulio's dresser, hair-stylist and their equipment, plus himself and baggage to the estate a scant three days ago and his driver had left it there for him.

He was always surprised when his fame as a super-star dancer, which gave him untold benefits in most cases, did not spill over to every sector of his life. Usually he got away with a lot because his many fans adored him and cut him a lot of slack. He rarely got stopped for speeding, was often let in places when he had no ticket, usually parked in other people's spaces near a theater without any problem.

"Bitch."

This had been an expensive year for him so far, what with Giazin's Specialist and his live-in sessions, paying for Eulio's luxurious Pre-wedding Retreat, (part of his job as Wedding Witness), the new custom made clothes for the event and the extra fee to his legal aces for getting them out on a Court Pause day. And now this! And who knows what Rio was going to cost him, once he found the little shit.

He knew the reason for this constant niggle of anxiety was the uncomfortable memories of being on the street, torn between his longing for beautiful things and his need for bare essentials. He pushed this down again and sat up. On one hand he knew it would take a lot to drain his finances, but on the other, he led a very lavish lifestyle. Maybe he could make this Rio nonsense pay off somehow.

He smiled thoughtfully. Yes. He would contact his manager as soon as the kid turned up.

Realizing the busybody Regulator was headed back in his direction, he revved the engine, sending a few pedestrians scrambling out of the way, and took off. Luckily the big car was very powerful and didn't need much room to maneuver in spite of its size. It was only when he was on his way that it occurred to him that something serious could have happened to Rio. To his surprise, this thought hit him hard.

"Shit," he muttered. He hadn't been wild about this sudden addition to his small family in the first place but now that he was committed, he wanted the kid to come home. "My sibling," he said, tasting the word out loud for the first time. "Where the hell are you?"

He headed for his town quarters, needing a shower, a nap and a change of clothes before going home. He was yawning when he walked up to his gold and white door and went inside.

"Where the fuck have you been?" shouted a high-pitched voice. "I've been waiting here forever and there's nothing to eat!"

"*Rio?* How the hell did you get in?"

"The door recognized my DNA, I guess."

"Yeah, well the whole city is out looking for you. Why didn't you contact me?"

"We're not allowed to have com-dev's. You know that!"

"I don't know that and stop shouting at me!" Triani strode over to the chair where Rio was curled up, hugging his knees and looking miserable. Triani handed him a tranq stick. "Here. This will calm you down."

"I'd rather have some pain blockers or something. I haven't had anything since yesterday before the performance and I can't find anything in this place that I recognize."

Triani sank down beside him and reached for his hands. Rio pulled away but Triani hung on tightly, feeling the waves of wringing pain roll into him. Then he slid his arms around the small figure, letting in the other's pain and fear and loneliness. Rio gradually slumped against him and began to cry. "I'm sorry. It wasn't supposed to be like this. Corvin has the drugs we stole."

Triani reached up to the shelf above his head and took down a small jeweled casket. Opening it with one hand he took a vial of pills. "Here, sweetie. Here's a red. It's the strongest thing I have and I only take it in dire emergencies. Judging from what I feel from you, this is dire."

Rio sat up and reached for the pill, swallowing it dry. "Could I have another one? I mean just to keep for later."

"No. Who knows how your system will react. You're smaller than an adult. Look, I've got to shower and change. I'll order in some food then we'll go home."

"This isn't home?"

"Shit, no. Just my town place for when I'm at the theater a lot." Triani switched on the news feed for Rio to watch and began taking off his top as he went towards his sleeping chamber.

"Oh no!" Rio was on his feet, one hand pressed to his mouth.

"Now what!" Triani turned and looked at the images on his wall. A group of the dark clad Guardians who looked after the Colony Dancers were shown searching through an alley Triani recognized as being near the theater. The voice over was saying there was still no sign of the two missing children and the authorities were getting worried for their safety. "What's the problem? Your Guardians are helping look for you two."

"No! No, Triani. Honestly they're not Guardians. I *know* all our Guardians. They're members of the Faisian Falanx. Soldiers. Everyone's afraid of them. Oh fuck! Grepion must have sent for them when we didn't turn up in a few hours. What'll I do?"

Triani watched the figures, how they moved, always in formation, the way they carried themselves, the suspicious-looking attachments to their belts. "Stunners, you think?" he pointed to the belts

"I don't know. I just know everyone's scared of them. *Mertsi* says they call them in when there's even a hint of trouble in the mines. Oh shit!"

Triani went to the wall on the other side of the large window and slid open an invisible door, revealing a small cupboard. He grabbed two protein buns, two bottles of pamayo juice and a few squares of honey, which he took to Rio. Then he pulled his top back on.

"Come on, sweetie. You can eat on the way. We're going home."

SEVENTEEN

Marlo was in his office watching the newsfeed intently. He, like Triani, had grave doubts about the sudden numbers of 'helpful' Guardians who were now joining in the search. He checked the SpacePort Office and found that his suspicions were correct. An unannounced super-fast transport had arrived that morning full of blue clad Guardians, wanting to help. But they did not look like the Guardians Marlo had met. They carried themselves like people with some sort of military training.

When he told his boss, Liviano just shrugged his bony shoulders. "The more the merrier, Marlo. You know as well as I do we can't keep this level of intensity in the search much longer. Two missing kids is a tragedy about to happen, I know, but I've already had to divert some teams back to traffic. It's a mess out there and we've had three accidents already. It's a miracle someone wasn't killed."

Marlo pulled his official badge on its wide ribbon over an inch or two to cover a stain on his tunic. He cleared his throat, wondering how much of an explosion there would be once Old Livid realized one kid was already found. He couldn't hold it back much longer. If Triani and Rio issued a statement, he would be in even greater trouble than usual.

"There are some very nasty rumors about the Colony, chief. And some especially nasty ones about how they treat those children. And they're not missing. They ran away, trying to escape the place."

Liviano leaned back in his seat and stared at his Investigator, his beady eyes like sharp lasers aimed at Marlo. "What have you been up to now?"

Marlo cleared his throat again. "They've been drugging those children. And they're not as young as they look. I don't know how they're doing it but one of them, Rio, should have had his *cimbola* ceremony two years ago. They're determined we don't find the kids first because once we have them, we have all the documentation we need against them right in the kids' bodies. Anything that may have been only a vague rumor, will be fact."

Liviano closed his eyes for a moment, drawing in his lips with a sucking sound. When he opened them again, he leaned forward and put his elbows on the imposing desk. "Start talking, Bogardini. And I mean everything you and your cronies have been doing."

Marlo began to talk, filling his chief in on his first faint thoughts about the red-headed child from the old missing person case, the stolen drugs in the silver valise, and the disturbing fact that it had now disappeared, having been given back by the night security guard who was promised tickets to the Colony Dancers' last performance. He told what he had seen and heard at Triani's apartment, how he had helped in the escape and what had gone so horribly wrong.

"Rio is now with his sibling Triani at his well secured estate," he finished up. "I heard from him a few hours ago. I still don't know where the other one is."

Old Livid looked more pale than usual. Silence settled in after Marlo had finished. Liviano reached under the desk and produced a bottle and two glasses. He poured out the clear liquid and handed one to Marlo. "This is the worst thing I have heard for a long time," he said.

Marlo took a sip. It was sweet and very strong. He felt the warmth reaching down into his stomach. He wished he had a pink biscuit.

"Why didn't you tell me?" Liviano said.

"Because then you would have had to do something to stop us."

Old Livid poured the rest of the liquid down his throat and slammed the glass into the desk. "I have to say this, Marlo, but don't think I don't love children, because I do. I have a few of my own, one of whom wants to be a dancer, may the gods protect him. But we are Cap City Regulators. We are responsible for the city and the airways directly above it and only that. Not the planet and certainly not a Merculian Territory planet which is the source of one of our main imports." He paused.

"The last missing child is in our city," Marlo pointed out.

"I have to release the majority of the search team tonight. The order came down from upstairs." Old Livid looked at the bottle, then put it back out of sight. "Until then, you have my full support. Find that kid." He paused and rubbed his chin. "And open a file on that damn dance company. But facts only, Marlo! No rumors or what you hear. Clear?"

"Crystal."

"And do it quietly." Old Livid made a dismissive wave of his hand and Marlo left the room. The blue privacy light snapped on at once. Marlo wondered if the bottle would make an appearance again.

Opening a file meant it could be turned over to the Merculian National Regulators, who had jurisdiction everywhere. That gave him some hope.

He was well into entering info into the new file when he got a call from Triani.

"Hey, sweetie, Rio wants to make a statement about leaving the company and living with me and all that shit. I said we should clear it with you first."

Marlo, still shaken from his sessions with Liviano, took a deep breath. "Please tell him to hold off. I have only a short time left with a full search party and I don't want to alert the Guardians yet. They'll redouble their efforts."

"Yeah, well Rio says some of those so-called Guardians are military."

"I know. All the more reason to keep quiet."

"The little shit is very determined," Triani said.

"So am I. Just give me today. I can't stop you after that." He snapped off the com-dev, wishing Triani would stop referring to his recently discovered sibling as the Little Shit, and made his way to the large room used as search headquarters. The room was lined with screens, projected from the latest team leaders. None of it looked hopeful. The area around the National Dance Theater had been endlessly searched, since this was the only area the kids knew at all.

"Wait," said Marlo suddenly, his eye caught by the image of Corvin's smiling face on one wall. If he actually was one of the missing children from fifteen years ago, as Marlo suspected, he might remember his old neighborhood. He had been a year older than the others. It was possible and Marlo didn't have any other ideas.

He hurried to his office and unearthed the file, kept out of circulation in paper in his desk because he wasn't supposed to be looking at it. He checked the name under the image of the five-year-old child: Berliti Cativo Alisis. The family who had moved out of town. Moved on. Fabulous. Even if the poor kid did find his old home, no one who remembered him would be there. Certainly not the parents he was seeking.

"What's going on?" Eldred stood in the doorway looking concerned. "You just yelled 'wait', and then rushed off."

"Can you search for the whereabouts of the Cativo Alisis family? Not sure if they have kids now. If they do they'll be under fifteen. Also I don't think they're in the city, but check just in case."

Eldred walked to his desk and began his search, asking no questions. He had worked with Marlo a long time.

Meanwhile Marlo searched for and found Berliti's birth registration and downloaded it to his con-dev. Hope was growing, spreading like the heady liquid he had consumed with Old Livid.

"Nothing in the city, nothing anywhere that I can find. Maybe they went off-world?"

"Maybe."

"What's this about?"

Marlo glanced at his old file, checking out the address where the little Berliti used to live before that fateful day.

"Keep looking for that family, and don't forget the transport passenger logs. I have to check something else. I'll fill you in later. And keep everyone else on track!" Marlo rushed out and grabbed an official air-car on the roof pad-park.

He was getting near the neighborhood the youngster had grown up in when he got a call from Cisorin. Marlo grimaced. He didn't have time for the grieving parent now. But he couldn't ignore him either.

When he answered, there was sobbing on the other end. "What's the matter?" Marlo asked, alarmed. The tears didn't usually come out till after a lot of talking face to face during his yearly visit.

Cisorin caught his breath and laughed. It sounded almost hysterical. "I'm sorry, Marlo, I know I should have called you way earlier but it's been...so...quite a day! Please come!"

"Look, I'm sorry but I'm in the middle—"

"*Please*, Marlo! It's so hard to explain but if you come you can see it all for yourself right away." He caught his breath and gulped.

Marlo glanced at his co-ordinates and realized he wasn't far away. "I can drop in for a few minutes, but then I have to go," he said, trying to sound firm.

He shook his head. Poor thing. Maybe the constant search news had brought it all back. Missing children. Lines of Regulators searching fields and gardens, clapping at doors. Were they sitting there gazing at images of their own missing child? Pictures made to show him aging through the years?

He landed ten minutes later and found the door wide open. From inside came music and the sound of conversation. Odd. Cautiously Marlo moved inside and clapped gently. And then he saw Corvin. The youngster looked very tired, his red hair drawn back from his face on top of his head, short corkscrew curls escaping over his forehead. He was wearing a plain black tunic that made him look even more pale, and had a dance bag at his feet. It looked as if it was turned inside out.

"Are you a sight for sore eyes!" Marlo exclaimed. He started over to him but the kid drew himself up, as if preparing for an onslaught. Perhaps he'd had enough from Pendorin's family. Marlo stopped and sat down instead. There were platters of food on the table. He took a pink biscuit absentmindedly.

"Isn't it a miracle?" Cisorin cried. "And Berliti here says Pendorin's alive!"

"He's alive, Marlo!" Dorli broke in, wiping his eyes. "And he's dancing in the company too, back on the Colony Planet!"

As they chattered on, Marlo watched Corvin. So far he hadn't said a word. He looked as if holding on with every fiber of his being. It must have been exhausting for him all this time. He had apparently found his way here to his best friend's house from his former home, having discovered his family had moved away years ago. He must have been through a long confusing time here trying to explain enough so that they could understand and not freak out completely.

Marlo glanced at his timepiece and stood up. He had to rescue the kid and fast. "I'm sorry to have to take him away so soon, but there are protocols, you know." He nodded to Corvin who picked up his bag at once and stepped over beside him.

"I'm ready," he said quietly. "I'll come back again to visit later," he added, turning and bowing to the tearful couple.

"Oh please do! Soon, dear, because we'll be getting ready to go the Colony Planet."

"It's not easy to go there now," Marlo said gently. "You have to go through a long screening process, I hear, mountains of paper-work and then pay a hefty fee as well."

"None of that matters!"

Marlo just smiled and promised to tell them how things went with the young Corvin, whom they knew as Bertili.

"That was clever of you, finding your way here," Marlo said as he and the youngster climbed into his air-car.

"Do you know anything about Rio?" Corvin asked at once, ignoring the compliment. "We were supposed to be together and I have...what he might need now."

"I know. He's with Triani. Don't worry. I'm taking you there now."

Corvin took a deep breath and exhaled, his whole body seem-ing to loosen. "I was so worried. And those poor people, going on and on. They have no idea, thinking they can go pick up their kid like he's just been away at school for a while! It's not like that. He's not...well, not who they think he is any more. It didn't help saying all those nice things about him. The kid is not that great a dancer, for one thing. He's in the third company as an understudy, and they rarely tour and never off-planet. And he's not...well, not popular like he used to be when we were kids."

"But he's theirs," Marlo said, "and he's alive. That's all that counts."

"Perhaps. I wouldn't know."

Marlo glanced at the bag, now on Corvin's lap. It looked as if lumpy things were inside, not soft dance clothes. Corvin was almost hugging it. Near the top was a large brown logo shaped like a bat.

"That doesn't look like the dance company's logo. Whose is it?" Marlo asked curiously. "I think I've seen it somewhere before."

Corvin looked down. "That's the Windfall Group symbol. They make lots of things back on the Colony. Rio says they even own the company now, but I don't know. They don't tell us anything." Corvin stifled a yawn. "Are we there yet?"

EIGHTEEN

Eulio and Beny lay side by side, naked on their floating blanket. Water lapped softly around them and water flowers spread their lulling fragrance nearby. They had decided on coming to the Bower Boats on Secret Lake because they both equated traveling long distances with work. They were content to go two hours away instead of two days to be together, just far enough away from the everyday world. This was one of the easiest decisions concerning the wedding they had had to make.

Eulio whispered in his ear and Beny obediently rolled onto his stomach. Almost at once he felt the cool trickle hit the sensitive area all Merculians have just at the end of the spine. He squirmed deliciously and smelt the sweet scent of the liquid honey-chocolate. When Eulio's warm tongue began long, licking strokes he squirmed more, moaning as he felt his sex begin to stir and the warm juices inside him leaking out. When the licking stopped, he felt his spouse's muscular body slide into place on his back, felt the warm pleasure as Eulio began to slowly enter him. It took longer from this position but that was all part of the exquisite emotional joy of joining this way. Warm tears slid down his cheeks as he moaned. Eulio seemed to be even better at love-making as his spouse then he had been as his lover,

When the shuddering ecstasy was over, Eulio slid off Beny's sweaty body.

"Just think," he murmured. "No one else will ever see this private part of you again, but me." He laid his hand possessively on Beny's sensitive diamond, low on his back.

Beny rolled over. "What if I get sick and need a healer?"

"Healers don't count." Eulio kissed him, then slid into the water and swam out of sight around the boat.

For a moment, Beny felt anxious. Then he, too, slipped into the water and floated, letting the water cleanse him. "Is that why you wanted to get married early?" Beny asked, when Eulio showed up at his side again.

"You have a wandering eye," Eulio said, climbing onto the boat deck.

"I do not!" Beny climbed after him. "What do you mean?"

"I'm just teasing, dear. You used to, you know."

"I wasn't jeweled then. And you had a few...escapades your-self as I recall, and who knows what you got up to when I wasn't around." He lay down beside Eulio who was reaching to touch the wall controls.

"Let's watch some more of the wedding video. Some of those from-the-heart presents were incredible."

"I loved the sand painting in the air that Didio did. An art form that disappears as soon as you finish."

"Like dance."

"Hmm. I hadn't thought of it that way."

"Triani's gift was amazing. Very clever, don't you think?"

"Hmmm. Very. He knows his audience."

"Always." Eulio laughed.

Beny reached into the box of delicious wedding balls which was nearly empty. He held one to Eulio's lips.

"Are you trying to get me fat? As it is I will have go on a diet when we get home."

"We have to finish them, you know. Otherwise it's bad luck."

"You eat them. I want to see if we're still in the news or already forgotten.."

The wall in front of them sprang to life. "God's teeth! It's Triani! He certainly is taking advantage of my absence."

"To be fair, you've been taking up most of the space lately. Look, there's Rio beside him. Turn up the volume."

"Chai Triani and his newly discovered sibling Chaisilin Rio, revealed tonight they are taking some time off to get to know each other. Chaisilin Rio announced that he is leaving the Colony Dance Company where he is a principal dancer, and is looking forward to some much needed rest and recreation with his new-found family."

"Bloody damn," said Beny, popping another wedding ball in his mouth.

Eulio absently took the last one.

"Also making headlines is the arrest of prize-winning architect Parla Serlini Adelantis, who is charged with a High Crime, endangering public safety, and possibly much more if the young Merculian who fell when the bridge in the Wave Entertainment Complex collapsed does not come out of his coma. Adelantis is being detained at the High Court Center.

"In other news—"

Eulio waved off the transmission and looked at Beny, tears in his large blue eyes.

"High Crime? What's that exactly?"

Beny hesitated, not wanting to frighten his spouse. "It's pretty serious, I'm afraid. It means anything that might cause danger to life or limb of a Merculian."

"God's teeth, Orosin! Parla wouldn't do that!"

"Of course not." Beny paused, watching Eulio's expressive face. "We can leave right now, love." He dusted sugar off his hands.

"But this is our wedding trip. We wanted the Bower Boats..."

"If we stay, there will be three people here. If we go home, only the two of us."

"And Dhakan, but I know what you mean."

"And we can do anything at home we can do here, though it may be messier," Beny added, noting the spilled jar of chocolate honey that had been washed clean by the water as they climbed into the boat.

"Thank you, *chaleen.*"

Beny reached for his com-dev. "I'll alert the Bower Boat people to come and get us in an hour and transport us to the air-car pad. You start to pack and we'll have a last swim."

"Do we need a whole hour?"

"We're both a little high, dear. It might take longer than you expect."

All the way home they listed the people they knew, or their family knew, whoever might prove useful in helping Parla. In the end they had to admit that with all their connections, not one was in the right place to make it all go away, something Beny had suspected all along but it kept them busy.

"It would be better if he had committed some interplanetary offence," Beny said distractedly. "All my connections are diplomatic and Inner Circle like *Tan* Pami. I'll try him now, though. It can't hurt."

"Most of mine are city related, not national judicial council. But I can try a few more."

After all their efforts they discovered, to Beny's astonishment, that Triani had arrived that morning with this famous law team and now Parla was back home under house arrest.

"Bloody damn," exclaimed Beny. "Triani, of all people."

"But he's still under arrest!" cried Eulio.

"Yes, but at least he's in his own home, and he has a great legal team. I didn't even think of that."

"But Triani did," said Eulio, shaking his head.

NINETEEN

Triani was feeling very pleased with himself as he swept into the theater later that morning to see the director of the company, Nevon Bantino. He didn't have an appointment, but he knew the director would see him anyway. They had had an intense affair years ago when Triani had arrived at the company. When it was over, Nevon pined for him for years but that was a while ago. Now Triani was simply a celebrity draw to keep bringing in the audience. But that was important to Nevon and it meant Triani still had the upper hand.

Triani put his head around the door of Nevon's office. Sure enough, the director was there, inspecting sketches with the young set-designer Triani had had a brief fling with recently.

"Hi sweetie. Can you spare me a few minutes?"

Nevon raised his head and smiled. "Come take a look at this. Tell me what you think."

Triani walked over and squeezed in beside Nevon, bumping the designer out of the way with his hip. He winked at the young Merculian.

"Hmmm. Stark, aren't they? Modern."

"Do you think it might work?"

Triani traced the pattern sketched on the stage floor. "Worth a try." He reached over and cupped the designer's succulent rear-end with his other hand.

"Okay, I'll give it some thought," Nevon said. "I'll get back to you, Belsani."

The designer moved away from Triani, who winked at him before Belsani turned and left.

Nevon snapped off the design. "Leave him alone, Triani. His

contract expires in a few weeks anyway. What did you really think about it?"

"Piece of shit," Triani said at once, throwing himself gracefully into the chair opposite Nevon. "Too stark and that complicated design on the floor idea is old-fashioned and only works for the cheap seats up high. Nice idea with the water feature, though."

"I agree. So, what's on your mind?"

Triani leaned forward. "I have a great idea for the short program opening in two weeks."

"That's all ready to go. Done. Finished. And you said you wanted more time off so I left you off the program."

"Just listen. This is for me and Rio. *The Dream.* The two celeb siblings making a stunning appearance together for the first time ever. Everyone and his lover will want to see this!"

"Except that the program's done. Finished. Ready to go."

"You don't even have to alter anything. Just add on ten minutes at the end."

"Alesio will set up a stink."

"Since when do you care about Alesio?"

"Since he won the TOSA Award."

"Small potatoes," sneered Triani, who had forgotten about that. "Think about it, Nev."

"Anyway, wasn't the idea for Rio to rest after all the touring?"

"And he will. After this performance. I know that series of shorts doesn't fill the house every night. Admit it! But if you add 'Triani and Rio in *The Dream*' on the marquee, it will."

"You haven't been coming to class lately. You'll be out of shape."

Triani laughed. "Did you see me dance at the wedding? Did I look out of shape to you? I have my own dance studio at home, remember."

"Does Rio even know *Dream*?"

"Yes, he does."

"Which role?"

For the first time Triani wavered. "The Spirit."

Nevon sat back in his chair. "You've never done the other role."

"I know but me as the Spirit and him as the Dreamer would look ridiculous because of his height. The other way around would be great. I'm a quick study, you know that. It will only take me about an hour to learn it and we have two weeks to rehearse."

"You must really love him," Nev remarked. "The Spirit is the best part."

"This is to showcase *him*."

Nevon looked out the window, picking at his thumbnail. "You know it'll be an adjustment dancing with someone so much smaller than you."

Triani had already thought of that and it did worry him but he wasn't about to admit it. "We've fooled around a bit in my studio. It'll work fine."

Nevon fiddled with a silver music cube. "This is going to cost me, isn't it?"

"You get what you pay for." Triani grinned. "I'll only charge what I would for any company."

"You have no loyalty?"

"I'm here, aren't I?" Triani revised the fee downwards a little.

"You have a contract with us, don't forget."

"But Rio doesn't."

"And won't if you pull any more stunts like this. What's the going rate for a sibling these days?"

Triani sprang to bis feet. "How dare you!"

Nevon felt around for his PortaPadd on his cluttered desk. "All right, I apologize for that last comment. Sit down."

Triani leaned over the desk and snarled, "What do *you* think a sibling like mine is worth?"

"I know his former company practically drained the coffers here. How much do you want, and be reasonable!"

Triani sat down again and crossed his legs. He was not ready for any sort of showdown with Nevon about this so he lowered the figure again before stating it. Nevon's expression didn't change but Triani knew him well. The director was relieved.

"And make that 70/30 in my favor when you send the contract," he added.

Nevon smiled. "My confidence in you is restored. I'll draw up the contract and send it this afternoon."

"Thanks, sweetie." Triani stood up. "And no last name for Rio. That's a deal breaker. When do you want us for rehearsal?"

"Tomorrow afternoon." Nevon stood too, too. "And I'll have to add two more matinees to cover this extra outlay."

"One," said Triani at once. "Add extra seats at the back." He leaned over the desk and gave Nevon a quick kiss on the mouth.

An hour later Triani walked in the door of his beautiful house at Hanging Rock and almost bumped into the Keeper.

"The Specialist Healers are already here, *chai*," he said dolefully. "They were surprised not to meet you."

"They'll get over it. Where's Rio?"

"With them, *chai*. As is *Chaisalin* Corvin.

"Could you bring Rio to my sitting room without telling the others I'm here yet? If Daisa's here, let him do it."

"Very good. That sort of thing is not my job. I'll relay your order to your assistant."

Triani shook his head. He was never quite sure what the Keeper considered his job to be exactly. It seemed to be a field that was continually shrinking, but he did keep the sprawling place running smoothly so Triani let this sort of thing go.

He changed into a loose silk tunic and silk stockings of the same changeable hue, belted on a flashy dagger and went to his sitting room where Rio was waiting. Triani had arranged for his hair stylist to come that morning to give Rio a shoulder length cut that suited someone going into puberty, someone just recently graduated from the senior circle.

"Sweetie you look really good like that," Triani said, looking at him appraisingly. "The new clothes fit perfectly, too." Daisa had bought them earlier.

"I saw to that," Rio said smugly. "I sew, remember? You're late," he added. "They're waiting."

"I wanted to talk to you first. I have a surprise. I've booked a performance of *Dream* for us with Nevon and we're doing it in two weeks. Isn't that wonderful?"

Rio looked at him silently for a moment. "Without asking me?"

"Come on. No one could turn this down. Anyway, there wasn't time. We'll be closing the program."

"What's the contract like?"

Triani told him the amount. "Of course it's 70/30 to me."

"No." Rio straightened his back. "50/50. I'm a principal too, and a star where I come from."

"Exactly. Where you come from. Look, you ungrateful little shit, I worked hard to set this up. And I'm doing a lot for you in other ways, too. Just look in the mirror!"

"I paid for all this," Rio said indignantly, pointing to his hair and new clothes.

"Yes, but I made it happen."

"Daisa did."

"He works for me, you idiot."

"Don't call me an idiot! And I am not dancing for 30% I *don't* work for you!"

Triani grabbed a glass and poured some wine. "You'd be dancing the spirit role." He took a sip of wine. Why was everyone being so stubborn today?

"So. Let me get this straight," said Rio, hands on hips. "You want me to dance the longer, more difficult part and get paid 30%. Is that right?"

"I'm the one who set up the deal. It's my contacts."

"You think he couldn't contact *Chai* Bantino and get a deal?" Corvin came into the room. He, too, had had a haircut. It made him look older.

"You keep out of this," snapped Triani.

Corvin walked over and stood beside Rio.

"And you didn't even think of Corvin in all this dealing of yours, did you?" said Rio belligerently

"Why should I?" Triani slammed his glass on the table. "Okay, you don't want to dance, fine. You don't have to. I'll call the whole damn thing off."

"Of course I want to dance," Rio shouted, "but I want to be treated fairly for once in my damn life!"

"And after today who knows what we will have to go through before we'll be able to dance again," Corvin said calmly. "Come on, Rio. The healers are waiting."

Triani suddenly remembered why the healers were there. In his house. With these youngsters. How important this day might be to the young dancers. "Shit," he muttered. He was about to go to his office to get the choreography chart for *The Dream* so he could study it when Corvin's voice stopped him.

"They need you there to give your permission for the exam for

Rio. *Com* Bogardini is standing in for my parents until he can track them down and he signed for me."

"But you're both of age. Why do you need that?"

"Technically, perhaps, but apparently it's quite complicated. And the whole process will be recorded," he added.

"What? Wait!" Triani grabbed the bottle of wine and a glass and followed them. "Why is Marlo here?"

"We need a record if we decide to sue the company."

"Holy shit," muttered Triani.

TWENTY

Marlo had been waiting in Triani's house for a while. With him was the Regulator Recorder, one of a team of officials who did nothing but meticulously record and make reports at any scene which might end up in a major legal case. Idlandrin was older than Marlo and had been at this same job when Marlo joined the Regulators. He was revered in his field, which was why Marlo had asked him to join their not exactly standard team investigating the Colony Dancers. As soon as Idlandrin heard it was about the possible abuse of children, he cleared his schedule and that of his assistant and declared they were both in. Marlo knew that if Idlandrin asked his assistant to jump off the Art Wall he would do it and never question why. The assistant wasn't really that much younger than his boss, but everyone always called him the Youngster. It always made Marlo smile.

They were all in Rio's small suite of rooms near the west garden. It was at the other end of the house from where Marlo had been before and he longed to wander into the garden and explore the wonderful flowers and bushes and trees shaped like dancers and animals he glimpsed out there, but he stayed put in Rio's sitting room, knowing he might be needed. He could see the sleeping chamber up two steps to the right and the arched window beyond. Light poured in from the dome above, shining on the neat space, with its walls tinted a pale sky-blue. There was nothing personal on the walls or tables scattered about, but there were two open boxes of small dance shoes and a large bag from an expensive boutique on the floor. Rio's colorful ribbon jacket was folded neatly on one chair but its owner had left about ten minutes ago.

Marlo went into the sleeping chamber where the three healers and two techs were finishing setting up medical equipment. Someone had stripped the large bed and covered it with a pale green striped sheet. Two others lay ready to hand on either side. Marlo already knew Charlo, of course, and he had met Pom, the company doctor and Triani's personal physician. The third specialist was Prandsini, an authority on hormones and sexuality. Pom had brought him in to help with diagnosis and treatment.

"Terrible. Terrible business." Prandsini cleared his throat. "Assuming it's all true," he added, noticing the Recorder.

"Don't mind me," Idlandrin said, waving his hand cheerfully. "Just pretend we're not here."

Marlo looked around at all the gleaming equipment lined up against the walls; the scanners and vials, trays of instruments, several high-power microscopes and boxes of who knew what. There was a faint smell of disinfectant in the air. Poor kids, he thought. The room, formerly a soft and welcoming chamber, now had been turned into a place for cool dissection, reducing the two young Merculians to mere objects, something they had apparently unwittingly been for some time for their so-called healers back on the Colony.

"I'm here." Triani put the wine he was carrying down on a table and went to the sleeping chamber. The two young dancers followed him. "Where do I sign?"

The Recorder showed him while the youngsters went behind a screen Pom had erected for them and got undressed.

Pom folded his hands and began to speak in his soothing voice. "Just so that everyone knows; this is what will happen. We will give Rio and Corvin a complete physical exam, including an internal. Much will be familiar to the young ones, I'm sure. Some things will not. I am sorry we cannot give any heavy medication because we need them both completely awake and able to respond to questions while this is going on. And all this will take about two hours, at the most."

"But it won't be painful, surely," said Marlo anxiously.

"Let's just say some of this may be quite...uncomfortable, but I assure you it is necessary if we're to provide a course of treatment for any possibility of growth and progress of puberty. We'll give them a mild sedative. Now, everyone not involved in the exam, please leave the room. Excluding the Recorder, of course."

"Triani?" Rio's voice came from behind the screen, sounding very young.

"I'm here, sweetie." Triani walked over and pulled the screen away, revealing Rio clutching a sheet around him. He was very pale.

"Promise me something," Rio whispered.

"What?"

"If…well, if this doesn't go well and I don't make it through—"

"Shit, Rio, it's just an examination."

"They don't really know what's wrong with me," Rio whispered urgently. "So promise you'll…talk to *mertsi* and tell him what happened."

"You think I'd speak to that—" He stopped suddenly and swore. "Listen to me. Nothing will happen except they'll find out how to fix you. That's all. But if you decide to be a little shit and have a heart attack, I'll contact our wonderful saint of a parent and tell him."

Rio looked up at him and blinked. "Swear?"

"Fuck, Rio! Okay, I swear." He was about to turn away when he paused. "But you fucking better not kick off and put me through all that shit! Promise?"

Rio smiled and even the pale Corvin who was now standing beside him, let out a chuckle.

"Promise."

"Okay, okay. I'll be right outside." Triani gave him a sudden hug, then turned away and left the room.

Marlo paused, wondering if he should reassure Corvin in some way, but one look at that closed little face and he changed his mind. He went back to the other room where he had been sitting before.

"The kid's terrified," Triani said. "How come the other kid isn't upset?"

"I'm sure he is, in his own way, but his trust is in Rio. He'll do whatever Rio wants him to do."

Triani shook his head. "Bad idea," he murmured.

The doorway darkened so that no one could see in, but they could plainly hear what was said. Mostly there wasn't much of interest, occasionally a childish voice would ask a question, or sometimes gasp, presumably at a cold instrument surprising or momentarily hurting. Triani left the room for a few minutes, came back with a large PortaPad and sat on the floor to study something on it.

Every now and then he would shift his position, point a toe, bend a knee, arch his back. Marlo was amazed by his total concentration. He himself was a bundle of nerves, every odd noise from behind the darkened door making him start.

Triani finally got up for a stretch and noticed Marlo. "You okay?" He poured some wine and offered a glass to Marlo.

Marlo took the wine but would have preferred a snack. Triani didn't seem to have any food around. In fact, Marlo had never seen him do more than nibble at anything. He wandered over to the window and gazed out into the garden, enchanted by the vivid and unusual blooms, some of which he couldn't identify. Triani must have an army of gardeners and 'bots to keep everything in such wonderful shape. He leaned out the window, trying to get a closer look at an exotic striped vine winding itself around the slender pillars of the stick trees.

"Push on the right side and it'll open," Triani suggested, watching.

Marlo tried but something was blocking the way. Large bags of something heavy were piled too close to the house, closing off the door.

"Stuck?" Triani came over to see. "Idiots," he muttered. "That's the material Parla ordered when he was finishing up the Wave building. He's going to build an extension right here, circling around and turning this into a private courtyard, see?" He waved his arms, tracing out the area in the air. "You could hop out the window and take a closer look," he suggested, but Marlo detected a wicked glint in his eye as he said it.

Marlo shook his head and leaned out to check the bright green lettering on the bags. Elutian, if he was not mistaken. Since when did they have anything to do with material like *troxite*? And there was that moth-like symbol he had seen before on Corvin's dance bag. Odd.

A sudden scream brought Triani dashing for the darkened doorway. Marlo caught his arm.

"Better not," he said.

"It was only supposed to be an exam!" Triani said angrily pulling away.

"An internal as well, though," Marlo reminded him. "They are seldom pleasant."

"You got that right." Triani turned back to the table and poured more wine. "Pom should have put them under."

It was another hour before the door brightened and Pom appeared, looking strained and tired. He was rubbing sweet-smelling cream into his hands.

"Let's talk outside," he suggested, heading for the garden. "I gave them a short-term sedative so they could sleep for a while before having to hear all this. It was rough on them."

Triani paced around the colorful paving stones where comfortable chairs were set out, Marlo thought, as if waiting for people to gather for an afternoon snack. If only that were the case. He took a seat.

"Please sit down, Triani. I'll make this as short and uncomplicated as I can. All the details will be available from the Recorder when he has finished his report."

"Get on with it." Triani sat down.

Pom spread his hands out in the air in front of him. "Corvin is in worse shape than Rio by far."

"He's two years older," Marlo pointed out.

"I don't care about him," Triani interrupted. "Tell me about Rio."

"I will tell this my way or not at all." The healer paused.

Triani dropped his eyes and reached for his wine glass.

"As I was saying, there may not be much we can do for poor Corvin except help with the pain. We can duplicate their pain meds without a problem. They both have to take a rest from dancing. Corvin will probably not be able to dance again. Ever. Certainly not professionally. The stress fractures on his frame are too severe. Rio, however may have more hope. His fractures may heal on their own with rest. His blood is clearing nicely from all the drugs those evil ones pumped into him night and day, may their eyeballs rot in their skulls.

"What is relatively easy to fix is the delayed puberty. Since they left the company, they haven't received any injections of the puberty blocker they've been on for many years. Their bodies are already responding to this and will slowly begin to move forward, with help from us. They will lose those babyish looks, begin to develop facial maturity, grow hair between their legs, that sort of things. It will be a slow process but in six months you will see quite a difference."

"So Rio will grow?" Triani asked.

"Unfortunately, in Merculians the onset of puberty has nothing to do with growth. This is what had us stymied for a long time. That's why I brought in the Specialty healer. He found the shocking reason for the complete stall in their growth that was so horrible I had never even considered it." Pom shifted uncomfortably.

Marlo winced, feeling the tension. He glanced at Triani who chewed his lip.

"Why the youngsters cried out near the end was because we had found the reason for the lack of growth. It's an internal issue and the manipulation was painful. Both have been mutilated, just to keep them short." Pom paused again and cleared this throat.

"Holy shit, Pom, just spit it out."

"Corvin, Rio and every unfortunate member of that tortured dance company has been castrated. And that cannot be reversed. And when those two wake up I have to go in there and explain that half of what makes us Merculian has been ripped away from them. They can never fully experience physical sex by joining with a lover, or propagate a child with a loved one,

Or—" He stopped abruptly and stared.

Marlo turned around and saw Rio standing in the open window, his face wet with tears.

TWENTY-ONE

Triani leapt past Marlo, hopped through the window into the room and put an arm around Rio's shoulders.

"Come on, sweetie. Everything will be okay." He steered the youngster out into the hall and through an archway into another courtyard.

"Wait." Rio pulled away. "I want to ask you something. Have you cancelled the *Dream* thing?"

"Not yet. Why?"

"I've changed my mind. I want to dance. I don't care what deal you made. Take all the credits, who cares. I just want to dance."

"But Rio, you're supposed to rest—and—"

"No! I don't want everyone remembering me as that precocious little kid dancer who suddenly disappeared like so many before me in that freaky company. *I want to dance!*"

"Okay, calm down." Triani tried to guide him towards his private sitting room. He needed a drink. A strong one, but Rio kept pulling away. Even with tears in his eyes he was determined, standing chin raised, hands on hips, looking up at Triani belligerently.

"Okay. I'll contact Nevon and confirm. We'll do it 50/50 but you have to do something for me."

Rio looked at him warily. "Maybe," he said. "What is it?"

"I want the marquee to read Triani and Rio. Period."

"Of course you get to come first, you're older, but why only one name for me?"

"It looks better."

"Sure. You're doing this because of *mertsi*, right? You're a shit!"

"Do it and you can dance."

"You...you fucker! Okay, but do the contract now so I know."

"You don't trust me?"

"Why should I?"

Relieved, Triani pulled out his con-dev, contacted Nevon and confirmed the deal, with the 50/50 change and single name, even though he knew that part was already in the contract.

"There. Satisfied?"

Rio seemed to wilt against the wall. He nodded.

"Come on." Triani gathered him close and together they walked to his private sitting room. "Nobody will bother us here. Unless you want to go back to Corvin."

"He needs a lot more sleep than I do. He'll be fine."

Triani poured a glass of *lim* and another of mint wine. Rio reached for the wine and took a cautious sip.

Triani sank down on the white settee and patted the spot beside him. Rio joined him. "How much did you hear?"

"Just that last bit. That was enough." Rio tossed back half the wine.

Triani pulled him closer. "You missed all the good bits," he said quietly.

"Like what?"

Triani could feel his sibling's muscular body beginning to relax against him. He tossed the fluffy throw he kept there for Giazin around them both. It always worked to calm his own kid, maybe it would help his sibling now.

"So what good bits?" Rio asked, tucking a leg under him and finishing off the wine.

"Well, you can grow, for one thing, and begin to mature so you won't look like a little kid anymore."

Rio laid his head on Triani's chest. "And?"

"And, those stress fractures will cure themselves over time, with a little help from Pom. And then—"

"What's *he* doing in here?" Giazin stood at the door looking windblown and tired and very upset. "That's *my* blanket!"

Triani cursed himself for not closing the door or putting up a blue privacy light. "Why are you home so early?" he countered.

"It's late. It's nearly time to eat." Giazin rushed over and began to squeeze in on the other side of his *tatsi*.

Triani gently pushed him away.

"If it's that late, you better go with govsy now and get ready for mealtime." He scowled at the figure who now showed up at the door, motioning him in with his head.

"Come on, dear," the governor said, swooping in and prying Giaz away.

But the child resisted, stamping his foot. "No! I want to stay here. It's not fair! How come—"

"Be quiet." Rio sat up abruptly and glared at the child. "Do as you're told."

Giazin stared at him, his mouth open. He was so surprised that govsy had a chance to lead him away without a word.

"Don't talk to him like that again," Triani said angrily when they were gone.

"Honestly, he's spoiled, you've got to admit. He walks all over you! And I'm his *tan*, after all. It's my job to help him, not just play with him, like he thinks. I've started teaching him the old variation routines we learned from *mertsi*, by the way. He needs the practice and the discipline."

Triani stared at the little face, looking only a few years older than Giazin and talking like a mature sibling only a few years younger than he was himself.

"And," Rio went on, "I think you should join us in your studio tomorrow morning and go through the variations with us. He only does it about 20 minutes so far. Shit, I used to do the full set at his age," he added, disgusted. "Didn't you?"

Triani had a long-forgotten memory of a sun-filled room, his parent patiently going through the long series of the variation exercises, correcting every minor mistake he made, hitting the floor with a long staff to beat out the time. Rio was right. He could do it all by Giazin's age and more. Much more. "Look, you may be right about Giaz but before you get carried away with more parenting advice to me, I want you to talk to Pom about doing the *Dream*."

"I will."

"I mean it, Rio. Today."

"Yeah." Rio laid his head back on Triani's shoulder. "You feel just like *mertsi*," he said softly.

No wonder, thought Triani, who knew his body was practically an exact replica of the hated parent's but he couldn't tell Rio that and shatter his idealized picture of his *mertsi* forever.

"What's 'castrated' mean?" Rio asked suddenly.

Triani froze. "You'll have to get Pom to explain all that," he said uneasily. He slipped an arm around his small sibling, who had been through so much suffering and hugged him fiercely.

"Ow," said Rio, but he didn't move away. "Something to do with love, isn't it? I thought you were the big expert on sex."

"Love and sex are not the same," Triani said shortly. "Come on, sweetie. Corvin must be awake by now and you can't keep the specialists waiting any longer."

Before they got to the corridor leading to Rio's rooms, Triani paused. "Listen, I'm going out now, but I'll see you tomorrow and yes, we can do the variations with Giazin. But you have to talk to Pom tonight."

"I said I'll talk to him." Rio turned back as he was about to leave. "So, is it love or sex tonight?"

"I don't know, sweetie. That's why I have to go."

Triani's smile faded as he watched the small figure walk away. Back straight, head up, shoulders back, he almost floated down the hall. A talented dancer, who might not be able to dance for much longer.

TWENTY-TWO

Music reverberated in the vaulted space of the old hall, sending waves of joy through Marlo and his fellow choristers. Hands clasping the singer on either side, they sang full-throated, heads back, bodies thrilling to the emotions elicited by the music as it bounced back to them through their touch. When the last note quivered into silence, they all stood there, overcome. Some, like Marlo, had tears glistening on their cheeks. Some, an expression of ineffable joy. Finally, they dropped hands and turned away, breaking the circle.

"Wow," said Marlo's neighbor, a willowy contralto, wiping his eyes. "Isn't it just grand?"

Marlo nodded mutely. This was why he loved choral practice; why he had headed here in an almost frantic rush after leaving the charged atmosphere surrounding Rio and Corvin and their tragic lives. It was a safe space, cut off completely from his daily life, where he could push away the worrisome and sometimes horrific things he had to deal with in his job and just wallow in something pure, cleansing, joyous. His singing friends knew little about him really. All they talked about was music. They teased each other about who was a bit flat, or sharp, or lagging behind; who forgot lyrics, or jumped in too soon, who needed to stand beside a stronger singer so they wouldn't get lost in the five part harmonies. He knew that some were politicians, some worked on the Bridge, the famous elite jewelry venue. Some were healers. One had a house full of children and some taught arcane subjects in the Scolariti. They knew he was an investigator who now and then was in the news when some case of his hit the interest of the news hounds. No one took advantage of this knowledge, even when they went out in groups after practice to a snack house or song bar. They never tried to pry into the details of a particularly juicy case. In return, he never asked for advice from them in any field. It was a safe place for them all.

Tonight Marlo felt purged of the grime that seemed to cling to his soul from knowing far too much about the Colony Dance group; about what went on in secret behind their closed doors. But as the others wandered off to collect their belongings or chat about the rehearsal, Marlo waved goodbye and made his way to his air-car, avoiding all invitations. All he wanted was to see Calian again after what seemed a very long time. He wanted to hear the stories about the SongFest, the new music, Cal's *Meshdravi* family and friends Marlo didn't know, down in the Lakeside country where he had never been.

It would have been more convenient for him to have Cal come to his house, but it seemed unfair to expect this after Cal had been away for so much time. He must long to be back in his bright, playful house again, to be back among his own things; the toys and games and puzzles he created with his large strong hands, the wonderfully equipped cooking space. Marlo was almost licking his lips by the time he got to the brightly painted building where Cal lived and worked. He stumbled out of his air-car and saw Cal waiting, his pale blond curls blowing in the breeze.

"Next time you're coming with me!" Cal greeted him. "I don't care who's getting married."

Marlo walked into his arms and breathed in that special scent he had been missing. "Nothing I would like more," he said and kissed the warm moistness under the pale hair.

Arms entwined, they went downstairs on the lift disk, descending into the welcoming aromas of spices and jam and a mixture that was delicious but indefinable. Marlo took in a deep breath and felt himself relax. It was as if he was coming home, even though his home had never smelled like this.

Calian presented Marlo with a basket of music cubes featuring the high points of the SongFest and one featuring his family performing a morning ritual chant and anthem of thanks. Something to look forward to, especially seeing Calian with his family.

"I have something for you, too," Marlo said sheepishly, presenting a painted box in the Adelantis-Benvolini colors. "I'm sorry there's only two wedding balls left inside. There were six but they were calling, singing, wailing late at night..."

"I understand perfectly." Calian took out one sugared ball and popped it into his mouth. He took out the second one and held it out for Marlo, who could not resist.

"And here's a Good Wish ornament from the wedding. Luckily it's not edible."

Calian laughed and took the beautifully carved object in his hands. "Lovely work," he said, running his finger over the delicately carved figures inside the circle, with its deceptively simple design. "This is the real thing, not produced in any factory but all handmade. I guess that shouldn't be a surprise from your classy friends."

"I was working security, Cal." Marlo wondered if he would have been invited anyway. Maybe, but certainly not for the third day.

"Thanks. I'll hang it up in the window now, even though I wasn't there. Hope that's not a breach of good manners or something."

"The idea is to remind people passing by to think good thoughts of the married couple so I think it's fine."

Marlo wandered after him as Cal went to one of his large windows and attached the ornament so it hung there, suspended by its red cord. While Calian fussed over getting it to hang just so, Marlo noticed a bag on the floor in the corner. Something about it looked familiar so he went to investigate.

"That should be downstairs," Cal said, coming to join him. "You know I'm always bringing things up from my workshop. It's *troxite*."

"How come you use that stuff? I thought it was just used in buildings."

"It's very versatile. It depends on how you mix it, what you add to it, if you heat or not and on and on. I use it to make those little figures for mobiles, like this one, see?" He motioned to a colorful mobile hanging nearby. "And those candlesticks. Also in the cases for the bigger games I make."

"There's no Elutian markings on this bag."

Cal wrinkled his forehead as he looked more closely at the bag of *troxite*. "Should there be?"

"The ones I just saw at Triani's place did."

"Hunh. Well, this bag is old. They could have changed the packaging. I don't use much at a time for the figures. There's more downstairs that just came in to provide the case for another one of those big walk-in game units. Want to check before we eat?"

Marlo nodded and Cal took his hand.

"Let's use the slide."

Marlo was out of breath, his cheeks pink as he landed on the soft cushions at the bottom of the slide on the first floor. Calian was right behind him, his arms around his waist.

"There. See? Right beside us. I just used some to make these tiles last night but I didn't notice. So this is the newer stuff. I remember it took an unusually long time to get here." Cal picked up one of the tiles and handed it to Marlo. "What do you think of—"

"No!" Marlo felt the tile slip though his fingers as it fell to the floor. And shattered. "I'm so sorry!"

Cal stared at the scattered pieces. "They aren't supposed to break," he said. "Don't worry. I must have mixed it wrong. I really was too tired and shouldn't have tried it but I had this idea. You know how I am."

Marlo just stared at the broken pieces, now being briskly sucked up by a cleaner 'bot.

"This is for a case, isn't it?"

Marlo sighed. "I don't really know," he said. "I just notice things."

"How about noticing some cookery magic? I whipped up a little family recipe."

"Whatever you whip up I know I'll enjoy," Marlo said with enthusiasm, following him on the lift disk back into the fragrant second floor. If Calian's family home smelled like this, he really wanted to visit.

Back in his hillside home next morning, last night's candlelight and sweet intimacy seemed a distant memory as Marlo prepared for his interview with Parla Serlini Adelantis. He didn't want to do this but Old Livid had asked him to gather evidence to see if there was enough to have a hearing and it was part of his job. The problem was he liked Parla, who had been a big help to him in another difficult case last year. These situations were always easier if he didn't know the person involved.

Marlo took more care than usual with his appearance, the image of Parla's arresting beauty strong in his mind, then set off for the architect's much-admired house on the cliff. It was difficult to see much of the interesting structure from the front. It had been designed to blend in with the surrounding grey-green rock but once you saw it, it was amazing, hanging there as if in mid-air.

Parla opened the door himself, which surprised Marlo, but perhaps the house was smaller than he thought and Parla didn't need or want a Keeper.

"Do come in," Parla said, standing back to let Marlo pass. "Eulio and Orosin are here to give me moral support. I'm sorry to be the cause of them cutting short their marriage trip, but here they are."

"Family always wants to help," Marlo said, making his way to the beautiful reception room. He glanced up in surprise to see the turquoise water of a swimming pool that was their ceiling. "How fabulous!"

Parla smiled. "Water is so soothing," he murmured.

Marlo greeted the others and sat down, wishing he was somewhere else with no embarrassing questions to ask anyone. He discreetly slid his official insignia with its tiny recorder onto his lap. "I'm sorry this has to be an official visit."

Parla merely nodded and sat down, crossing his legs at the ankles.

"Don't mind us," Beny said. "Or would you rather we left?"

"No need," Marlo said. "This is just a few questions so I can get the feel of things." He glanced at his hands for inspiration.

"You do realize Parla had nothing to do with the accident," Eulio said, leaning forward.

Marlo looked at the lovely tense face. "According to the law he is responsible as the person in charge."

"And I realize that," Parla snapped. "Now let him get on with it, Euli!"

"You know, as I recall from the few times we talked last year when you were in the middle of the project, you seemed to be having a few problems."

"There are always problems in a big production," Eulio said, scowling. "And tell him about all those envious jealous rivals!" Eulio added. "Tell him."

Parla got to his feet. "Why don't we go to my office so I can show you the models. It'll make it easier to explain."

"Good idea." Marlo was relieved to follow him out into a corridor that seemed to go under a waterfall. He noticed a large image of Parla and Triani apparently at some gala outside the completed Entertainment complex. They were smiling at each other and holding glasses of pale green wine.

"If I was seen on camera pushing someone off the building Eulio would swear I didn't do it," Parla was saying as they entered a large bright space, obviously a workroom of some kind.

"Loyalty is a wonderful quality," Marlo murmured, looking around. There were images of buildings on the pale walls, some looked like private homes, some larger. Several 3D models lined the deep shelves. The largest one was the Wave Entertainment Complex.

Parla offered him one of the plain black chairs which turned out to be surprisingly comfortable. Marlo leaned back and folded his hands across his ample stomach, ready to listen.

"Eulio's right about one thing," Parla began. "Every project has problems and this one had more because it was so big. But most of it was with the work crews: people not showing up on time, people not showing up at all, others getting sick and then we needed to hire new people."

"Was this more of a problem than usual?" Marlo asked.

"Yes. And frankly I suspect that Eulio is right about this, too. My competitors, some of them, have never come to terms with the fact that I won this contract. Some have never welcomed me with open arms, shall we say, and after that, things escalated." Parla was pacing slowly, weighing each word, obviously aware of the possible repercussions of what he was saying.

Marlo said nothing, sensing this was the best tactic at this stage.

"They resent me, Marlo. They think, and even say from time to time, that a First Order Merculian has no business taking up space in their profession." Parla sat down again, seeming relieved to have gotten that off his chest.

"Are you the only one?"

"At the moment, but there have been others before me who encountered no such problems."

Probably not one your age with such astonishing good looks, Marlo thought. Who would have ever dreamed that being born into such beauty and privilege could have a down side.

"So I gather you suspect some of these people were behind these problems with the work crews?" Marlo suggested.

Parla nodded. "More than suspect. I know. At least in a few cases. Some of the crew admitted to me they had been paid off. It was all to delay the work so I wouldn't come in on time, something I pride myself on doing. I think that might have been one of the reasons I was chosen."

"So it slowed things a bit."

"A lot. We had to find new workers skilled in whatever aspect of the field was needed, and then had to teach them about the new way we were doing things."

"New way?"

"Oh nothing to do with the structure. That was all standard, even if a little different on the outside. The problems were all cosmetic, like mixing color in with the *troxite* along with a little sand to give it texture." Parla gestured to the nearby model.

"I see."

"But this has nothing to do with why the bridge collapsed."

"Any theories on that?" Marlo asked.

Parla looked down at his hands. "Sabotage," he whispered.

TWENTY-THREE

"**S**weetie, I just wanted sex, not your name." Triani turned his back on the young Merculian, who was still half undressed in the twinkling blue lights of the Labyrinth, and walked briskly away, ignoring the soft looks and offered caresses of those looking for a little sex in the misty morning before their day began.

Once out in the Pleasure Gardens Triani turned towards the parking pad and slowed down, tossing a buzzer in his mouth. His brief visit to Parla late last night had been unnerving. Parla's paranoia seemed to be growing and the endless plaints were irritating. Over and over again, no matter what Triani said or how he tried to change the subject. Didn't Parla realize that he had already done everything he could to help? "What do you want from me?" he muttered. "I'm your lover, not your legal advisor." Dissatisfied, Triani had left Parla's house early and come to the Labyrinth for the carefree release he craved.

Much more relaxed now, he swung into his late model air-car and punched in the co-ordinates for his country home. He wanted to get back well before Rio was up and do some work on *The Dream*. The more he thought about it, the more he wished he had not suggested this whole thing in the first place. He wasn't even sure that Rio was up to doing this, since he was no longer on all the drugs his old company had been feeding him all those years. How was his abused system reacting to this drastic change, not to mention whatever new stuff Pom was now shooting him up with? It all sounded good when the healer had explained it, but no one had asked how this might affect his ability to dance right now. The audience would be there, but would Rio still be good enough to dance with him? Triani the perfectionist never wanted to be seen in any but the best light on stage.

He lay back against the welcoming upholstery and closed his eyes, going over the choreography in his mind, taking note one more time of what would have to be altered, changed, or cut completely to accommodate their differing heights and strengths. Certainly no lifts for Rio. Triani sighed and opened his eyes. Of course he had realized this part earlier and had come up with a lot of ideas to get them through it, if only Rio was still up to it.

"We are approaching your destination, *chai*," the sultry voice announced. "Would you like to take over?"

Triani sat up and placed his hands on the controls, guiding the air-car smoothly onto the landing pad. The place was very quiet this early in the morning. Even the rope tree blossoms had not opened yet and were making no chirping sounds as Triani moved past them, through the gate in the wall and into the house.

It was blissfully quiet in here, too, the distant splashing of the fountain in the main courtyard the only sound. Until there was a crash nearby, followed by an angry shout.

"It's not my fault!"

Giazin was obviously up early too.

Triani veered towards the noise, then stopped, turned back and continued through to his own part of the house. Let Govsy do his job, the idiot. Fifteen minutes later Triani was down in his studio, dressed in rehearsal tights, leg warmers and dance shoes. He waved on the lights and took a drink of wake water, then popped a stim. For a long moment he stood staring at himself in the mirrored wall. This was going to be either a monumental disaster or a huge success. After warming up, he turned on the music and took up his position for the opening solo.

The next time he looked in the mirror, he saw a small figure watching intently from the doorway, hand on hip. He stopped and snapped off the music.

"Not bad," said Rio, sauntering into the room.

Triani bit back an acid reply. Instead he said, "Did you ask Pom about doing 'Dream' like you promised?"

Rio adjusted his slipper. "Honestly, Triani, you fuss too much. Yes, I did and he said since it's so short it's okay but after this no more, so my body has time to adjust to all the changes." He began to go through his warmup routine and Triani watched for a moment, then went back to his own sequence of steps near the end of his solo.

"Okay, you start your opening solo now until you sit down to sleep, and then I'll do mine, and we'll figure it out from there," Rio announced when he was finished.

"Yes, great one," Triani mocked.

Once the music started, Triani forgot about his annoying little sibling and melted into the part, until he glided over to the plain chair he had pulled into the studio to represent the couch. Then he watched Rio spring nimbly into his role, stop, peer around with a mischievous look on his face and leap across to circle the chair. It certainly wasn't the way Triani danced the role but it was charming and worked beautifully. Triani sensed things might not be so bad after all.

"Okay, this first partner section should work alright," Triani said. "Let's try it." He stepped forward, reaching out to his small partner. Rio swung around into place, and kept going smoothly for the next section of the music.

"And now I leap!" And Rio did, from across the room right onto Triani's arms.

Unprepared, Triani caught him and took a step back, barely resisting the urge to fling his sibling partner against the wall.

"What the fuck do you think you're doing!" he shouted, dumping Rio on the floor. "Do you have any idea how many dancers are dying to dance with me? And you do this...this stupidity! And you call yourself a professional!"

"I trusted you and you dropped me!" Rio shouted, enraged. "And I *am a* professional! I have it all mapped out."

"And I'm supposed to read your mind? Look, how much choreo have you done?"

"Some." Rio picked himself up and blinked away tears. "Okay, so next you can just leap over me and for your lift two bars later, I can spring onto your shoulder. What do you think?"

"I'm surprised you asked me," said Triani sarcastically. "I thought you might be planning to dance both roles yourself."

"You don't have to be so mean."

"You think this is mean? Shit, Rio, grow up!"

"I'm trying to! That's why I'm here!"

"So take advantage of my experience, you little shit. Learn something!"

"I've been dancing this role for five years," Rio said, hands on hips. "And I went through hell to get here," he added.

"Fuck." Triani bit his lip and walked over to get a drink of water. "Okay, look, we need a rehearsal director or we'll be sniping at each other all day and get nowhere. I'll call and see if I can get Mal or Daravini to meet us in the small rehearsal hall in the theater as soon as possible to help block it out. You okay with that?"

Rio shrugged. "Okay, I guess. But I have a lot of ideas—"

"Shut up."

"You wouldn't say that to Eulio!"

"If he's wrong, I would." Triani paused. "Let me ask you something. Would *you* behave like this with Eulio?"

Rio looked away. "Well, if you put it like that…"

"And?"

"Okay, Sorry."

Triani shook his head and walked out.

TWENTY-FOUR

Marlo didn't like to get his hair wet, especially since he had just had his highlights done to celebrate Calian's return. Besides, his bag of *chaico* chips was also damp, threatening the crispness of one of his favorite snacks. It wasn't supposed to rain today, yet another mark against the soothsayers of the Merculian weather network.

By the time he arrived upstairs and was settled in his small office just off the main investigative unit hall he was feeling more optimistic, at least about the weather. The Adelantis case, however, was not looking up. In fact, things were much worse. This case, which had at first been reported as someone falling off a bridge, had become progressively darker. Now the poor soul had died and everyone would need a scapegoat.

Marlo munched on a chip as he looked over the images of the fall, trying to get a sense of what might have happened. Had it been sabotage? Surely not. He could see the petty things, the luring away of workers, the cutting of cables, stealing materials, but this? Since that day there had been a lot of people touring through the newly opened building. There could have been more deaths or at the very least injuries, since that day there had been a lot of people touring through the newly opened building.

He paused, remembering that just last year he had been involved in another Adelantis case that turned out to be much more complicated and dangerous than anyone could have imagined.

Sensing someone approaching his desk, without thinking he tried to hide his bag of chips under some files.

"Too late!" Eldred laughed. "You never were good at subterfuge."

"I thought you were Old Livid," Marlo retorted. "Anything new?"

He stuffed some more chips in his mouth.

"On that Corvin kid's parents," Eldred began, sitting on the corner of the desk. "your hunch was right. It seems they left Merculian about six years after the kidnapping. I have a few people on it, sifting through all the passenger lists at the SpacePort around that time. There are a lot so it may take a bit longer, but we'll find them."

"Thanks, El. The poor kid has been through enough. He deserves to see his parents again. Are the bastard Guardians still here?"

"Old Livid has ordered a round-the-clock, off-the-books surveillance on them, but so far they haven't moved. They say they're giving the dancers time to rest up before going home."

"Because they're so thoughtful that way," Marlo said disgustedly. "Fabulous." Then he remembered the Nat Regs. Had Old Livid contacted them? Or was this undercover surveillance to assuage his conscience because he had done nothing. On the other hand they now had the Official Recorder's report on two of the poor kids. The terrible abuse was official, so the Nationals must know!

About to go in to get confirmation from Old Livid he remembered in time that he was supposed to be assembling notes on Parla's case for the High Crimes Court.

"Do you want me on this now?" Eldred had been studying images of the scene of the supposed accident. "The others can track down the kid's parents without me."

"I need that deep background on Adelantis—his credit accounts, his work history, what his workers think of him, his standing in the work community. Everything!"

"I know you had the rest of the team on it. Let's go see what they've found out."

In Team Room 3 on the other side of the unit, a surprise was waiting for him. The full breasts and a not-quite-slim waist attested to the fact this old teammate had recently had a child and was still nursing.

"Oslani! What are you doing here?" Marlo hugged his tech specialist and was immediately reminded of his Terran female friend Boothby. Must be the "boobies" as she called them.

"Oh Marlo I'm going completely lalagogs at home!" Oslani cried. "Babies can be quite boring, I've discovered. How come nobody tells you that? Maybe I'll take my baby leave later when he's older, talking maybe."

"Or ready for tech school?" suggested Ferdalyn.

"How about you say you need me on this case?" Oslani went on, ignoring his young colleague. He clasped his hands in mock supplication.

"Of course I do," Marlo spluttered, laughing, "but what about… well…you know…feeding the boring baby?"

"No problem. All figured out! My lover has plenty of time off. He might as well be useful." Oslani settled down at his familiar place at the end of the table. "Anyway, Old Livid says it's fine with him as long as you agree. To cinch the deal, I brought you some pink biscuits." He pushed a small box across the table towards Marlo.

"Well, why didn't you say that earlier!" Marlo pounced on them playfully and passed them around. "I hope you didn't make these," he added looking at his friend, who was a notoriously bad cook.

Oslani shook his head but he was already absorbed in what looked like a scan of something.

Marlo looked around the table as he crunched on the last pink biscuit. "How are Parla Adelantis's accounts?" he asked, looking at Tabor, who had a head for numbers.

The youngest member of the team pulled up a chart and began to explain it. "You can see he is very well off, but there are many weird withdrawals which I tracked down to credits paid directly to workmen and for materials. He apparently was trying to cover vastly overspending by using his own money to cover up mistakes, or whatever."

"Or covering up sabotage," Marlo suggested.

"Possibly, but it seems he has done this before, though not this much."

"This was his biggest project so far," Ferdalyn pointed out. "It seems he usually comes in on time but over budget."

"Everyone goes over budget, don't they?" Marlo asked.

The discussion went on for a while, with Parla looking a little less experienced than Marlo was expecting as far as the financing was concerned. It was almost as if he knew he could make up any short fall with his own money every time. Maybe this was why his rivals were envious, but jealous enough to sabotage a completed site in a way that might result in injury or death?

"Why did he go over budget so much on this latest project?" Marlo wanted to know.

Ferdalyn scratched his head, his floppy curls falling over his eyes. "Well, it's mostly materials. He started out using *troxite* from the Merculian mines but that was too slow and more expensive so halfway through he switched to the Planet Colony. That worked for a while but then there was a slow-down until work almost stopped on the site. See? They were waiting for weeks at one point. Then, the supplies started flowing again." He pointed to the file on the wall, moving his finger to the different columns.

"Look at this," Oslani said, sitting up suddenly. "This is a blown-up scan of the interior of the bridge wall. Here's another scan of the interior of the same building but the opposite end, where the other bridge is."

They all stared at the two images, now projected onto the wall.

"They look a bit different," Eldred ventured. "What does it mean?"

"I'll have to check this out with the lab but I think it means someone, somewhere, is watering down the *troxite*."

"But aren't you supposed to mix it with water?" Tabor asked.

"Yes, but I mean it's been rushed through the primary process when it's washed and then crushed before the extreme heating which leads to the final coarse powder. Too much water was used at their end."

Marlo remembered the tile he had dropped at Calian's house, the fine powdery dust that covered the floor.

"So, it's the stuff from the Colony Planet mines," Eldred said. "Now all we have to do is find out which ones."

"Which one is controlled by Elutians?" Marlo asked.

TWENTY-FIVE

On the way to the theater, Rio was quiet. Then suddenly he asked: "What happens when you go to court?"

"Which court? What do you mean?" Triani frowned at him.

"There's more than one?"

"Of course! Shit, Rio, don't you know anything?"

"I told you! Once we joined the company, there was nothing but dance in our lives. No school. Just dance. Morning, noon and night. Honestly, we thought that's what it was like for all dancers."

"Holy shit! And *mertsi* knew about this?"

"Not really. It just never came up."

"Fuck. Okay, what's this sudden interest in the court system?"

"I was just reading about what happens if you sue someone like we want to get lots of credits, but it seems complicated. Can't you just write down what they did wrong and send it in to the court place, or what?"

Triani took a deep breath. "You have to be there yourself. You have to say everything that the person or group of people did to you and how it has affected you, and you have to say it in front of the whole court and the people you're accusing."

"Shit," said Rio. "I never thought it would be like that! A whole room full of people?"

"And news hounds," Triani added.

"So everyone would know," he said slowly.

"Sweetie, I wouldn't do it, if I were you."

Rio didn't answer but his face was red and there were tears in his eyes.

Triani wordlessly offered him half a tranq stick. He had completely forgotten about this scheme but was glad Rio had asked.

Maybe now he would forget the idea once he realized he would make himself and Corvin into objects of prurient interest. Victims, not stars.

Triani was relieved to get back to the grand old theater that had been his home for so long. He paused before getting out of the air-car and looked at Rio.

"Honestly if you give me another lecture I will just scream!" said Rio.

Triani began to laugh. He couldn't help it. The expression on Rio's face was so much like Giazin's. "Let's go," he said, grabbing his dance bag and leading the way inside.

Mal and Nevon were both waiting for them in the rehearsal hall.

"Hi Mal, sweetie. Thanks for doing this at such short notice." Triani went over to Nevon and gave him a quick kiss. "Looking after your investment?" he murmured.

Nevon smiled. "Wouldn't you in my place?"

Triani stripped down to his dance clothes and began to warm up. He noticed Rio had reverted to the silent respectful youngster he had seemed at the beginning, bowing deeply to the two directors before warming up.

When they were ready to start, Mal introduced the accompanist who had just come in and was sitting at his *klavalo* in one corner.

"I have some notes here," Mal began, "but I'm sure you have already given this some thought, Triani."

"I have some ideas—" Rio began, but Mal walked past him and went up to Triani. "Your notes?"

"Sure, sweetie." Triani handed over his porta-pad.

Mal read the notes quickly then held his hand out to Rio. "And yours?"

Silently, Rio handed his over, with a resentful look at Triani.

Mal ran a hand through his sparse hair and cleared his throat. "Triani, you've done your usual thoughtful work on this, I see, but Rio has a few flourishes that might work well to combine both your styles." He paused. "Look, Triani, this ending is spectacular, but are you sure you can do it?"

"Of course, as long as the couch thing is attached to the stage. We'll need something similar to practice with."

"What ending?" Rio asked. "You didn't tell me!"

"Trust me, you'll love it," said Triani.

"Trust *you*? You dropped me!"

"Because you're an ass! You don't leap at your partner without sharing your plan!"

"Enough!" Mal's voice was unusually sharp.

"Sorry *chai.*"

"Mal, sweetie, he drives me crazy."

"I can see that, but if you two primo donnas have finished carping, we need to get down to work. I have limited time."

He went on to explain his vision of the altered choreography and began with the two solos, Triani first, then Rio, making minor corrections as they went along to make the piece more of a whole. This went on, only more slowly, as they began their dance together.

"Triani, you're giving more of a seductive interpretation. Could you make it lighter? More playful? Remember this is a young spirit you're dancing with this time. Good…Good…And Rio, slow down on the lyrical section. Give your partner time for those extra steps we added. Nice…"

And so it went, until they could dance the whole thing smoothly, with barely a hitch.

"And now I have to go," Mal said. "I'll see you tomorrow. Good work, both of you."

"Thank you, *chai,*" said Rio, bowing.

Over his head, Triani exchanged a wink with the director.

Tired and hungry, both dancers were silent on the way home. Triani was going over everything in his head, pleased that things had gone as smoothly as they had, with Rio accepting from Mal some of the same things Triani had tried to tell him earlier. But at least they had proved it was possible, he thought, as the house came into view. Of course they hadn't tried the ending yet.

They landed smoothly and Rio jumped down, pulling his dance bag with him.

"I'm going to eat with Corvin," he called over his shoulder.

"Like I care," muttered Triani, heading for his shower and a change of clothes.

He was sitting down to a solitary late afternoon meal in the garden, and was shouting at his manager on his com-dev, calling him every kind of moron for double-booking him twice in a month's time, when Rio rushed up to him.

"I can't find Corvin," he said "I've looked everywhere."

Triani gave a final excoriating insult to his manager before turning to Rio. "Holy shit, Rio, this is a big place," he said, gesturing to the vast gardens surrounding the sprawling estate. "Check the beach or the other side of the lake."

But Rio was back thirty-five minutes later, out of breath this time and still no Corvin.

"For fuck's sake," muttered Triani, getting to his feet. "Come on." He hunted down the Keeper, who at this hour was usually checking the house 'bots at the 'bot station near the gardeners' area to make sure all were running well.

"Have you seen my friend Corvin?" Rio asked, almost breathless.

"I do not keep track of the comings and goings of the people in this house," he said stiffly, standing tall so that he was able to look down his nose at Rio.

"Look, sweetie, I know that's not your job but you're observant, so, just tell me if you noticed him leaving."

The Keeper looked up at the ceiling, as if the answer was written up there somehow. Then he looked at his employer. "There was an air-car," he said thoughtfully.

"What air-car? Spit it out!"

The Keeper looked hurt. He sniffed. "It was an air-cab, actually, sent to pick up the red-headed one to visit the parents of his old friend."

"What old friend?" exclaimed Triani. "He doesn't know anyone here."

"He must mean Eulari's parents," Rio suggested. "They call him Pendaron. Corvin told me he promised to go back and visit them again. But why today?" Rio looked at Triani questioningly.

"How would I know!" But Triani felt uneasy. Corvin was not the adventurous type. "Was there anyone in the car to greet him?" he asked.

"Just the driver, *chai*, and that's all I can tell you."

Triani turned away and pulled out his com-dev to contact Marlo. The Regulator knew these people. He could check to see if Corvin was still there and Triani could send his driver to pick him up. He remembered the so-called Guardians who were looking for the kids early on. Were they still around?

But Marlo checked and told him Corvin had never been invited to visit Pendaron's parents. Nobody there had sent an air-cab.

Corvin had just vanished.

TWENTY-SIX

Marlo was sauntering back to work after taking an extended break from the exhaustive research into *troxite* mines on the Colony Planet. There seemed to be far more of them then he had expected. He was smiling, thinking fondly of the new Terran treat his female friend Boothby had introduced him to called 'ice cream'. He licked his lips, remembering the smooth, cool feel of it, the rich velvet-cream taste on his tongue.

And then Triani called on his private line, no less, and pulled him abruptly out of his trance.

"Leave it with me," he told Triani, when the dancer had run out of steam. "I'll find him."

Inside HQ he informed Eldred of Corvin's disappearance. "Ordinarily a youngster of Corvin's actual age would not be a matter of concern, but he looks really young, remember, and has no street smarts. None."

"Shall I get a search team together?"

Marlo shook his head. "Is Oslani here?"

El nodded.

"Okay, get him and join me in the reg car." Marlo was worried enough to think of telling Old Livid, but since there was nothing concrete to report, he changed his mind.

As he and his two top team members sped towards the Theater Residence where the Colony Dancers were staying, Marlo explained why he was so worried, just touching on the official report from the Recorder, careful not to go into details of a case liable to go to the court of High Crimes with a Top Secret label.

"I'm afraid this may be the first step in their scheme to get Rio back," he said.

"But if there's a surveillance team on them there's nothing to worry about," Oslani pointed out.

"I know, I know, but I want to talk to those Guardians. You two cover the exits. I think there are two."

"Or we could call the surveillance team," El pointed out.

"I want to be there," Marlo said stubbornly.

But all seemed quiet when they arrived and met the eager surveillance duo.

"We take turns patrolling all around the building," the younger one said. Marlo couldn't help noticing he was holding a honey stick behind his back.

"And nobody has gone in or out?" Marlo asked. "No children?"

"Not while we've been here," the other answered quickly.

"Guess he's not here then," said Eldred. "He disappeared late this morning, so these two would have seen him if he came here."

"True." Marlo went to the main door and clapped. He wanted to see the reaction of the Guardians.

"I remember you," exclaimed the caretaker, who had been there the last few times Marlo had visited. "So nice to see you again."

Marlo smiled broadly, a little surprised at his enthusiasm. "I'm pleased to see you, too," he said, "but I must confess I really came to see the Colony people."

The caretaker backed away shaking his head. "I am so sorry but they've gone. I can't understand such rudeness. Fled in the middle of the night sometime. And why? They were all paid up, so they weren't skipping out on the credits. It's a mystery." One hand went to his chin. "A real mystery."

"Could I see their place?"

"They left it a total mess, too. I don't understand it." He opened the double doors to show a scene of complete mayhem. Chairs were overturned, bits of clothing scattered about, a glass bowl lay broken on the floor, colored beads tumbled among the shards. "Just look at that, now."

"What in the world were they doing?" Oslani asked, looking around in amazement.

"When did you know they were gone?" Marlo asked.

"I don't remember, exactly. They were here last night. I could hear them talking and running around like they do. Then this morning

I was out doing errands. At noon I noticed it was very quiet but I didn't think much of it. Then, about an hour ago, I clapped because I had a lot of extra cinnamon twirls I'd made for our Epicantare Appreciation club but the meeting was cancelled so I thought the children would enjoy them."

"I'm sure they would have, too." Marlo's mouth watered at the very thought.

"So when no one answered, I went in and found…all this." He looked around at the confusion sadly.

"So you have no idea when they left," Eldred asked.

"I told you, they were here when I retired to sleep. That's all I know for sure."

"Thank you." Marlo walked outside, followed by the others. He looked searchingly at the two Regulators of the surveillance team. "What time exactly did you arrive?"

"We were on time," the younger one said.

"Answer the question."

"We had trouble parking, *Com*, but we arrived almost exactly on time."

"Almost. And the first shift was still here?"

"Well, they had just left. One of them got sick and was throwing up, you know."

"Fabulous." Marlo turned away angrily.

The next thing he knew he was knocked to the ground and felt Oslani's soft breasts pressing into his back as two large hover-bikes swooped past so close he could feel the wind lifting his hair. He looked after them and had the impression of pale green and a long yellow sash streaming out in their wake before they disappeared around a corner.

"Hoolee!" exclaimed the young Regulator. "That was a close one!"

Oslani jumped to his feet and dusted off his leggings. "That was deliberate," he said, helping Marlo to his feet. "He aimed right for you."

Marlo nodded. "Is that some sort of uniform?" he asked, rubbing one bruised knee.

"Yes, *com*," piped up the young Regulator. "I used to collect images of all the different uniforms I could find and then paint them. I remember this one because it was hard to get that golden yellow color just right."

"So what is it?"

"It's the Faisian Falanx. They're a private army from the Colony Planet."

Marlo sat down abruptly on the edge of a convenient statue. "Of course," he said quietly. Poor Corvin.

"They shouldn't be wearing their uniforms here!" Eldred said indignantly.

Marlo was talking to his chief, filling him in what had happened. When he was finished he turned to the others. "They locked down the SpacePort hours ago so the Guardians and the kids must still be there. They probably took Corvin there directly so he must be there too. Somewhere. Oslani, go back and see if you can find any trace of him on the public area cams around here. Let me know if you find anything useful. El, let's go."

"Can we come too?" asked the young Regulator.

"Go home," said Marlo.

TWENTY-SEVEN

Triani had a glass of *lim* in one hand and his com-dev in the other. He had contacted everyone he could think of who might help track down the kid but there was no sign of him yet. He had even called Eulio, though what he expected from him he didn't know.

"It's all my fault!" wailed Rio. "This whole thing was my idea! Coming here. Getting better medical aid. You."

"I thought it was *mertsi* who gave you the idea," Triani said, taking a drink.

"Yeah, well, I talked Corvin into coming along with me."

"That wouldn't take much." Triani looked through his contact list one more time and paused. "Shit. There's one more person I haven't tried. Not that he was much good to me the last time, but still. He owes me." He punched in a code and waited.

"Fan is here, *Chai* Triani. Is nice you call."

"Look, you snuffling Elutian miscreant, you owe me! That's why I called, not for social chit chat. I need a Searcher to do a job for me. For free."

"Fan no work for free." The Elutian snorted loudly in indignation.

"You owe me from last time!"

"Last time is last time. This time, who knows? So what missing?"

Triani described Corvin and the danger he might be in from kidnapping. "He was one of the Colony dancers."

"Ahah. Planet Colony. Bad things happen there. Some of my people, not so good."

"No kidding," said Triani acidly.

"No worry. Me and Tuli, we find. But not free," With a parting snort he was gone.

"Not free. I can believe that." Triani was surprised Fan hadn't done any hard bargaining, the sort Elutians were famous for. That was either good, or really, really bad. Why was he possibly bankrupting himself for this kid he barely knew? One look at Rio's tear-streaked face gave him the answer.

"Did you try him on his com-dev?" he asked.

"I tried, but it was turned off."

"Try again."

Rio pulled out his small device and pushed Corvin's code, one of the few he had programmed so far.

"Hello, Rio Porvan Erlindo."

Rio dropped the device, his face suddenly drained of color.

Triani snatched it up at once. "Who the hell is this?" he demanded.

"It's the head Guardian of the company," Rio whispered. He grabbed the device from Triani. "Where's Corvin?" he asked, his voice shaky.

"Corvin is right here where he belongs. He's just waiting for you to join him before we go home."

"Our home is right here! Neither of us is going anywhere!" Rio's voice was gaining strength as he went on. "You can't do this!"

"Don't you want to see your parents again, Rio? Don't you know your *mertsi* is not well and may get much worse? Or that your *tatsi* might lose his great job? Don't you care about them?"

"What are you talking about?"

"Life can be very difficult on our home planet. Just come with us and all will be well."

Triani had been listening, his head close to Rio's. He grabbed the com-dev.

"Now you listen to me, you vile snake! You low-life drek of a Merculian! Don't you dare threaten a member of *my* family! Release Corvin at once or there will be consequences."

The only response was laughter. "The SpacePort, Ramp 15, in an hour." And the connection was broken. Triani tried to open the contact again but the device had been turned off.

"Fucking shit!" he shouted.

"You shouldn't have said that! Now they'll hurt *mertsi*!" Rio beat against his chest with his small fists.

Triani caught his wrists. "That was just a threat, Rio. They're trying to get you back the only way they can. As long as you're here, they can't get at you."

"They got at Corvin."

"Because he left. He fell into a trap."

"I'm going."

"You're doing no such thing. That's exactly what they want you to do and you wouldn't get anywhere before being scooped up."

"Not if you're with me."

"Holy shit! You want me to wade into the middle of this?"

"You fucking are in the middle of this! Come on!"

"Shit!"

Giazin was on a school field trip of some sort and Govsy would be picking him up in time for the late meal, so that was fine. Triani looked around as if trying to find some reason why he couldn't go anywhere. Then he called his driver.

Vandari had been working for him for some time, apparently immune to his employer's frequent moods when in frustration he would fire some member of his staff. Perhaps it was because he was unusually silent for a Merculian. Perhaps because he had been trained in aggression and had served as a bodyguard for his superstar boss from time to time. This would be one of those times.

"Hey sweetie, you armed?" Triani asked, before climbing into the air-car with Rio.

"If I need to be."

"You need to be."

"Then I am," he said enigmatically.

"Okay, sweetie. The SpacePort, VIP entry."

Rio chewed a tranq stick Triani had given him. "They're not really going to hurt *mertsi*, are they?" he asked again.

"No sweetie. Of course not." But *I* might, Triani thought as they headed to the city and the SpacePort high up in the south-east edge of the city.

TWENTY-EIGHT

The Cap City Central SpacePort looked like a gigantic glittering mirage built on the side of a cliff. The vast glass building jutted out into the air, forming a massive arch from the east side of the cliff to the west, sheltering the smaller shuttles now parked on their cradles beside the long silver landing ramps on different levels below. Coming from the city through the main entry, the gigantic Port Concourse in front was usually bustling with Merculians and aliens of all sorts, some hurrying to catch a shuttle out to the larger ships docked at the Hub Station in the sky far above, or waiting to welcome family and friends returning home after a long trip off-world.

Today the huge space was jammed with jostling crowds, mostly Merculians. Many had colorful luggage piled on floating carrier pads beside them. A few babies were crying lustily, red-faced and angry at the noise and confusion. Some of these people had obviously been waiting a long time and were becoming very impatient. The SpacePort guards struggled to keep the unusually large crowds back behind the thick red braided cord that formed a fragile temporary barrier but it was getting difficult.

By the time they arrived, Marlo was frustrated from trying to get information on his com-dev about starting a search of the shuttles and small ships for the children of the Colony Dance group. Tired of being passed from one office to another, he had given up and decided to try the face-to-face approach.

"I didn't think it would be this bad," Eldred said as they pushed their way determinedly through the immense crowd with a litany of apologies, finally arriving at the long row of gleaming scanner passthroughs at the front. Each one led to a moving slip-walk that mounted slowly through the air to the boarding platform high above the crowd. Once up there, the passengers would have access to the shuttles beyond through rows of numbered gates. But the normally translucent passthroughs were now completely opaque, which meant they were locked. No one could get in or out.

"Now what?" Eldred asked.

"No guards down by the far wall," Marlo pointed out, motioning to the vine-covered wall at the other side of the vast concourse that supported that end of the huge building housing the lounges and offices.

"That's a long way, Marlo. Sure you can make it through this mob?"

As if to illustrate Eldred's point, the crowd surged forward and Marlo almost fell.

"Flying farts!" he muttered, righting himself and hanging on to Eldred for a moment to get his balance. "Look, I know there's a service stairway by that wall over there leading to the boarding platform and if we go up that way we can get into the building. It's the only way to get to the people who know what's going on here."

"Why are we worrying about the guards?"

"Because, El, I have no authority in the SpacePort. It's a Merculian National Regulator zone. Didn't you know?"

"It's never come up before," said Eldred defensively. "Anyway, I don't see any of them around."

"You will soon," muttered Marlo, edging in the direction of the wall.

It took them a long time to get there and Marlo was soon tired from the constant effort to keep his balance while pushing steadily forward. Finally the crowd thinned out a little and they were able to reach the shadow of the wall, where Marlo sat down on the bottom step for a moment to catch his breath.

"Are you okay?" Eldred asked, looking at him solicitously.

"I'm not that fragile," muttered Marlo. A little annoyed at his colleague's concern, he got back up and began to climb.

The two Regulators made their slow way up the long narrow flight of stairs to the platform where Marlo paused to catch his breath. Glancing down from this vantage point high above the jostling crowd, he caught sight of a troop of National Regulators in their distinctive maroon and black braid uniforms marching in from the Guard House far away at the other end of the concourse. Someone must have called in reinforcements.

"Fabulous," muttered Marlo, backing closer to the building so as not to be easily seen from below. "Next they'll call in the Serpian Raiders." He didn't like military displays of any sort. The Nat Regs were bad enough, but the Serpians could inflict real damage.

"Remember, the Raiders are on our side." Benvolini appeared beside him.

Marlo jumped in surprise.

"I didn't mean to startle you," Beny said apologetically. "I came because Eulio asked me to."

"Why?" Marlo asked, giving Beny a keen look.

Beny waved one hand in the air. "Well, there's nothing mysterious about it. To make a long story short, Triani called all upset because Rio was insisting on coming here to try to get his little friend back. I'm sure you know all the details."

And you probably do too, Marlo thought, his mind going back to times when Beny seemed to know things he had no right to know. "What did he expect you to do?" he asked, always trying to pry out some details of Beny's source of odd power.

Beny just smiled. "It's my *tan*, who has the real power, Marlo," he said, as if reading his mind. "Pamiano is a member of the Inner Council. He deals with the InterPlanetary Alliance all the time, and he's the reason there's an imposing star-ship of their fleet way out near the travel lane to the Colony Planet. Look. You can just make it out from here."

Marlo shaded his eyes as he looked up and saw the wide-winged vessel glinting silver in the sun. He wondered what their orders were.

"Luckily they were in the area," Beny said casually.

Marlo shook his head in bewilderment. "I don't understand why they don't just search all the shuttles in the inner harbor." He frowned as he checked in his pocket for the last bit of pink biscuit he had thrust there earlier in the day. "Who can I contact about that? I can't seem to find out who's in charge."

"Good question. I suspect there's a squabble over who has the authority and who wants to take the risk with no actual proof to back it up. No one wants to be responsible for riling up a foreign power if nothing is found. Most of these shuttles aren't Merculian."

Eldred, who had ducked into the control center behind them while Marlo was talking, arrived back at that moment to report that the captains of freight barges and passenger shuttles alike were getting very fractious. "Luckily one of my old friends from the Health Club works there. He says the powers that be insist that there's no proof Corvin or the other children are even here. There's no sign of them on any passenger lists."

"There wouldn't be if they're trying to sneak away with a kidnapped kid," Marlo said crossly. "They're all here. I *know* they're here. But they aren't going to be anywhere obvious." Marlo turned around and walked over to look through Gate 1, trying to make out the shuttles which were now so close. He couldn't see much. He turned back again to Beny and El. "Can you find out if there are some Elutian ships out there," he asked, thinking of the Elutian marks on the questionable *troxite* packages.

"Well, there are two, but why would the kid be there?" Eldred said. "According to my friend, they're not even carrying passengers."

"Just a thought."

"And a good one," Beny said, raising his voice to be heard over the rising din from the mob below. "The Elutians on the Colony have gradually moved into positions of power in their government, and at the same time have bought up several of the mines. Windfall is theirs, for one."

Marlo looked at him. "This is why you came," he said. "To give me intel."

"Knowledge is power," Beny remarked. "Excuse me. I have to make a call." He turned and disappeared inside the glass building.

Windfall. Their bat-like symbol on the children's dance bags. Did they own the dance company? All Marlo's research showed the company had been what looked like a real children's group for more than two hundred years, putting on charming shows for the residents of their small town. Nothing like the going concern it was now, touring all over their planet and branching out to ever farther regions, charging huge fees for professional level shows, the 'children' always guarded and kept to themselves. This sudden and increasing focus on credits was very Elutian.

"Can you find out how long the Elutian ships have been here, El?" Marlo asked. "And while you're at it, find out what ships have been here longest, from early this morning, say."

Eldred nodded and set off to talk to his friend in the control room again.

Something caught Marlo's eye, right across from the stairs. Triani and his small sibling were standing in a circle of admirers on the VIP parking pad's upper level, the only area still open. And there was a silent someone standing beside him and slightly to the back, his eyes scanning the restless crowd. As Marlo watched, a large Elutian lumbered off the lift-disk and ambled over to Triani.

"Fabulous," Marlo muttered.

Several yellow-jacketed Port guards had also noticed the group and soon rushed up to them, one gesticulating wildly. Triani tossed his head and motioned the silent one back to the air-car. No parking in the VIP area today, Marlo decided, smiling at Triani's obvious annoyance. But his smile melted away as Triani caught sight of him, jumped onto the lift-disk and once on the ground, dashed up the stairs to join him. Rio was right behind him. So much for staying inconspicuous now. Although the security guards would probably not come up to the platform, the Nat Regs would.

"Where's Corvin?" Rio shouted.

"What are you doing here?" Marlo countered, looking at Triani.

"The little shit insisted. He thinks it's his fault Corvin got tricked into this."

Rio hit Triani's chest. "It *is* my fault! I talked him into this...all this..."

"Fan need action now." The Elutian had arrived, snuffling loudly to lend weight to his words. "Kid you want, he here."

"How do you know?" Marlo asked sharply.

"Tracking from him, com-dev. But now gone," he added sadly, hanging his big head.

"So you can't prove he's here, either," Eldred said, rejoining them.

"They said to come here, that Corvin was here." Triani pushed the dark curls out of his eyes. "There's nowhere else he could be!"

"'Here' is a big place," Eldred remarked.

"Who is 'they'?" Marlo asked.

Triani explained about the threat from the guardian when Rio had tried to contact Corvin. "Ramp 15," he concluded, looking up at the numbers over the gates.

"Still not enough to make anyone here activate the search order," Marlo said. He didn't bother mentioning that Ramp 15 had many levels.

"Two Elutian vessels and the Uzois have been here the longest," Eldred reported dutifully. "And next longest here are the two Merculian shuttles."

"Cross off the Uzois. They never carry passengers not their own race if they can help it. The Merculian shuttles. When did they arrive? More importantly, when were they scheduled to leave?"

"Hours ago, Marlo. It can't be them. They're scheduled to offload on the *Myranis*, a Serpian ship."

"Don't write them off yet." Marlo noticed several National Regulators heading their way. They had finally been spotted. He glanced down through the gate behind him and this time saw a vessel he hadn't noticed before on the docking area. It was small and neglected looking, but it had faint Merculian markings on one side, and some other nearly illegible ones on the cracked and peeling dome. It was also the right shape for a Merculian runabout.

"I'm sorry, but everyone must move away from this area, *chais.*" The maroon uniformed Regulator bowed but looked serious.

"I'm a colleague," Marlo began, but he was cut off abruptly.

"You have no authority here, *Com.* Please move. You too, *Chai* Triani."

"It's nice to be acknowledged, sweetie, but I have to wait here for my driver."

"No one is allowed in this area now, *chai.* Please move away from the Port Area. You can contact him to pick you up outside the Port gates."

Several other maroon-clad ones had arrived to back their chief.

Triani was just opening his mouth to protest when Marlo grabbed his arm. He gave a sketchy salute and began to lead Triani and Rio towards the stairs the way they had come.

"No," interrupted the guard. "The other way, please. Down the stairs way at the other end and then leave the area at once through the east entrance. The port is closed indefinitely."

Marlo grimaced but couldn't do anything but turn around and start out on the long trek to the other end of the platform, where there were steps similar to the ones they had recently climbed up. The Regulators started to follow them until several in the crowd made a rush for the closest stairs, distracting them.

Realizing they were no longer being followed, Marlo sped up and reached the ground with record speed. He caught Rio, who was about to charge into the crowd and turned back, ducking through an opening beneath the platform, right underneath where they had been. It was cool and shadowy behind the wall that separated them from the now angry crowd. Fuel supplies, replacement couplings and other bits of machinery and tools were kept back here in bins against the high wall on one side. The other side was open, with only a simple railing to protect them from the steep drop to the ground barely visible far below. At intervals, long, moving walkways led out to where many shuttles and runabouts were parked on cradles until released by the authorities. Far in the distance, flashing streaks of light indicated the legal line between the port and outer space.

Rio leaned over the railing gazing down with interest. "Wow. This place is massive!" he said. "Look! This is where we came in when the company arrived. Only it was down on the fifth level, I think. Underneath where we are, which is level 2, right? Us four principals were allowed up on the bridge to watch the landing. Honestly, it was the most super thing ever!"

"Get back on the path, you idiot," said Triani, pulling him by his jacket.

"You're right about all the levels, Rio," Marlo said. "I think there are twenty of them, and which one you land on depends on how big the shuttle is. We're halfway between 1 and 2 now. And stay on the path, please."

"It's icky back here." Rio brushed a long-legged bug off his sleeve as he walked along.

"Keep mouth shut," Fan glowered, loosening something that hung from his wide belt.

Marlo didn't say a word. His hasty plan might backfire but he had to try something before they really were run off the property. The Nat Regs were right. He had no authority in the port. He just hoped most people didn't know that. He kept walking, glancing out at the shuttles now and then, searching for a glimpse of the oddly shaped Elutian ships with no luck. All he could make out were rows of blinking red lights in the shadow cast by the looming building above. He sighed and kept going. It seemed to take a lot longer to get to the other end down here than it had on the platform above. Then they would have to get back to level 1 again. He sighed. This was all very exhausting.

"That Regulator person was really cute," Rio remarked.

Marlo almost stumbled. He glanced back at Triani, eyebrows raised.

Triani shrugged. "All those new hormones," he explained. "I had to peel him off one of the gardeners the other day."

Marlo nodded. Puberty held off for so long was apparently rushing back with a vengeance. Poor kid.

When they finally came to the end, everyone stopped.

"Now what?" Rio asked.

Marlo looked up. The old runabout was still docked farther out along Ramp 1. It didn't look any better from underneath, deep scrapes showing where some landings had gone less than smoothly. Once they were out from under the protection of the platform high above them they might be spotted, assuming anyone was looking this way. Steps came down from the gate above but there was also a disk lift. Marlo smiled with relief. As long as it worked. The walkways along the ramps were not moving as they usually did so maybe...He stepped on the disk and it emitted a satisfactory hum. Good. Of course they ran the real risk of being seen once they emerged on level 1 behind the gate. He just hoped the National Regulators were all focused on the rebellious crowd in the square, some of whom were now chanting rude slogans at the people trying to control them. Then they just had to get into the shadows cast by the arch of the enormous building above them.

Eldred pointed to the old shuttle. "Is that your plan?"

"We're going to commandeer it for government service."

"Oh goody," said Triani.

"Is Corvin there?" Rio asked.

"For fuck's sake!"

"They said to go to Ramp 15. This is 1." Rio pointed to the sign.

Marlo looked at him for a long moment. "This is how we get to Ramp 15," he said at last. The people on board, assuming there were people on board, would know how to maneuver around the inner harbor. He hoped.

"This is what's going to happen," he began, hoping he sounded a lot more confident than he felt. "We all get on this lift-disk. As soon as it stops on Level 1, we rush along the walkway to the that small shuttle. We will have to run since the walkways have been turned off. That shuttle is our transportation. Everyone must go as fast as possible through the open space into the shadows by the vessel. Ready?"

"What if somebody sees us?" Rio said.

"Pray to the gods of the universe."

They were all silent as the lift-disk rose slowly to the first level and stopped with a creak.

Without a word, Marlo started off down the walkway at a fast trot, Fan and the others right behind him. Almost there, Marlo's foot slipped through a gap in the railing and he lurched forward, only saved from falling by the bulk of the small ship. Pain ripped through him as his leg jammed between the shuttle on its cradle and the walkway. Unperturbed, Fan stepped over him. Marlo stifled a scream as Triani and Rio crashed into him, jerking his leg.

"Shit! Move!"

"I can't!"

Four of them were safely behind the high wing of the runabout, but there was no room for Eldred to get past Marlo who was stuck in a sprawl on the narrow track.

"I'll go back," he whispered. "You might need a decoy."

He was gone before Marlo could stop him.

"You down there! Freeze!"

Marlo clutched his leg, gritting his teeth. Fan abruptly reached down with his long arm and somehow, one-handed, freed Marlo's foot. Close to tears, Marlo peered around the launch to see Eldred, his hands in the air, marching up the stairs with a National Regulator on each side.

TWENTY-NINE

Rio knelt on the ramp, pulled off his white silk scarf and wrapped it around Marlo's leg. He had already wiped away the blood from the long, angry-looking gash and seemed surprisingly skillful at this sort of thing.

"Thanks," Marlo said, standing up slowly.

"Accidents happened all the time in my company," Rio said shrugging. "Not always from dancing, to be honest."

Triani silently offered Marlo a yellow pill but Marlo shook his head. He was gazing after Eldred worriedly. There was nothing he could do. Eldred would not be back.

Marlo moved farther into the shadow cast by the launch and sent an update to Old Livid. There was no response, but he hadn't really expected any. He knew he was on his own. The noise from beyond the barrier had changed to a frightening roar. An explosion rocked the walkway, reminding him of Big Stendi's exploding balloon when the children from the Colony first arrived. Was the notorious villain of the River District at it again? This time he had perhaps reckoned without the presence of the Nat Regs, who did not put up with such nonsense.

"Fabulous," Marlo muttered. It was time to make a move before someone from one of the other vessels came to investigate.

Unfortunately Fan chose this moment to remind Triani that he had now done his part. If he was expected to do more, he would need payment.

"You slimy reptile!" shouted Triani. "You haven't finished the job!"

Marlo laid a hand on his arm to calm him down.

"Deal is *find* kid, not *get* kid. Different deal." Fan snuffled and tossed his scaly head from side to side.

"No! Find includes delivery," Triani argued, but at least he had lowered his voice.

"Already I do favor," Fan said. "Big favor."

"I realize that, but you owed me."

"No more."

"So, what?" Triani glanced down at his rings, but he wasn't wearing his usual flashy jewelry. He slipped off the one valuable ring from his thumb and held it up so it flashed on the light. "This is a very fine stone."

"Tuli like jewels. Me, no. Credits only." He named a number that made Marlo gasp.

"I have credits," Rio piped up.

"Shut up, you little shit. Half of that number, Fan, and only when we get the kid back."

"Need danger pay."

"Come on! You're a soldier! You all are."

"You get nowhere without me."

"We have Marlo."

"Hah. He not Elutian. Kid on Elutian ship." Fan grinned triumphantly, showing long yellow teeth.

"We have to go, and soon," Marlo said, peering anxiously towards the ships parked farther out along their ramp. He had just heard the keening wail of Regulator emergency cars. Perhaps Big Stendi had gone too far this time! More troops would be arriving and his little group could be discovered.

"What a rip off," Triani muttered, checking his cred ring. "Here. Half now, rest later."

Fan hesitated, then extended his talon-like hand and clicked off the agreed number of credits onto his large ring.

"Let's get the hell out of here," said Triani.

"The only entry I can see is on the top," Marlo said worriedly. "It's very small." It was obvious that neither he, nor Fan could possibly fit. Not even the slim-hipped Triani could make it.

"Kid go. Open lower hatch down there." Fan pointed to the small loading space outside the hatch.

Marlo blinked. It seemed a long way down to him and there was no ladder, nothing to hang onto. He had a sudden vivid image of his round body falling down, down between the levels of silver ramps to land eventually—

"Wait!" Triani grabbed Rio who was about to leap up on the top of the launch. "We have no idea how many people might be in there. It might be a trap of some kind. The point is we don't know!"

Fan shook his head and snorted several times in annoyance. "Is only two peoples inside. I check." He waved a small instrument he took from his belt. "Mercs in cockpit," he added, slipping the tool back into place.

"Mercenaries?" Marlo asked.

"Merculians." Triani was obviously more used to Fan's vocabulary.

Fan was tall enough to be able to reach the hatch top and in two minutes he had the cover off, using another tool. "Hop now."

Rio did and swiftly disappeared inside the old vessel. Moments later his dark head appeared at the stern of the ship, sliding back the entry doors. Triani leapt down beside him and Marlo sat down, shifting himself closer to the narrow platform. The longer he stared at it, the worse he felt. How solidly was the launch attached to its cradle? Might a sudden increase of weight dislodge it?

His stomach lurched unpleasantly. "I think—"

But before he had a chance to suggest another possible way, powerful scaly talons under his armpits lifted him away from the safety of the walkway and dropped him onto the center of the platform. He sprawled forward, winded and upset. His leg throbbed.

Fan landed beside him, surprisingly light footed. The launch didn't move.

Marlo struggled to his feet. He turned his back on the alien and limped after Triani through the doorway inside the old runabout. "Wait!" He moved ahead of the small group and looked around. Rows of shabby, patched seats filled the area, seating for a dozen or so. Above, the luggage area had a section marked off 'not for use'. Marlo put his insignia of office around his neck as he turned towards the cockpit where Fan had said there were Merculians. The official symbol made him feel better even if it meant nothing out here.

Marlo moved towards the cockpit door which was suddenly thrown open. Two scrawny Merculians stood there staring at them open mouthed.

"How did you get here?" one asked, hitching up his stained work pants.

"Just dropped in for a chat, sweetie." Triani moved up to stand beside Marlo, who sighed in exasperation.

The one who had said nothing broke into a big smile, gazing at the super-star dancer with awe.

"We need transportation to the Elutian ship on Ramp 15," Marlo said, stepping ahead of Triani again.

"No can do. Whole place is locked down."

"Not the inner harbor," Marlo pointed out. "We can still move around in here and that ship is still in Merculian space. We don't need to go out to the Hub Station. It's about rescuing a child," he added, moving closer.

"He's my—" Rio's voice stopped abruptly as Triani clapped a hand over his mouth.

"It's his best friend," Triani explained with an engaging grin. He undid a few buttons on his shirt. Slowly.

The second pilot was now nearly swooning with emotion as he gazed at his idol. "We can do it," he said, his voice hoarse.

"No we can't!" The other one, who looked so similar Marlo was sure they were related, turned on him angrily. "*I* am in charge and I obey the rules."

"I'm *Com* Dasha Bogardini and I apologize for our sudden appearance here in such an unorthodox way, but this is an emergency. The child has been kidnapped and speed is of the essence here before the lock down is lifted."

"I'm Morsini. This is my cousin Ludian. We're tolerated here because we're small, have steady customers and can use the docking station back here close to the entry on Ramp 1. But we don't want to draw any attention, know what I'm saying?"

"On the other hand, sweetie, you'd be doing me a huge favor." Triani oozed closer, his striking face wreathed in seductive smiles. "I can be very nice to those who do me...favors." He winked at the cousin who looked about to faint.

"Shit," murmured Rio.

"I can take care of any problems with the Port Authorities," Marlo said, edging Triani out of the way. "Just FYI, this is a covert action to rescue a child. Please cooperate."

"See? It's to save a child and it's Regulator business," Ludian said. "I'll disengage the cradle."

"Wait! Then what's *he* doing here?" Morsini pointed at the Elutian.

"He's assisting us in the mission, as is often the case in these matters," Marlo said airily.

Morsini shrugged and waved to his cousin to rev up the motors.

Marlo moved back and sat down in the front row of seats to rest his throbbing leg.

"So what's the plan?" Triani asked, sitting beside him.

Marlo looked at Fan.

"Plan come," he said and snorted as if affronted at the question.

I hope it comes soon, Marlo thought.

THIRTY

The floor of the small craft thrummed beneath their feet as the vessel moved steadily off the cradle and dropped underneath Ramp 1, staying as close as possible to the deeper shadows until they were forced to veer away to avoid collision with other docked ships. Marlo tried to read their official markings without success.

Rio sat hugging his knees while Triani paced, pausing now and then to peer out of a dusty porthole and frown.

At last he threw himself down beside Marlo. "You don't have a plan, do you, sweetie?" he said, quietly.

Marlo glanced at the big alien, who stood behind the Merculian pilots, probably making them very nervous. "Can you trust him?" Marlo nodded to Fan.

"As long as I keep paying him," Triani said. "My supply of credits is not limitless, though. So, about that plan?"

"The plan does not involve you," Marlo said firmly, getting to his feet. He took a step forward and almost fell on his face, his foot entangled in the scarf Rio had wrapped around his leg that was now unraveling.

"Flying farts," he muttered, pulling the bloodied scarf off and throwing it behind him. All I need now to make my day complete is to fall on my face. No dignity, no weapon, no real authority, no plan. Perfect. He glanced down to see a smear of blood on his pant-leg but at least it wasn't gushing.

He motioned to Fan to join him in the corner by the biggest porthole. Outside he could now glimpse the Elutian ship, dangerously close to the outer harbor where they could be spotted by the vigilant SpacePort traffic controllers in their glass tower. It was about four times their size at least, with the odd, bulbous silhouette at the back, common on short-haul Elutian craft.

Fan tramped over and snuffled loudly. "One of C class ships," he said. "Carry much freight and sometimes passengers. I know."

"You have a plan?" Marlo asked in a low voice.

Fan snorted and went back to speak to the pilots.

Marlo watched tensely as the alien ship loomed closer until they inched into the shadows underneath her flat bulk. Fan came back and shot his neck up about a foot to look out the porthole. He made a motion to the pilot who moved the launch up on the other side. Fan made a cutting motion and the small vessel shuddered to a stop, baffle engines straining to hold the stabilizers in place. It wasn't very efficient and the craft kept lurching. Marlo tensed and hung on to the pole next to him as the noise seemed to increase.

Fan turned back to the cockpit and Marlo followed as the Elutian cranked up one of the yellowed windows and leaned outside. Marlo shivered. The air was colder this far out but still bearable. Glancing back along the way they had come, the Port was an indistinct blur of blinking red along the ramps and dark shadow underneath the walkways wide silver ribbons.

Fan pulled out a long wide tube from his belt and aimed it at the wall of the ship that was so close they could almost touch it. He flipped up a screen on one end, grunted at what he saw.

"Like I think," he said, showing Marlo the glowing lines and smudges.

The Merculian knew enough to realize the gist of what he saw: several decks, and people in bunches on these decks. The details Marlo wasn't sure of, or really why some of the bunches were more yellow than red. Differences between Elutian and Merculian heat signatures, he supposed.

"This ship have big loading dock. Us use as lube shower during breaks. We go in that way. Bay doors recanize Elutian like me. Then find kid. Leave fast."

Marlo nodded, though he thought the plan a little short on detail, even for him. "So...the Merculians on board are the red smudges? And which deck are they on, exactly?"

"Deck B." Fan pointed out the area of the ship he meant on both the vessel in front and the heat camera. He closed the window. "Go now. End, end. Then wait." He gave this cryptic message to the confused pilots, who simply stared at the alien, uncomprehending.

Marlo went over to stand beside Morsini. "The plan as I understand it is to try to maneuver the craft so that we are back to back with their ship, you see. That way both loading docks will be facing each other so we can step from one to the other. They won't expect anyone to come in that way."

"And we have to dock to them? Won't they notice that part?"

"No dock. Just…hover."

"Ah come on!" cried Morsini. "We're port jockeys, *com!* Not space aces!"

"But we can try. For *Chai* Triani we'll try, right, Morsini?"

Marlo glanced back at Triani, who had slouched lower in his seat and was now undoing another button lower down on his tight-fitting embroidered shirt. At least he was trying to help, Marlo supposed, turning back to see the effect of this on the pilots. To his surprise, they both began pulling out charts and checking manuals.

"We can't hover," Morsini said, shaking his head. "This old tub just can't do it. But we can stop briefly, then slip down underneath if you give us a signal when to come back up to get you and the child. But no hovering."

"But it's not so different from what you're doing now," argued Marlo.

"It is! Hovering means holding the vessel in place with scarcely any movement up or down. We can't do that."

Marlo staggered as the ship dropped a few feet abruptly, illustrating the pilot's point. "Okay. Have you got charts of the alien crafts usually coming in and out of here?" Marlo asked. "I need to see exact drawings with measurements, entrances, exits etc., to judge timing."

"I know this." Fan snorted in annoyance.

"But I don't."

Ludian poked around under his seat and soon plugged in a data cube. He keyed through the various schemata of odd-looking craft and stopped at last at one of the Class C Elutian ship above them.

Marlo studied it carefully, noting stairs, lifts, separated areas marked off as storage. It looked like a very large shuttle, not meant for long distance hauling, so there wouldn't be protection probes or anything like that. A Deck seemed to be a games room of some sort.

"So most of the Merculians seem to be on B Deck," he said, looking at Fan.

"Yes!" He snuffled, obviously miffed. "Us go in here." He pointed to the aft section where the platform jutted out for loading. "Need go! Now!"

Morsini glanced down at the controls and then back to the manual. "We can't hover," he repeated.

"But we can get close for a few minutes and you jump," Ludian suggested, his face glowing with enthusiasm. "Then we'll drop back here. When you have the child, give us the signal and we'll come back for you."

"How many minutes, exactly?" Marlo asked.

"Three. Four at most," Morsini said. "It could work."

Marlo grimaced. It could work with two athletes. He glanced at Triani, but he couldn't send a civilian. "Let's go."

He turned towards the aft doors and noticed Rio getting to his feet. "Triani, keep him here."

"How am I supposed to do that exactly? Sit on him?"

"If necessary!"

The craft shuddered as it began a slow turn, then rose and backed towards the Elutian ship.

"Aren't they going to see us?" Rio asked, but at least he remained beside Triani.

"There are no significant portholes and no probe outlets back here," Marlo said. "Besides, they don't expect us."

"But they told me to come!" Rio said. "They'll be expecting me."

"Not coming in from the loading bay. They expect you coming along the walkway to the main gangway on the other side."

"I guess."

Ludian rushed past them and out onto the loading area. He was wearing a headset and began issuing a series of instructions to his cousin, guiding him closer to the looming alien craft. When Marlo and Fan joined him, he covered the mike and explained that their rear view screen wasn't working very well.

"So now you tell us," murmured Marlo. His hands were clammy with fear as he stood beside Fan, shivering in the cold air.

"Close enough," shouted Ludian. "Go!"

"I don't think—"

A vice-like grip clamped onto his arm and yanked him into the air. He landed hard on the Elutian deck, sprawled on all fours and panting heavily to get his breath back. He blinked in shock and saw the launch sinking rapidly out of sight.

THIRTY-ONE

The hard landing had opened up the gash on Marlo's leg and it was bleeding again, but this wasn't the time for first aid treatment. As he hauled himself painfully to his feet, he saw Fan running some gadget up and down the seam in the bay doors. Then the alien pressed his large-taloned hand against the panel right above his head. To Marlo's surprise, the doors gradually opened a crack. Fan braced himself, sturdy scaly legs wide apart, and forced the doors open just enough to pass through. Marlo followed and the doors snapped shut behind them.

The hot damp air hit them in the face. To Marlo it was an almost physical blow making him gasp, but Fan straightened up and took in deep, joyful breaths.

"Like home," he murmured.

Marlo decided never to visit Fan's world. He took shallow breaths, trying to get accustomed to the sudden change in atmosphere. His nose wrinkled in protest as the smell hit him; the heavy earthy scent. Mold. As his eyes gradually adjusted to the dimness, he took in the wide-open space of C Deck, crammed with shadowy bundles on flats, tied into place with green cords against the bulwarks and in large crates attached to the pillars up and down the middle. Hammocks hung from the ceiling, filled with smaller parcels. Marlo recognized the familiar logo of the Colony Dance Company in the pile of luggage near a flight of steep stairs to the left of the bay doors. At least they were on the right ship. About twenty feet in front of them was what looked like a lift system of some sort but Fan made for the stairs on the other side of the dim space. Marlo panted after him, switching on his camera as he went.

The Elutian slid stealthily up the steep steps. Marlo found it easier to go on all fours, as if climbing a ladder. Through the heavy, damp air came murmurs and coughs and a faint sound of crying. A light childish voice asked sleepily, "When are we going home?" No one answered. Marlo's heart beat faster. He wiped the sweat out of his eyes.

Cautiously he raised his head enough to see about half of B Deck. Sure enough, a group of the Colony children sprawled on big cushions on the floor, their faces shiny with sweat, their eyes heavy, long curls hanging in damp snaky tendrils. They were all wearing the short lacy tunic things they had on when they had arrived that first day in Cap City, but now they were dirty and crumpled. They had obviously been here for many hours. Small food boxes and bottles of water littered the floor around them. Most of the children were asleep. Marlo recognized some of the tired faces but didn't see Corvin. Maybe they had taken him somewhere else on the ship?

"The one I'm looking for isn't here," he whispered to Fan.

The Elutian stretched his neck up higher and twisted his head all around. "More Mercs in other room."

Marlo climbed higher, then ducked down hastily as he saw Corvin in between two blue-clad Guardians. One had a heavy hand on the youngster's shoulder, guiding him towards the others.

"You keep that brat, Sutini, quiet and we'll leave you alone. Here's some honey milk. Just feed it to him and he'll be fine."

"How much has he had already?" Corvin's voice, sounding a little hoarse.

"Obviously not enough. Don't worry. He'll be fine once we get home. If that smartass buddy of yours doesn't arrive soon, our friends are going to lose patience with you. I won't be able to protect you then."

"He won't come. I *told* you."

"So much for love. Hah." He gave a light slap to the back of Corvin's head. "Now, do as you're told."

There was silence for a moment, then Corvin's voice again, but so softly Marlo couldn't hear the words. He peeked up again to see Corvin pushing the damp hair off little Sutini's flushed sweating face.

"I want to go home," Sutini said. He started to wail but Corvin thrust the bottle with a nipple on it into his mouth. At once Sutini began to suck on it. He closed his eyes.

Taking a closer look, Marlo noticed the difference between Corvin and the others. Even though he was dressed in the same lacy outfit, he looked older, more mature. It wasn't just the shorter hair, either. The medical treatment he had been receiving at Triani's was actually beginning to work. Marlo could see the lace tunic was a little shorter on him. He was growing.

Fan walked into the room and motioned to Marlo. "Quick."

Marlo hurried over to Corvin. "Come with me, dear." He held out his hand.

Corvin stared back at him, a stunned look in his tired eyes. His usually vibrant red hair hung to his shoulders in damp spirals. "What about them?" One hand motioned to the apparently drugged young dancers around him.

"Others are coming for them," Marlo said. "I had to make sure they're all here first. Now give me your hand. Our ship's waiting." Marlo punched the contact button to summon their launch and reached for the youngster's hand, trying to pull him to his feet.

Corvin stifled a cry. "It's okay. It hurts, is all. I'm coming." He laid Sutini's head gently back on the cushion and fastened the child's hand around the bottle. Then he ran after Marlo and Fan, holding his arm as he scurried down the steep stairs.

"Ho! Take thems back." A strapping Elutian in black overalls with a yellow stripe of office on the bib stood by the bay doors, staring across at Fan.

"We just need some things from our luggage," Corvin said, reaching into the pile of Colony Dance Company belongings.

"Let me help." Marlo started rummaging around beside Corvin as he whispered instructions about the waiting launch. It was a good thing the Elutian officer was all the way over by the bay doors and they were all in deep shadow, he thought.

Fan grunted amiably. "Back up there soon."

Marlo heard the doors open and felt the rush of welcome cool air. He peered up over the hump of baggage and saw the Elutian step out of his clothing, pick up a pail of lube and stride outside, his greenish scales gleaming in a sudden burst of sunlight. The doors snapped shut.

"What..." Marlo looked up at Fan, but he seemed unfazed by

this behavior. But now the naked alien was on the platform and any minute their scruffy little shuttle would shudder into sight, in response to Marlo's signal.

Meanwhile, above their heads a thumping of big feet shook the floor. A high-pitched whistle split the air.

"Them cast off cradle," Fan said, striding across to the bay doors.

"They're making a break for it?" Marlo rushed after the alien. Corvin bent down, unbuttoned his scuffed red shoes, kicked them off and ran after the other two.

They all stopped at the bay doors, just as they began to open. Marlo grabbed one of the buckets, ready to fling it at the enemy's head. Before he had a chance, Fan leapt forward, grabbed the startled Elutian officer and spun him around. The broad back gleamed wetly, green lube mottled with yellow highlights dripping to the floor. Fan grabbed the wide knob-like proturberance on the end of the alien's spine and twisted with both taloned hands. The alien howled and struggled to turn around. Fan held on, feet planted wide for balance, and suddenly the enemy alien crashed to the floor, right across the entryway.

"Is he dead?" Corvin whispered.

"Him sleep."

Marlo doubted that, but outside he saw a flash of silver and red speeding towards them. Someone was about to hail, board or attack and they didn't want to hang around long enough to find out which!

"Jump!" shouted Fan as their dilapidated escape craft lurched into view just below them.

Corvin tried to run toward the edge but slipped on the lube, falling on his side with a cry. Marlo reached out to catch the youngster's arm but Fan hauled the kid up, clasped him against his broad chest and without a moment's hesitation, leaped, disappearing onto the loading deck below.

Marlo heard the heavy tread of at least two Elutians behind him, probably coming to investigate why the bay doors were not closing. Panicked, Marlo turned around and flung his bucket of lube, then shuffled to the edge, closed his eyes and jumped.

THIRTY-TWO

The news of the near riot at the SpacePort was almost eclipsed by the constant loop of announcements about the exoneration of 'renowned young architect' Parla Serlini Adelantis in the death of the Merculian who fell from the Wave Entertainment Complex.

The on-going news flashes added more and more information on the real culprit—the two Elutian-owned *troxite* mines on the Colony Planet:

After a serious cave-in in the main Windfall mine, there was a major shortage, which threatened production and filling of their many orders. It has been established that the company began diluting the troxite to keep up with the heavy demand.

"The Merculian department of Territories apparently had no idea the governing Signet of Seven had been infiltrated to such an extent by the Elutians hired to help with the mining," Thar-von remarked that evening, stretched out in Beny's garden sipping *siva*.

"But why bring them in in the first place?" Beny asked.

"They have good eyesight in the dark and, unlike Merculians, have no fear of being underground, so it seemed like a good idea at the time."

"And nobody was keeping an eye on them?"

"So it would seem."

Eulio had fallen asleep beside Beny, his dark-blond curls spilling over his spouse's shoulder. They had spent most of the day doing their post wedding visits and were both tired. Luckily the tradition was to visit only those who had given creative presents and this did not involve family members which shortened the list Manolin had left for them considerably.

Tradition also required them to spontaneously drop into at least three houses displaying their Wedding ornament in the window to thank them for their good wishes. These were the most enjoyable since it was a complete surprise and everyone was delighted to have Eulio in their home. Beny just smiled and bowed and drank sherry, basking in the reflected glory. By now he was a little tipsy, but still wanted Thar-von's take on what was going on.

"Eulio was so relieved to find out Parla's exonerated!" he said now. "We didn't know until late this afternoon when we came out of Dario's place and I glanced at my com dev. I think that's one reason he's so tired. The relief, you know?" He smoothed Eulio's hair back from his face. "By the way, do you have any background on the children? I know about the Serpian Raider Strike Force team boarding the Elutian ship but what happened after that?"

Thar-von paged through his PortaPad. "Some of the so-called Guardians were actually soldiers, members of the Faisian Falanx, and they and the other Guardians are in the main detention rooms at the National Regulator building. The children are all under the care of healers in the VIP wing of the Central medical center, it says here, except for that friend of Triani's sibling."

"Corvin. His name's Corvin." Eulio sat up abruptly. "You shouldn't have let me sleep," he went on accusingly, looking at Beny. "I'm sorry, Von. I didn't mean to offend."

"No offense taken, I assure you." Thar-von rose to his imposing height. "I must go. Meeting at the embassy in half an hour." He bowed and left abruptly through the garden gate.

"Well, talk about rude," Eulio said, twirling a curl around one finger.

"If Von says he has a meeting, he has a meeting."

"If you say so." Eulio stood up and stretched. "I'm awake now. Let's go see Triani."

"Why?"

"Wedding visit." Eulio smiled sweetly.

"Isn't it a bit late?"

"There's no rule you have to do it at a certain time," Eulio pointed out. "Anyway, it's still relatively early. Come on."

"You're just curious."

"Aren't you? He was there, you know. At the SpacePort when the riot broke out. Besides, I want to find out how Corvin is."

Beny sighed and finished off his sherry. "But we won't stay long," he said. "And I'm driving," he added, leading the way to their sporty sapphire blue Dashen-8 two-seater, their wedding present to themselves.

When they arrived, Beny was surprised to see several other air-cars on the parking pad outside Triani's sprawling home.

"One of them belongs to Pom, the healer looking after Corvin," Eulio said, recognizing it. "He has a team assisting him, so I guess they're all here."

"Maybe we should just leave," Beny suggested, but Eulio was already through the gate.

The Keeper frowned. "It is late for a visit,' he said reprovingly.

"Nonsense." Eulio motioned him back with an imperious wave and moved past him. "Where's Triani?"

"I do not keep track of the whereabouts of my employer." The Keeper snapped the door to so sharply Beny had to jump into the hall.

Eulio stared at him. "Could you hazard a guess?" he suggested icily.

"Perhaps in the studio, but I do not state this as a fact."

"Thank you. It's a start."

Sure enough, they found Triani and Rio both in the studio, rehearsing *The Dream*. The visitors stood side by side in the doorway watching as the beautiful music swept the two dancers through to the spectacular finale. Eulio caught his breath as Triani sprang onto the back of the chair and Rio leapt up onto his hand, instantly lifted high in the air to be suspended for what seemed like nearly a minute. Then he jumped to the ground and Triani turned around.

"What the fuck are you two doing here?" he demanded, wiping sweat out of his eyes.

"Wedding visit," Eulio replied with a smile. "And that was amazing, by the way."

"Just don't expect me to do that final lift with you. Look, if you insist on staying, I need a shower. I'll join you in the sitting room in a few minutes. Help yourself to whatever."

"How's Corvin?"

"Pom says he has to stay in bed for a day or so but he'll be fine." Rio smiled, bowed and followed his sibling into the shower.

"Those two dancing together are spellbinding," Eulio said.

"What they can do because of Rio's small stature is astounding."

"What happens when he grows?"

"He'll give us all a run for our money, if his health holds up."

In Triani's sitting room, they found Parla, reading through a set of documents and making comments here and there. Beny thought he looked a little thinner, but still strikingly beautiful. Hard times seemed only to have given him more of a glow.

"This is a nice surprise," said Eulio, embracing his cousin.

"Such a relief to get my life back." Parla embraced Beny, who felt nothing but contentment from the touch. "Now that the inspectors know what to look for, I can soon get back to work fixing up the eastern wing of the building."

"I'm so glad for you," Beny said.

There were bowls of fruit, a dish full of buzzers, some pastries on a platter and a bottle of Crushed Emeralds on the table in front of Parla. Eulio helped himself to a drink and handed a glass to Beny.

Triani walked in at that moment wearing a loose crocheted purple top and matching leggings. He threw himself on the couch and stretched his legs over Parla's lap. "Pour me one too, sweetie, will you?" He popped a buzzer in his mouth. "So, is this a wedding visit or are you really looking for gossip about the SpacePort riot?"

"Both," said Eulio.

"From what I could see it wasn't much of a riot," Triani remarked.

"What were you doing down there, anyway? I saw the images of you and Rio and some Elutian. What was going on?"

"When Rio finally noticed that Corvin was missing, he tried to contact him on his com-dev but one of the shitty Guardians answered and threatened him. I had to do something."

"It wasn't quite like that," Rio said, coming into the room and helping himself to pastry.

"If you gain one ounce, *Dream* is off," Triani said.

Rio ignored him. "The Elutian seemed to do all of the work."

"He worked for me," Triani pointed out.

"And Marlo was there. All Triani did was seduce the pilot."

"And a good thing, too," Triani said. "The other damn pilot wanted to leave when things got dicey. Guess who talked him out of it?"

It took a while to get the whole story out of them but finally

Eulio was satisfied he had all the details worth having.

"And then you came home and rehearsed?" Beny asked, trying not to sound surprised.

"Of course," said Rio.

"Don't you want to be with Corvin?"

"Why? He's being looked after. Honestly, he doesn't need me there while he sleeps."

Beny shook his head but said nothing.

"Guess what?" Rio said, jumping to his feet again. "Triani said he's going to give me a *cimbola* party."

"It's a ceremony, dear," Parla corrected him.

"Whatever. We never learned about it at home. I mean in the company."

"I didn't mean it, anyway." Triani sat up. "I was high at the time."

"No you weren't," Rio objected. "You promised. Will it be just like yours?"

Triani swallowed. "No fucking way."

Eulio exchanged a look with Parla. The atmosphere had changed completely and Beny hoped they could soon leave.

Parla began rubbing Triani's back soothingly. "Listen, Rio. This is not at all like throwing a big party. You have a part to play in this. You have to learn some Mercoli, and chants and a section from the Epicantare Epic. A song needs to be composed for you. It all takes time."

"Oh," said Rio.

"I have a headache." Triani stood up abruptly and stalked out of the room.

Parla watched him go, a worried look in his beautiful face.

"So it's not a party," Rio went on, oblivious, "but I can invite some people to come, right?"

"Of course."

"*Mertsi* and *tatsi* have to be here, and some of my friends in my old company," Rio prattled on.

Beny grimaced as Eulio's fingers clutched at his thigh, sending a message louder than words. "Rio, about travel from the Colony Planet right now. It's very difficult."

"Yeah, but Triani knows people, right? And what about you, Parla? You can help too?"

"Even the Adelantis family can't help when martial law is

concerned," Beny said firmly, prying Eulio's fingers from his thigh. "Now, if you'll excuse us, we must go. Wedding visits are not supposed to linger so late."

Once back in their air-car, Eulio exhaled in one long breath. "This will not end well," he said.

"It's a family event. Rio has the right to have his parents there."

"All parents are not equal," Eulio said darkly. "You have no idea how much Triani hates the 'Bastard Parent', as he calls him. I don't even know the whole story behind it but I suspect Parla does, judging by how he reacted. God's teeth, Orosin, this could be very bad!"

"You worry too much, *chaleen*. I meant it when I said travel was difficult there right now, so relax."

"Even so, if what I suspect about Triani's *cimbola* ceremony is true, it's going to be a very difficult time for him."

THIRTY-THREE

Triani paused to check his messages on his way down the corridor from the costume department where he had had his final fitting for the *Dream* costume. He deleted a few from Pom with a scowl, then paused, cocked his head and listened. He was beside the door leading to one of the cupboards holding dance shoes, but no shoes made those kinds of noises. Voices. Panting. A burst of laughter. He was about to pass on when he recognized a raised voice. Rio?

He pushed the door open so fast it banged against the wall. Carondi, the second soloist with the company, jumped back, his mocking laughter gone as he pulled his tunic on, while Rio, half naked, tried to push out of sight among a pile of dance shoes that had been dislodged when Triani flung open the door.

"Holy shit!"

"He said he was of age," said Carondi sullenly.

"So you jumped him."

"It was the other way around, *chai*. But then I saw his smooth pubes so I wasn't sure. And he got mad."

"Listen, you imbecile, if you want to keep dancing in this company or any other company in the city, you will never mention this to anyone. Get it?"

Carondi swallowed. "I didn't do anything."

"And you won't. Ever." Triani's long finger poked the young soloist in the chest. Hard. "And if I get even the faintest whisper of this you will be out of a job. If you don't think I can do it, just try me. Now get out."

The kid took off down the corridor.

"And as for you," Triani went on, whirling around to face his young sibling. "How could you be so stupid!"

"I just want sex! What's wrong with that?" Rio struggled to his feet and pulled up his pants. "But he laughed at me. It was humiliating."

"You're going to have to learn to judge people better, sweetie. And wait till you get some hair down there. Remember, you still look very young."

"Shit! I hate this!"

"Come on. Let's go to my dressing room so you can wash your face and calm down."

On the way, Triani wondered if he would have to go through some version of this with Giazin down the road. At least his child had not been tampered with. He would be able to perform all aspects of sex, including joining with his partner, whereas poor Rio never would. Triani suspected the kid didn't quite understand the ramifications of what had been done to him or he wouldn't be throwing himself at people like the older assistant-gardener or the worldly Carondi.

"I thought he liked me," Rio said now, drying his face.

"Carondi likes playing with people," Triani said. "The only person he actually likes is himself."

"Maybe I can go to the Pleasure Garden," Rio suggested, brightening. "Like you."

"Fuck no! Haven't you heard a word I've said? You have to wait!"

"Like you have such great self-control," Rio muttered.

"I never said I was a role model in sexual matters." Triani reached for the bottle of mint wine. "Don't you have an appointment with the costume people for a final fitting for *Dream*?"

"I know! I'm going." Rio slammed out the door.

Triani took a long drink. The Bastard Parent had a lot to answer for, he thought savagely. Ruining two kids in different ways by abandoning them. And what was he supposed to do with Rio now?

Someone clapped at the door. With a sigh, Triani got up and opened it. Taken aback to see Pom standing there, he opened it wider so the healer could enter the dressing room.

"Do you no longer pick up your messages?" Pom asked, walking in and sitting down in a comfortable chair. "I had to finally track you down in person."

"Look, Pom, I know I've been cancelling check-ups lately but——"

"I don't understand why you're doing this to Rio. Why are you ruining his future?"

Shocked as much by the words as the anger in Pom's voice, Triani stared at the old healer. Pom had looked after his physical health for a long time, handling some very sensitive problems with gentle finesse. He often didn't agree with Triani's choices in life but he had never attacked him like this before. Why? What had he done?

"I don't know what the hell you're talking about," Triani said at last. "I'm doing my best to look out for his future. I got this performance added to the program for him."

"Exactly, without any thought to the consequences."

"What the fuck, Pom? He talked to you about it, didn't he?"

"Oh yes. We talked about it at great length."

"So why this attack?"

"Because I said no!"

"That little shit!" Triani sat down and poured wine for both of them. "Look, he told me you said it was okay. That it was a very short performance so it was fine. That it would be his last performance before the rest period."

"That last part, unfortunately, might be the truth. It may be his last performance ever."

"Holy shit. That's what you told him?"

"Yes. Exactly that. I also told him it might be too late already."

"I had no idea."

"You should. I gave you the full report."

Triani ran a distracted hand though his dark curls. He didn't want to admit he had never actually read the full report, relying on what Pom had told them after the examination, before they were interrupted, and that was bad enough. But not this bad. Not ruined-by-dancing bad. But the idea of never dancing again was like a blow, a cold stone in his stomach. Maybe a last performance would be better than no performance at all as an adult.

"Pom. I'm really sorry but in the end it's his decision. He is, in spite of his looks, an adult."

"Brought up in isolation as he was, with little or no education? How can he be considered an adult?"

Triani stood up abruptly. "I'll talk to him, Pom, but it's his decision."

Pom shook his head sadly. "Don't do something you'll regret for the rest of your life, Triani. Think about that poor child."

"I am."

After Pom left, Triani switched on the blue privacy light, sat on his divan with his head in his hands and stared at the colorful floor that had just been installed recently. After a while he sat up and accessed the file Pom had given him weeks ago. If he was to have a say in this, on either side, he needed to know everything that was in it. Pom was right. He probably didn't have the whole picture.

For the next twenty minutes he read through the long difficult file, pausing now and then to drink more wine or just to take a deep breath. "Those bastards," he muttered from time to time. "Those fucking, evil bastards!" At last he was finished and switched off the text. His first impulse was to contact Parla, but he was not a dancer. It was another Adelantis he needed to talk to. But at the last moment he changed his mind and dropped the com-dev back in its case on his belt. The only one he really needed to talk to was his poor, mutilated sibling who wanted so much to have one more chance to fly that he had lied and put his own life on the line to dance *The Dream* just one time as an adult, even if most of the audience wouldn't understand.

THIRTY-FOUR

The theater filled with the illusion of a starry night, the velvet sky dropping down suddenly over the expectant audience who filled every seat, including the extra ones Nevon had added for the occasion of Rio's debut as a soloist away from the Colony Dance company. The glittering stars looked near enough to touch. The sky had descended abruptly, moments after the last performance by the company danced their way off-stage, led by Alesio.

Triani stood in the wings waiting for his music cue. Out in the audience, Eulio, Benvolini, Parla, Corvin and several of the Colony kids were crowded into the VIP box. Above the stage, he could just make out the small figure of Rio, sitting on the golden rope suspended between the twin moons that would descend just as he, the Dreamer, was falling asleep on his blue velvet couch. The dream. A dream he had worked harder for than Rio would ever know. And it wasn't even his dream. It belonged to his young, talented sibling who, he realized, was very much like himself.

One of the first things he had done, after talking to Rio (who refused to give up the event, just as Triani had expected), was to go to see Nevon, the director of the company. He found him in the theater bar, having a drink with friends. They welcomed the star dancer with open arms and Triani smiled and flirted as usual, but after about five minutes he asked Nevon for a few words in private.

"What can I do for you?" Nevon asked. "And how much will it cost?"

"You never used to treat me like just an expensive commodity," Triani said, watching Nevon's expression.

"Well, that seems to be the way things are going with you and me these days." Nevon took a sip of the drink he had brought with him.

Triani lounged back against the soft pillows of the sofa in the small salon where they had retired for their private conversation. He let the loose red silk top he wore slip off one shoulder and twirled the glass in a slender hand. "I'm sorry you feel that way," he said, his voice soft. "So sorry." He felt Nevon shift uncomfortably but his expression did not soften. Triani dropped his eyes and realized this tactic was not working for him. He straightened up, deciding on the direct approach. "What will it take for you to drop a few performances of *The Dream*?"

"You talked me into this thing and now you're trying to talk me out of it? There are only five as it is! You already vetoed one matinée."

"Not drop the whole thing, sweetie, no. Just one matinée and one evening."

"You are a piece of work, Triani," Nevon said angrily. "Get this through your head. You cannot play me the way you used to, so stop trying."

Triani felt a stab of intense dislike for this person whom he used to twist around his little finger and now held so much power over him. Shit. How far was he willing to go for Rio? This member of a family he had refused to acknowledge most of his life?

"I need this to happen," Triani said. "Please, Nevon."

The director shook his head.

"Shit! Is it a question of credits?"

"Of course it is! Adding you two onto an already complete program took a lot of them. Mostly to you," he added. "So no. I need to get back my investment. We're done here."

"No we're not," said Triani, standing up. He was taller than Nevon and that came in handy now. "If you don't do this for me, you will lose a lot more credits next season without me."

Nevon laughed. "Don't try that on me, either. I know you won't walk out on Eulio."

"He's a great partner, yes, but Rio is family. I *will* walk out with him." Triani hoped his nerves didn't show. He had never gone so far with Nevon before. If it didn't work, Rio wouldn't be the only one not dancing for a while.

Nevon leaned back and smiled up at Triani. "*You* putting family first. This is a surprise." He took a thoughtful drink then placed it on the table and turned the glass around in his hand. "I can possibly cut one matinée."

Triani shook his head. "Matinée and one evening. Your choice."

"Oh, how generous of you!" Nevon barked with laughter. "What will you give me in return for this magnanimous gesture of mine?"

Triani perched on the arm of his chair. "The credits you were going to pay me for my performance."

"Return *all* the credits, yours and Rio's, and you have a deal," Nevon said.

Triani scowled. He could win but at what a price. "On one condition: Rio never knows."

"If you want to pay the whole thing that's fine with me. Nothing will get back to the kid."

"His name's Rio," said Triani stiffly "and he's not just a kid."

"You always were touchy," muttered Nevon.

Now Triani felt the excitement of opening night and the expectations of the audience who had come to see something new, someone new, in what was essentially a brand-new production of an old favorite.

The houselights dimmed, the stars winking out all over the theater. The music began and Triani glided onto the stage, the colorful ribbons of his costume fluttering around him. Dance fans knew he had never danced this role before. It was part of what had brought them here, to see Triani dance this familiar part for the first time; to see his young sibling interpret the part that had been Triani's for years.

As he lay in graceful sleep on his couch, the audience burst into applause as Rio descended to the stage, poised gracefully between the two moons. Through his eyelashes, Triani watched him leap and glide, his sparking costume of deep blue and silver enhancing his every move.

It went by so fast, their duets graceful, punctuated with the new and exciting lifts that brought the audience to its feet. But Triani could feel his partner's growing pain, feel the slight tremor in the muscled legs as they went into the last specular lift with Triani seeming to balance him on the palm of his hand long seconds until the curtain fell.

"You okay?" he whispered, as Rio jumped to the ground.

"Everything's wonderful."

As they joined hands to take their bow, Triani could feel that, too. The pure joy of the performer who has given his all and loved every dangerous minute.

The next night was an even bigger success, since news of the first performance had spread. People were clamoring for standing-room only tickets and Nevon obliged, even going above the prescribed limit for seating. The possible fine would be worth it. Just looking after his investment, Triani thought with a wry smile. Rio danced his heart out but by the end Triani knew he was in more pain than on opening night.

"You can stop now," Triani said, as they walked back to their dressing rooms. "You've made your point."

"No." Rio turned and stared at him as he reached Eulio's dressing room, which the star had kindly loaned to the young dancer. "It's bad enough I let you talk me into cutting the number of performances. I won't walk off before closing night."

Triani shrugged.

In the end he was glad Rio managed to make it to the last night, when the crowd threatened to deafen them with their cheers and shouts of *"toori!"*, smothering them with the bouquets and message packages that rained down onto the stage during their final bows. But Triani knew what it had cost Rio. He had felt the taped ankles, smelled the familiar scent of numbing gel that Pom must have rubbed over his knees and hips to mask the pain. And the tremors were more pronounced. But the audience had no idea what his young sibling had gone through to give them the performance of his young life. He might never dance again but he would always have *The Dream*.

THIRTY-FIVE

Marlo went back to work a week later. When they had arrived back at the docking station, their scruffy craft had been met by the emergency healer team, who had carefully patched up the gash on his leg, numbed the pain with a Green Strip along the length of the wound and taped the sprain on his left wrist. He was given strict instructions to rest, mostly because of the jolt given his whole body when he had landed so inelegantly after leaping off the Elutian ship. He was lucky nothing was broken, they told him sternly. "It's all that padding," Triani remarked, with a grin.

Back home, he sat on his garden shelf, talking to his plants and enjoying the feeling of the rich earth as his fingers kneaded their roots. It was another way of talking to them, he thought and was convinced they enjoyed their massage. On his last day off, he made notes about the events surrounding the rescue of Corvin, which he then turned into the report he was about to give to Old Livid in his office right now.

Old Livid's huge desk was piled high with report cubes and Marlo dropped his on top. "This is everything, chief," he said, waiting for the cue to sit down.

"Thank you for your help identifying the ship the kids were on," Liviano said. "Next time, try to do it without *Chai* Triani and *Chaisilin* Rio. That family gives us too much publicity and it was supposed to be a covert op."

"Well, they came along with the Elutian, and I really needed him. Sort of a package deal."

"I suppose it doesn't matter now." Liviano got to his feet and started around the desk. "I need to bring everyone up to date on this complicated case. I was waiting until you got back." He touched the wall which emitted a loud bonging noise.

Out in the investigative unit room, Regulators began streaming out of their offices and team rooms, chatting amongst themselves, speculating about what was going on. Marlo joined Eldred, Oslani and the others.

"Who's getting fired?" Oslani whispered.

"Probably Marlo." Eldred grinned wickedly.

Marlo ignored them, watching Old Livid wind himself up to make a speech. He was familiar with the different stages of his chief's speech-making process. It began with a sort of shoulder shake, then a small neck stretch, followed by much throat-clearing. Then he clasped his bony hands together and looked around the room, waiting for them to settle down, as they leaned on walls or sat on desks so everyone could see their diminutive chief.

"Each and every one of you has contributed in some way to breaking this difficult and highly disturbing case," he began, "so I thought it only fair to bring you up to speed and fill in part, at least, of the big picture.

"This whole thing started out as part of Marlo's 'hobby case', a file on the missing children from fifteen years ago he kept pecking at for years, in spite of being ordered to leave it alone."

A ripple of gentle laughter greeted this comment.

"It was Marlo who made the possible but seemingly very unlikely connection between the Colony Dancers and one kidnapped child, and this led to other shocking discoveries about the unusual and talented company. Then there was a terrible accident, ending in death for a poor soul who fell when the bridge collapsed on a new building. Seemingly random, this, too, surprisingly, fed into our investigation and was eventually connected to the Colony Planet and the new and malignant powers that have taken over there.

"The visiting children are now all being cared for by our healers and are doing as well as can be expected. I don't have any details because the 'veil of privacy' rule has been invoked so nothing is being released and no newshounds are allowed anywhere near them. What I do know is there'll be a High Crimes court case indicting all of their supposed Guardians, company healers and the owners of the company. The trial will be held in the strictest secrecy to protect the children but rest assured, justice will be done."

"What about the children still back on the Colony?" someone asked.

"I was coming to that." Liviano sniffed and looked around balefully. He did not like to be interrupted. "The latest news coming across my desk this morning is that the rest of the children will go into care under a team from Merculian who left this morning. The whole planet is in a state of martial law, the military part being supplied by Serpian Raider troops and Black Circle soldiers and the legal part our own Merculian Inner Council who are taking over the government for a while at least. The rogue Elutians have been banished."

Marlo grunted. He knew what that meant and it wasn't much. They would be sent back to their own planet in order not to upset the fragile alliance with Merculian. Even Fan had known the Elutians who had taken such power in the Signet of Seven had been bad to the bone. By Elutian standards, that must have been pretty bad.

And then there were all the children whose names had been changed, Marlo thought. He for one, would keep looking, checking every missing person report all over Merculian and the Colony Planet to see if any links could be found to their real names. He was determined that as many parents be reunited with their kidnapped offspring as possible.

At that moment, a young Regulator from the Drugged, Drunk and Disorderly squad rushed in the door. Many of them had been seconded to work on various aspects of the case, too, sifting through mountains of data in search of links, names, birth records, anything useful to add to the mountain of evidence they had accumulated against the Colony.

"I found something!" the new arrival shouted.

Liviano glared at him.

Undeterred, the young officer made his way through the crowd to Marlo's side. Marlo put a finger to his lips to stifle further interruptions.

"It is seldom that we get to celebrate what we do," Liviano went on, "but I think, and those higher up agree, if ever there was a time, this is it. Unfortunately it will be a subdued celebration because there is still a lot to do, but let's celebrate when we can, and then move on."

Bottles of mint wine began circulating around the room, glasses appearing on desks as if by magic. Someone even brought Marlo a small box of *rolinis*.

"Courtesy of Liviano," Ferdalyn said, grinning.

Marlo felt overcome by emotion at this small gesture. It was not usual for his boss. He raised his glass in a toast, but it was too late. Old Livid had retired to his office.

By now, the level of chatter had risen to a clamor when Marlo remembered the young DDD officer and looked around for him. In the crush, he had been pushed further into the room. Marlo ploughed after him.

"You have found something I should know?" he asked.

The officer had a glass in his hand and appeared to have forgotten the important message he had come to deliver.

"Ah, yes, right," he said, gathering his thoughts. "I've found the parents."

"Which parents," asked Marlo, patiently.

"The parents of the red-headed child who was dancing with the company. The one who was kidnapped."

"*Corvin?*"

"Yes, that's the name he was using."

"So, where are they? Come on!" For someone who was so anxious to report that he had interrupted Old Livid, the kid now seemed not to care much about the new info.

"They've been living in Adpian on the Colony Planet for many years. It's a medium sized city near one of the major mines."

"Flying farts! They were right there. All this time, they've been right near their kidnapped child, thinking he was dead. That's so sad!" Marlo was about to add more about poor Corvin's ruined life but thought better of it. "Did you contact them?" he asked.

"No, *com*. I knew it was your case so I thought I'd better tell you first."

"Good call. Thanks. Just leave it with me." Marlo put his glass down and made for the door, clutching his box of *rolinis*.

THIRTY-SIX

Triani was not usually an introspective person but these days he was finding his life forcing him to examine his own reactions and feelings. Thinking about the performances of *The Dream* later on, he realized that Rio was not the only one who had suffered. What must it have been like for Corvin, sitting neglected and alone, watching night after night as Triani danced the part that used to be his alone? One among many he would never dance again? Watched Triani swing Rio effortlessly into lifts that had been impossible for him. Triani remembered him standing on the sidelines at the opening night gala and again at the closing night party, where Rio, high on pain killers, had barely acknowledged his presence. That was when Rio had leapt up on a table to make a speech of thanks and had ended by inviting everyone there to his coming-of-age ceremony which was "coming soon". Luckily no one took him seriously, since the date had not even been set.

The age of maturity. But was Rio ready for this? Parla reminded him that few young Merculians were really ready. "He'll learn," he said, and Triani leaned back against his patient lover and wondered why he was so worried about this kid he hadn't known existed until a few months ago.

Now that the performances were wrapped up, all the activity switched over to planning the next event in Rio's life. Triani wondered briefly what to do about Corvin, who was older than Rio and should have a ceremony too. Perhaps at the same time? But that didn't seem fair either. He knew Rio wouldn't want to share the stage with anyone else on his special day any more than he would himself.

Things were falling into place much more quickly than he had expected, people coming forward to offer their services once the event became widely known. Benvolini had offered to spend some time with Rio so he could know enough about him to write his *cimbola* song. He also suggested he could teach Rio about the *Epicantare* Dragon saga and the storytelling technique that went along with it, since he had studied that art years ago and Rio would have to choose which section was most appropriate for him to recite. A *meshdravi* who had been at their final performance of *Dream* stepped forward and offered to sing the chants. His name was Calian something and he was apparently Marlo's lover, so at least he knew a little about the kid. Best of all, they were doing it for free. Flowers and such would come from his own gardens so that left food. The band. Decorations. And drink. Wine flowing like water in the fountains of the main courtyards. If he was throwing a party it had to be great. He had a reputation to uphold. Triani sighed.

Once committed to actually hosting the ceremony, he spent many anxious nights with Parla, asking him what to expect, details about Parla's own ceremony and how to handle questions from Rio. Triani always prepared well for every role, but he had no experience in this department and had to hide this fact from everyone but Parla. This made him nervous and more irritable than usual.

"But surely you've been invited to friends' ceremonies?" Parla asked.

"Invited, sure." Triani looked away. "I never went. I always had an excuse: on tour, in rehearsal, had another engagement, anything."

"Why?"

"I felt everyone there belonged to a sort of secret society and if I went I would give myself away somehow as not belonging. I don't expect you to understand, but I just couldn't make myself go."

Parla was silent for a moment. "Well, after going through this one, you'll know everything anyone else does. You will belong."

The one thing Triani was sure about was buying the dagger. He had made an appointment with Drelin's, one of the best known and most prestigious jewelers on the legendary Bridge. As expected, he had no trouble getting an appointment with the renowned old artist who had made his own dagger. He hoped the oldster would not remember that no member of his family had ever been in the store with him back then, no one had ever shown up to pay for it, either. Just him.

Rio was excited about the dagger, which he had seen so many adult Merculians wearing. He was very impressed when they arrived at the crowded bridge to find out the whole store had been closed down during the time of their appointment. The crowd outside waited patiently, watching through the store windows as the two dancers looked at patterns and Rio tried on a few samples to get the feel of the different styles.

"Might I suggest something with a slight curve," old Drelin said at last. "Just in case you do not grow as tall as your sibling." He looked at Triani and smiled.

In that moment, the star realized the old artisan did remember him but would never mention what he suspected to anyone. As they were leaving, he turned at the door and made a formal bow of thanks to the oldster.

The trouble started with the guest list. It had never occurred to Triani to consult Rio about the invitations. The day after the trip to the Bridge, Triani came back from the theater where he had been rehearsing a new production with Eulio and went to his office to draw up a provisional list. Giazin was out with Savane and Rio was supposed to be with the tutor Triani had hired to teach him what he needed to know for the ceremony. Corvin was studying too, just because he loved learning things, or so he said.

Triani had just settled down for a drink in his sitting room when Rio appeared.

"We need to talk about who's coming," Rio said, pouring himself a glass of mint wine.

"Aren't you supposed to be studying?"

"I'm finished for the day, and Corvin paid him to stay on and teach him about how the government works and the courts and that shit."

"It wouldn't hurt you to learn that shit, too," Triani said.

Rio shrugged. "So here's my list so far." He settled back and shone the list on the wall in front of them.

Triani scanned down the names, most of whom were on his list, too. And then he stopped.

"There is no way in hell that person will darken the doors of my house," he said, anger making his voice shake.

"Who?"

Triani underlined the name with his finger. "That bastard has ruined my life. And yours," he added.

"This is my ceremony. It's a family thing and both my parents are going to be here!"

"I have no problem with your *tatsi*, but that's as far as I'll go."

"I don't know what the hell happened between you and *mertsi* and I don't care. Just get over it. *Mertsi* is coming."

"Over my dead body!" shouted Triani, beside himself with rage. He should have seen this coming and nipped it in the bud, he thought to himself now, grabbing the Crushed Emeralds and filling his glass. This could not happen.

"Triani, this is supposed to be about me, not you."

"But it takes place in my house!"

"Then move the venue!"

"Holy shit! It's too late, you idiot!"

"Then leave, if you can't stand seeing him here!"

"You little shit! Now you're trying to kick me out of my own house? After what I've done for you?"

"If you're talking about *The Dream*, that started out being all about you, as I recall, and more credits in *your* pocket."

"Yeah, which I–– had to—" Triani seemed to stumble over his words for moments. "Which I fucking well need these days with you around!"

"Shit! If it's credits you want take mine!" Rio flung his cred-ring at Triani, who caught it and flung it on the floor scornfully.

"As if there's enough there, thanks to your wonderful *mertsi* skimming off most of it. That wouldn't even pay for the band that will be playing at *your* event!"

"You take that back! It's all there! *Mertsi* kept it *all* for me!"

"Excuse me." The voice from the door made them both turn around. Marlo stood there with two older Merculians looking a little shell-shocked right behind him. "I'm looking for Corvin," Marlo went on, now that he had their attention. "I've found his parents."

Triani took a quick drink and stepped forward with a bow. "Please forgive the commotion, *chais*. Just a little family disagreement."

"*Chai* Triani, it's such an honor to meet you. And we're the ones who should apologize, barging in like this without warning, but we're so excited to see Berliti again. All these years we hoped he was still alive, but it seemed…almost impossible. Nobody else…But now…I'm sorry. I'm babbling."

Rio rushed out of the room, shouting Corvin's name. Moments later he was back, with an astonished Corvin in tow.

"You really did find them," Corvin said, staring at the parents he could barely remember but speaking to Marlo.

"Well, it took a whole team, and thanks to a few spelling errors on the paperwork, it took much longer then expected. We also had to arrange for their special passage back from the Colony Planet along with Pendorin, and that wasn't easy, let me tell you. We dropped him off at his parents' place on the way here." Marlo stopped talking. No words were needed now.

One of the parents fell to his knees, his arms around the child he thought he had lost fifteen years ago. The other was crying, bending over, trying to embrace them both while he babbled the child's name over and over. After a moment he straightened up and flung his arms around Marlo.

"Thank you! Thank you! I can't begin to find the words to thank you enough!" he babbled though tears.

"You don't need to say a word, *chai*. I know."

"Oh Berliti! Your hair got to be such a lovely dark red! You're so beautiful!"

Corvin wiped his tears on his sleeve and hugged his *mertsi* tighter. "But I'm short," he mumbled.

"We don't care, dear. Short runs in the family, anyway."

Triani watched impassively. This is how it's supposed to be, he thought bitterly, how it can never be for me. If, by some horrible twist of fate, he ever met his parent face to face again, there would be no tearful reunion, no heart-felt embrace.

He noticed Rio watching the reunion, a strange expression on his face. It was probably just dawning on him that Corvin would soon be gone with his parents, leaving Rio behind. It would be hard on both of them, but Triani expected it would be far worse for Corvin. Rio would find someone else, eventually. He wasn't sure Corvin would even look.

THIRTY-SEVEN

Marlo sat in the small park behind HQ with Calian, who had brought freshly baked cinnamon twirls as a special snack to eat during morning break.

"Thanks for offering to sing the chants at Rio's ceremony," Marlo said. He moistened his finger and gathered up all the sugar hiding at the bottom of the box.

"I didn't think Triani would know any trained *meshdravi* singers, and as you know, we are the best."

"Even ones who are now making toys and not singing?"

"Once a singer, always a singer." Calian took the box away from Marlo and collapsed it between bis hands.

"I wasn't finished!" protested Marlo.

"Trust me, there is nothing left in there." Calian gave it a final tap and it disintegrated in his hand.

Footsteps made them both turn around and look towards the bushes that masked the corner of the building. A uniformed Regulator appeared, shepherding a group of three youngsters ahead of him. They all had the shoulder-length hair and simple tunics of the senior circle but they looked too young for the style. Something about the way they held hands and kept close together, and their faces looked years younger than senior circle students.

"Is this the one you were looking for?" the officer asked, smiling kindly at the little group.

All three nodded vigorously.

"*Com* Bogardini, they want to speak to you. Nobody else will do."

"That's fine. Let's talk here, shall we?" He made more room on the bench.

Calian buckled his shoulder bag. "I'll see you later," he said, touching Marlo's hand.

The three youngsters watched him go then sat down in a row beside Marlo.

"You're with the Colony Dancers, aren't you?" he said conversationally.

The one at the end cleared his throat. "We used to be. We're not sure who we are now."

The one in the middle, who was shorter than the other two, whispered; "We have to go to school and we can't dance. When we get home everyone will be ahead of us. We'll lose our places." He blinked.

"That's not why you want to talk to me, though, is it?" Marlo asked gently.

They shook their heads in unison.

The one beside him let go of his friend and clasped his hands together. "We know you helped Rio and Corvin. And Varsili too. We need your help now." His voice was tentative, rising at the end of sentences.

"And what do you need my help with, exactly?"

"We heard all our Guardians are locked up waiting for trial. Is that true?"

"That isn't really my department, dear, but yes, I believe that's true."

"But that's wrong!" the middle one piped up.

"How so?"

They looked at each other. Three youngsters with little experience of the outside world, trying to make sense of the Merculian justice system. It must have taken a lot of courage to come in search of him. Did they remember him from that first visit with the silver case holding their special boxes? But what did they want?

"It's wrong because all the Guardians are *not* bad. We love some of them. A lot. And Varsili…"

"He's the one with the straight white-blond hair?"

They nodded again.

Marlo remembered taking that child back to the Theater Residence after the wedding; how he had leapt into the arms of the guardian who was his lover.

"Anyway, when they took Bledsi away, Varsi got really sick. He won't eat, can't sleep, won't do anything for anyone."

"He's dying for love," the one on the end said, his eyes welling up with tears.

"And there's nobody we know taking care of us anymore!" That was the one beside him.

"That's very sad, but what can I do about it?"

"We need to tell the court people that Bledsi and four of the others are good, kind people. They *never* hurt us. They comforted us and said they loved us. Not like Grepion and the rest."

"We don't want to desert them now!" said the middle one.

Marlo sighed. These 'good' Guardians must have known what was going on though, he thought to himself. How could they not know? Still, the children had made a big effort. The least he could do was give them some of his time. This case was not over yet.

Marlo took down the full names of the Guardians the kids were trying to have released and gave them a ride back to the Theater Residence where they lived now. "What you can do is write a petition and get everyone to sign it. Then we can present it to the court with our arguments."

That cheered them up, though it did little for Marlo's spirits. A petition wasn't necessary but at least it would give them something to do and let them think they were helping.

Just as he was about to leave, the young spokesperson ran back and called out to him. "How do we get Rio and Corvin to sign?"

"I'll look after that. You just write it out and get the others' signatures. Everyone who knew him, not just kids, remember."

Marlo had never thought about this aspect of the case, that the Guardians might not be equally guilty. He wondered about the charge, how it read, what it might mean. And, most importantly, how he could find out.

On the way back to the office, he contacted Rio, then Corvin. Both agreed that the Guardians mentioned by the kids were warm and caring, though Rio had reservations about one of them. When Marlo asked Corvin about that, he dismissed it. "Rio couldn't get his way all the time with that one," he said. "But he was fine. Really caring, just strict."

Marlo paused, looking at the pale intense face watching him

from the screen. "Did anyone ever come in from outside to visit, or inspect the place that you remember? Health check, maybe? Or housing?"

Corvin shook his head. "Not that kind of visit, no. But I remember years ago we were paraded out to meet the new owners. After that, more Guardians were sent in and they were not nice to us."

"Were they cruel? Physically, I mean?"

"No, no. Nothing like that! I just meant they were short with us and didn't even bother to learn our names. I was always just Red, and Rio was Blackie. Sutini they called Baby and it made him cry."

"And these mean ones came with you here?"

"Some of them, yes."

"Thanks."

The new order, Marlo thought. The changing of the guard. Out with the kinder, gentler approach. But he reminded himself that the children had been abused long before that. Who knows how long, once greed set in and the prospect of decade after decade of brilliant 'child' dancers brought in the big numbers of credits real children dancing could not hope to equal.

Back in his office, he tried to find some reference to the charges brought against the Guardians, the others picked up in the raid on the ship, and the members of the Faisian Falanx. The Elutians were not his concern. He kept thinking of the Guardians who stayed, probably knowing what had been done but staying to show the children affection and real care. That's who the kids were trying to save; the only adults who had given a damn. But no matter how hard he tried, he could find no trace of them. What was going on? Was this some kind of conspiracy?

One name came to mind—Orosin At'hali Benvolini. Beny. He might be able to help, but would he? And another thing, did he, Marlo, have any right to ask? He was still not clear as to the boundaries of their relationship, but the enigmatic Merculian with the red-gold hair was the only person he could think of who had the right connections.

Not wanting to overthink things, Marlo contacted Beny and told him what he was trying to find out. There was silence for a few moments and Marlo thought he had made a mistake. Perhaps it was some kind of conspiracy after all; something to do with that shadowy connection Eulio's spouse seemed to have with the powers that be. But after a moment, Beny asked if he could come over in an a few hours. "Right now I'm in the middle of composing the song for Rio's ceremony, you know. It's proving difficult. But I'll see what I can do for you, Marlo. No promises, though."

Marlo thanked him profusely and broke the connection. The time moved slowly since he couldn't settle to anything else while he waited, but two hours later he was at the Adelantis-Benvolini home, walking under the arch of the two trees that were entwined over the entrance to signify this was the home of a married couple. Beny and his Serpian friend Thar-von Del were in the small sunken courtyard surrounded by narrow pillars of brightly colored tiles topped by hanging greenery. A table was covered with data cubes and paper.

"Thank you for seeing me," Marlo said. "The poor children seemed so desolate and needy."

"I want to thank you, Marlo," Beny said with a slight bow of his head. "I'm so glad your questions have forced the legal powers to take a closer look at this document. It was drawn up in haste, as you may imagine, and there are several errors and one big loophole that might have led to the whole evil crew going free and never being brought to justice, so you see why I'm grateful to you."

"It was a joint operation," Marlo said slowly. "Sometimes things go horribly wrong and communications can be…misinterpreted."

"I myself have no direct input into this, but my *tan* Pamiano does. He sits on the Merculian Inner Council, as you know, and between him and what Thar-von managed to dig up for us over at the Serpian Embassy we now have a much clearer picture of what happened."

Thar-von shuffled a few papers with his large pale blue hands, then stacked them neatly together in front of him. "I hate to admit it but I'm afraid the trouble started on our end. The Serpian Raider teams understood their orders as 'pick up all the Merculians on board the Elutian ship and bring them all back to the High Crimes Building for incarceration.' Consequently, they lumped them all together; children, members of the Faisian Falanx, Guardians, baggage handlers, the lot. They turned the children over to the healers and took the rest to be incarcerated."

"That seems reasonable," Marlo said. "They should have been sorted out there."

"Except, they weren't," Beny explained. "That unit isn't used to such large numbers being dumped on them. They don't have the staff, for one thing. They have managed to get names but some are not cooperating at all."

"I expect they're not the ones I'm interested in," Marlo said.

"I expect not." Beny laughed. "Anyway, *tan* Pami contacted the High Crimes containment center and a team will be there tomorrow to sort some of this out. Your five have already agreed to testify against the others and I expect they will be released with tracking bracelets so they can be with the poor children."

"Strangely, things seem to be working out much better for the combined forces sent to the Colony," Thar-von said. "The Signet is in Merculian hands, the Elutians have been sent home and the so-called healers in the dance company have been arrested, along with everyone working in their experimental lab hidden away behind high walls near the school."

"And *they* will most definitely be severely dealt with." Beny stood up, indicating the meeting was over.

I sincerely hope so, Marlo thought, as he walked along the street, keeping an eye out for a Snack House.

THIRTY-EIGHT

Triani's country home was rarely a sea of calm but now it was a storm of activity. Daisa the ex-assistant, was hired again, as was the gardener who had been fired after the incident with Rio.

Savane was proving useful, since he was not in rehearsal with his company at the moment so could be there most afternoons. But it was Parla who was a steadying presence during all the stress and tumult. Unfortunately he had to check on the rebuilding of the east wing of the Wave building from time to time so wasn't always there and Triani had to rely on his assistant more and more, since he himself was in rehearsal. They were in constant contact; during breaks, while he was resting during Eulio's solos, even during costume fittings. Everyone in the company would be glad when Rio finally received his dagger!

Triani had a frenzied session with his manager about this time, going over finances and demanding higher fees for several special appearances. The harried manager set up a guest appearance at the Halabion outpost for an outrageous amount, and Triani settled down and decided not to fire him after all.

But when the wine delivery was late by half an hour, Triani paced about, one hand slapping his thigh. When he saw the labels on the crates that began piling up in the food prep courtyard, the tension erupted in fury.

"I wouldn't serve that piss to the slugs in my garden, let alone give it to my guests," he shouted. "It's a *cimbola* ceremony, you cretins! Take it back! This is not what I ordered."

"But *chai*, it says right here—"

"Take it back!" Triani pulled a bottle out of the closest crate and threw it at the hapless creature who dodged aside. The bottle shattered, a green stain spreading over the slate walkway.

"Let me take care of this, dear." Parla arrived at that moment, moved smoothly in front of Triani and took a look at the order. "There's an error, see? It plainly says Polini 5 Star, but you brought plain Polini. No star, see? Just return all this and come back with the 5 Star."

"Okay, *chai*."

"Can't you read?" Triani shouted after the retreating delivery floats.

"Calm down, dear. It's a wonder anyone works for you at all."

"I pay well and I always tip."

"That's a very good idea." Parla slid and arm around his waist and guided him back inside. "Keep doing that."

The great day finally arrived. Rio was so excited he could barely stand still. He had chosen his white outfit carefully and spent a great deal of his own credits so he could get the jeweled buttons he wanted down the front and the silver lace at the wrists. He had also decided on white satin slippers with small heels, to give him a bit more height, since his brief growing spurt seemed to be over for a while. Corvin had come with him to buy the sparkling belt with its dagger clip. He was now living with his parents in the Theater Residence and would be going back to the Colony with them after the ceremony where he would have his own *cimbola* at last. After that, he would join a special school that was being set up for former dancers from the disgraced company where they could try to catch up on all the years of study they had been denied, plus all the little things children usually learn at home. And after every day, Corvin would return to be with his family.

The house was filled with flowers; bunches and sprays and huge arrangements in colorful urns on the floor. The prevailing shades were white and green, the traditional *cimbola* colors. Long ribbons with tiny bells attached hung from bows hooked to the tops of arches leading to the main courtyard where a tall white and silver candle stood marking the spot where Rio would recite his Epicantare story, hear his song and receive the dagger. Each guest would bring a candle to help light the path of the youth into his maturity and when everyone had arrived, and they lit the candles at the start of the ritual, the place would be full of soft golden lights. After the ceremony the fountains would be turned on, running with wine. The refreshments would appear, the band would begin playing and the party would swing into high gear.

Triani prided himself on throwing great social events, but he had had to scale back on this one, thanks to Parla's constant reminders that this was about Rio, not him. Traditionally *cimbola* affairs did not degenerate into all night revelries, and fun as these might be, there was a time and a place. Tonight, Parla said, was not the time. "Which is why there's only one band," Triani pointed out.

People began arriving as the sun slid closer to the horizon, first in small groups, then as if in a flood. Triani had invited the whole company, although Rio had demurred seeing Carondi's name. He did, however, agree that leaving him off the list would cause gossip. Rio had invited the Colony kids who were back staying in the Theater Residence along with the five Guardians he liked who had now been released. Corvin and his parents came early. So did Marlo and Calian, and Marlo was now inspecting the refreshments with interest. Beny and Eulio arrived at the same time as some of the backstage people Rio had made friends with. Pom and the other healers also came, of course, and some of the designers Triani and Parla knew well.

As the house filled with cheerful conversation and laughter, Triani popped another buzzer in his mouth and took a sip of wine as he watched Rio talking animatedly to his friends from the Colony, Corvin, as usual, by his side.

"He's come a long way," Parla said quietly. "You've done well."

"He's done most of it himself," Triani said, but he was pleased Parla had given him some of the credit.

Half an hour later, Triani was in the courtyard, flirting with one of the young servers hired for the event. "Your hair smells divine," he breathed, his face so close to the youth's he could feel the heat from his flushed skin. He paused, cocked his head, listened. An unusual buzz was coming from the main reception room. The whole energy of the place had changed. Laughter burst out. And then he heard it. A voice so like his own, stirring a long dormant memory into life.

"Holy shit!" He pushed the kid roughly aside and grabbed a drink from a passing bot. It couldn't be. The little shit wouldn't dare! Or would he?

At that moment, Rio rushed up and hugged him. "Thank you! Thank you!" he cried, his face flushed with joy.

"You think *I* invited that piece of shit?" Triani cried, pushing him away.

"I invited him," Corvin said, joining them.

"*You!* You stabbed me in the back like this?"

"It was the one thing Rio wanted to make his night perfect. I have to leave him but before I go, I wanted to give him something he would never forget, because I love him and always will." Corvin turned and walked away.

"Traitor!" Triani shouted after him.

A few people turned to stare but he didn't care. He slammed down his glass and headed across the room where his hated parent stood, the center of attention. It was obvious that everyone knew who the newcomer was. Tall and straight, he looked the picture of elegant ease, a long carved staff in one hand, a silver candle in the other. That face, so like his own, had aged some over the years but he was now even more attractive, the black eyes bright, the sensuous mouth curved up in amusement, softening the harshness he remembered. Triani felt acid twist in his stomach. "You bitch," he muttered, pushing past the crowd.

But just as he came face to face with the despised parent, Eulio sprang in front of him and grabbed the candle out of his startled parent's hand, passing it to Beny.

"Lorsadan Mavini Erlindo!" he exclaimed, steering the surprised parent towards the small courtyard. "Such a pleasure, isn't it Parla?"

"It is indeed." Parla took a firm hold of Lorsadan's other arm. "We know you and Triani have a lot to catch up on, so let's go somewhere more private."

"But *mertzi*—"

"Later, Rio," Parla said sternly. "Mingle with your other guests now. Wait your turn."

"Where's *tatsi*?" Rio asked plaintively.

"I invited them both," Corvin said and shrugged.

Triani restrained his fury long enough to chat with a few guests in passing, then followed his parent to the room on the other side of the courtyard. Eulio and Parla were just leaving. Parla touched his hand as he passed by, a gesture cautioning restraint, but Triani's anger had been simmering far too long to be stifled by a loving touch.

"Triani, darling! It's been so long! Let me look at you!"

"Look in the mirror, you bitch." Triani slammed the door shut and snapped on the privacy light.

"You invited me here just to insult me?"

"I wouldn't invite you to your own funeral! I told Rio that."

"You told Rio?"

"Not the reason, you putrid piece of shit! He loves you, for some reason, even though you managed to fuck up his life, too!"

"I tried my best with him!"

"You didn't even tell him I existed until I was useful to you."

"I wanted to put the past behind me so I didn't tell my lover Piansi. So after that I couldn't tell Rio either when he came along, could I?"

"Some excuse."

"Anyway, that school was the best in the Colony when I put Rio there. I even taught there myself for two years and everything was fine."

"And then you left him, just as you left me."

"Piansi got a wonderful post with the Windfall mine company and I went with him. But I came back to visit!"

"And you never noticed that your precious offspring wasn't growing an inch? You expect me to believe that?"

"I didn't notice at first. Why should I? His father was short. And later on, they began to find excuses why I couldn't see hm when I came to visit. He was on tour. He was sick. He was in rehearsal or out. It's not my fault!"

"Nothing is ever your fault!" Triani noticed the bottles of Crushed Emeralds on the table and poured himself a large glass. "Wait a minute. I've seen the image Rio has of you two together and his *tatsi* is almost as tall as you are. So you're telling me—"

"No, Triani!"

"Someone else is Rio's real *tatsi*. You shit! And he doesn't know!"

"Piansi loves him!"

"Then why isn't he here?"

For the first time, Lorsadan looked away, fiddling with the long crystal beads around his neck. "He's not feeling well."

"Sure. You left him too, didn't you?"

Lorsadan raised his head imperiously. "I am not made for small towns," he said grandly.

"You're made for moving on, for leaving people behind, for abandoning kids you have just for your own pleasure."

"I wanted you, Triani!"

"Then why didn't you have me the legal way so I would have the three names every child has a right to?"

"You fixed that! Your one name is legal!"

"I shouldn't have had to if you weren't so selfish and self-centered and—"

"It wasn't like that!"

"It was exactly like that! How else could it have been? Normal people would have stopped short of carrying an illegal child but not you. Why?"

Lorsadan went over to the table and poured himself a drink. "All right. I was wrong but in my defense my long-time lover had just left me and I was broken-hearted. Looking back I think I had a bit of a breakdown, I missed him so much. Self-pleasuring was a comfort."

"Yeah, yeah. We all do that from time to time but we don't fucking let it go so far we conceive, for shit's sake!"

"Plus, I was on heavy tranqs then, so it took quite a while to realize..."

"Oh please."

"And then I was so lonely. I wanted the baby I was carrying. Someone to love! Someone to love me!"

"Look how well that turned out!"

"It was good for a while. It was! Don't you remember me teaching you how to dance, all the old variations? Singing our special songs? Taking you to the theater with me? I remember you getting up at one rehearsal and trying to repeat some of the dances you saw the soloist doing and doing it pretty well, too. You were so talented, even then. Taking you—"

"Enough! I can barely remember any of that!"

"You have a selective memory, I'm sure! Don't you even remember my horrible accident? The one that ruined everything?"

"What I remember is having to look after you when I was six years old! You so out of your head on drugs you hit me! Often."

"I was in terrible pain! I got addicted, I know, but you're an adult, Triani. Can't you understand now? I still have some pain and need a staff to walk with."

Triani looked around for a bowl of buzzers but there weren't any. He poured another drink. What was the point? They could go on all night like this. But there were some things he just couldn't let go.

"And then you got better and left me."

"Oh for fuck's sake!" Lorsadan sank down in a chair and stretched out his bad leg. "I got tired chasing after you when you ran away. "

"I ran to get away from a house full of chaos and sickness and one lover after another whose names I never had time to learn."

"I made sure you were in a good school before I left."

"That seems to be your pattern, doesn't it? I was ten! I needed love and a home!" His eyes filled with tears.

"Oh Triani, I loved you! I did, in my own way."

Triani laughed bitterly and dried his eyes. "I believe you, *mertsi*. Thousands wouldn't, but I do." He took another sip of his drink, feeling the warmth calming his nerves. "Fuck, I'm tired."

"Me, too."

There was silence in the room for a few moments. The hum of the party came through the round window, mixed with the heavy scent of the rope tree blossoms heaped in a colorful container in one corner.

"I can't forgive any of it,' Triani said at last. "I really can't."

"Can we at least call a truce, for Rio?"

"Glad you're finally thinking of one of us."

"It will be time to light the candles soon." Lorsadan tried to lift himself out of the chair without success.

Triani went over and offered his hand. "Come on, you old reprobate. Heave-ho."

Lorsadan stood up unsteadily and paused. One long hand touched Triani's *cimbola* dagger gently. "I'm so, so sorry."

"Yeah, yeah. Don't go there, okay?"

"There's one thing I gave you both, don't forget. Talent."

Triani paused, then started for the door.

"Wait a minute." Lorsadan pulled out a mirror from the pouch at his waist, checked his make-up and handed the mirror to Triani. He fluffed his hair with one hand, smoothed his eyebrows then handed the mirror back.

"Shit. If I looked any worse they wouldn't be able to tell us apart." Triani took his parent's arm. "Come on. Let's put on a show for Rio."

THIRTY-NINE

The great airy rooms buzzed with laughter and chatter of the many guests as Triani and his parent entered the main reception room. Eulio appeared almost at once, watching them both closely. Parla was right behind him.

Lorsadan looked at Triani, and whispered, "I think your grand friends expected one of us to come out feet first."

Triani burst out laughing.

Rio's face flooded with relief when he saw them. "I thought you'd forgotten about lighting the candle," he breathed.

Triani noticed Giazin edging his way through the crowd and had an impulse to shield him from Lorsadan. Instead, he held out his arms to his child and then introduced them.

"How come I never saw you before?" Giazin asked, holding onto the carved staff.

"Because I live far, far away, child."

"Exactly, so you'll probably never see him again," Triani added.

Lorsadan sighed.

Triani gave the signal and the Merculian pipes played the opening notes to the ceremony. Triani and Lorsadan walked behind Rio to the tall candle that stood in the main courtyard with the small stand beside it holding the brand-new dagger and a silver bell. When the music died away, Triani reached out and lit the tall candle that came up to Rio's shoulder. At once all the other candles crowding the courtyard sprang into life, emitting a soft golden glow. Triani stepped back, glad to note that Parla was now close by, holding Giazin by the hand.

As Calian moved into the spotlight, a hush came over the guests, many of whom were now reliving their own ceremonies.

Triani knew what was coming since Pala had told him, but he was not prepared for the beauty of the singer's voice or the waves of emotion coming to him from the crowd as the ritual phrases rolled over their heads. It was all about opening the doors to adulthood and music, and light guiding the way. He glanced at his parent and saw tears gathering in the black eyes, so like his own. Moved by some emotion he didn't recognize, he reached out for Lorsadan's hand and held it for a long moment. He felt lips graze his cheek. As the music died away he pulled his hand away. It's not enough, he thought, but it's something.

Rio stepped into the spotlight now and cleared his throat. "I have chosen the 'Tale of The Child Who Was Lost'. He was all alone and cold, but a young dragon found him and stayed with him, warming him with his dragon breath. He was too small to carry the child to safety, but when night came, he opened his mouth and flung a beacon of fire into the velvet sky so his rescuers could find him." He paused while the musicians played the dragon theme. When it faded away, Rio began the short tale, his voice taking on a rhythm and tone Triani had not heard before, something he had obviously learned from Benvolini. It was oddly mesmerizing, and so were the movements and animated manner that accompanied it.

"He's very good," whispered Lorsadan. "Who taught him?"

"Obviously not me," muttered Triani.

Everyone knew the story but they hung on every word as if it were a brand new tale, and at the end they applauded lustily, even shouting *"Toori! Toori!"* as if they were in the theater. Triani could see Rio's chest puff with pride.

Triani glanced at Parla, uncertain in all the emotion if it was his cue next, but Parla shook his head. Calian again stepped forward from his place beside the portly Marlo. The crowd quieted at once, people practically holding their collective breath.

Calian announced, in his surprisingly deep speaking voice, that he was about to sing Rio's song for the first time. "It was composed by the renowned musician Orosin At'hali Benvolini as a gift to celebrate Triani's young sibling's coming of age."

"Your friends are famous," murmured Lorsadan.

"So am I." Triani moved over to stand beside Parla.

Gradually the lights dimmed, the coughing and rustling died

down and complete stillness settled over the crowd. Calian took a deep breath and opened his mouth to release beauty. A long-sustained note, then trills, swoops, a slow, rhythmic happy beat and suddenly, a jagged quick slide into the minor key. Then it was as if the sun had risen early in the morning after a night of rain and a beautiful melody floated over their heads like balm.

I get it, Triani thought, his eyes wet with tears. It's his life, which suddenly slipped into a minor key and is now back in the sunshine.

When the music stopped, there was the utter silence of respect. It was not usual to applaud after a *cimbola* song, Triani had learned, so this was fine. Only one thing remained. He stepped forward and reached for the dagger. "For my sibling Rio on his coming of age," he said simply, lifting it into the air. Then he clipped it to Rio's sparkling belt and kissed his cheek. It was the first time he had ever done anything that intimate to his sibling.

Rio flung his arms around him. "Thank you," he said, his face wet with tears. "Thank you for everything."

Parla stepped forward and rang the bell that turned all the white ribbons green all over the courtyard and reception rooms. The celebration was complete. Let the party begin!

ABOUT THE AUTHOR

CARO SOLES's novels include mysteries, erotica, gay lit, science fiction and the occasional bit of dark fantasy. She received the Derrick Murdoch Award from the Crime Writers of Canada for her work in the mystery field, was short listed for the Lambda Literary Award, the Aurora Award and the Stoker Award. Caro lives in Toronto, loves dachshunds, books, opera and ballet, not necessarily in that order.

Curious about other Crossroad Press books?
Stop by our site:
http://store.crossroadpress.com
We offer quality writing
in digital, audio, and print formats.

Enter the code FIRSTBOOK
to get 20% off your first order from our store!
Stop by today!

CPSIA information can be obtained
at www.ICGtesting.com
Printed in the USA
LVHW080721090621
689715LV00007BA/310

9 781637 899496